LESLIE -
Get well fast!
Love you!
Dad & Sharon

Greasy Lake

& Other Stories

Greasy Lake

& Other Stories

T. Coraghessan Boyle

Viking

for Vivian Martin

VIKING
Viking Penguin Inc., 40 West 23rd Street, New York, New York 10010, U.S.A.
Penguin Books Ltd, Harmondsworth, Middlesex, England
Penguin Books Australia Ltd, Ringwood, Victoria, Australia
Penguin Books Canada Limited, 2801 John Street, Markham, Ontario, Canada L3R 1B4
Penguin Books (N.Z.) Ltd, 182–190 Wairau Road, Auckland 10, New Zealand

First published in 1985 by Viking Penguin Inc.
Published simultaneously in Canada

LIBRARY OF CONGRESS CATALOGING IN PUBLICATION DATA
Boyle, T. Coraghessan.
  Greasy Lake and other stories.
  I. Title.
PS3552.O932.G7   1985   813'.54   84-23427
ISBN 0-670-80542-4

The author wishes to thank the National Endowment for the Arts for its generous support.

Page 231 constitutes an extension of this copyright page.

Printed in the United States of America
by R. R. Donnelley & Sons Company, Harrisonburg, Virginia
Set in Caledonia

Contents

Greasy Lake

& Other Stories

Greasy Lake

It's about a mile down on the dark side of Route 88.
—BRUCE SPRINGSTEEN

There was a time when courtesy and winning ways went out of style, when it was good to be bad, when you cultivated decadence like a taste. We were all dangerous characters then. We wore torn-up leather jackets, slouched around with toothpicks in our mouths, sniffed glue and ether and what somebody claimed was cocaine. When we wheeled our parents' whining station wagons out into the street we left a patch of rubber half a block long. We drank gin and grape juice, Tango, Thunderbird, and Bali Hai. We were nineteen. We were bad. We read André Gide and struck elaborate poses to show that we didn't give a shit about anything. At night, we went up to Greasy Lake.

Through the center of town, up the strip, past the housing developments and shopping malls, street lights giving way to the thin streaming illumination of the headlights, trees crowding the

asphalt in a black unbroken wall: that was the way out to Greasy
Lake. The Indians had called it Wakan, a reference to the clarity
of its waters. Now it was fetid and murky, the mud banks glittering with broken glass and strewn with beer cans and the charred
remains of bonfires. There was a single ravaged island a hundred
yards from shore, so stripped of vegetation it looked as if the air
force had strafed it. We went up to the lake because everyone
went there, because we wanted to snuff the rich scent of possibility on the breeze, watch a girl take off her clothes and plunge into
the festering murk, drink beer, smoke pot, howl at the stars, savor
the incongruous full-throated roar of rock and roll against the pri-
meval susurrus of frogs and crickets. This was nature.

I was there one night, late, in the company of two dangerous
characters. Digby wore a gold star in his right ear and allowed his
father to pay his tuition at Cornell; Jeff was thinking of quitting
school to become a painter/musician/head-shop proprietor. They
were both expert in the social graces, quick with a sneer, able to
manage a Ford with lousy shocks over a rutted and gutted blacktop road at eighty-five while rolling a joint as compact as a Tootsie
Roll Pop stick. They could lounge against a bank of booming
speakers and trade "man"s with the best of them or roll out across
the dance floor as if their joints worked on bearings. They were
slick and quick and they wore their mirror shades at breakfast and
dinner, in the shower, in closets and caves. In short, they were
bad.

I drove. Digby pounded the dashboard and shouted along with
Toots & the Maytals while Jeff hung his head out the window and
streaked the side of my mother's Bel Air with vomit. It was early
June, the air soft as a hand on your cheek, the third night of summer vacation. The first two nights we'd been out till dawn, looking
for something we never found. On this, the third night, we'd
cruised the strip sixty-seven times, been in and out of every bar
and club we could think of in a twenty-mile radius, stopped twice
for bucket chicken and forty-cent hamburgers, debated going to a
party at the house of a girl Jeff's sister knew, and chucked two
dozen raw eggs at mailboxes and hitchhikers. It was 2:00 A.M.; the

bars were closing. There was nothing to do but take a bottle of lemon-flavored gin up to Greasy Lake.

The taillights of a single car winked at us as we swung into the dirt lot with its tufts of weed and washboard corrugations; '57 Chevy, mint, metallic blue. On the far side of the lot, like the exoskeleton of some gaunt chrome insect, a chopper leaned against its kickstand. And that was it for excitement: some junkie half-wit biker and a car freak pumping his girlfriend. Whatever it was we were looking for, we weren't about to find it at Greasy Lake. Not that night.

But then all of a sudden Digby was fighting for the wheel. "Hey, that's Tony Lovett's car! Hey!" he shouted, while I stabbed at the brake pedal and the Bel Air nosed up to the gleaming bumper of the parked Chevy. Digby leaned on the horn, laughing, and instructed me to put my brights on. I flicked on the brights. This was hilarious. A joke. Tony would experience premature withdrawal and expect to be confronted by grim-looking state troopers with flashlights. We hit the horn, strobed the lights, and then jumped out of the car to press our witty faces to Tony's windows; for all we knew we might even catch a glimpse of some little fox's tit, and then we could slap backs with red-faced Tony, roughhouse a little, and go on to new heights of adventure and daring.

The first mistake, the one that opened the whole floodgate, was losing my grip on the keys. In the excitement, leaping from the car with the gin in one hand and a roach clip in the other, I spilled them in the grass—in the dark, rank, mysterious nighttime grass of Greasy Lake. This was a tactical error, as damaging and irreversible in its way as Westmoreland's decision to dig in at Khe Sanh. I felt it like a jab of intuition, and I stopped there by the open door, peering vaguely into the night that puddled up round my feet.

The second mistake—and this was inextricably bound up with the first—was identifying the car as Tony Lovett's. Even before the very bad character in greasy jeans and engineer boots ripped out of the driver's door, I began to realize that this chrome blue was much lighter than the robin's-egg of Tony's car, and that Tony's car didn't have rear-mounted speakers. Judging from their expressions, Digby and Jeff were privately groping toward the same inevitable and unsettling conclusion as I was.

In any case, there was no reasoning with this bad greasy character—clearly he was a man of action. The first lusty Rockette kick of his steel-toed boot caught me under the chin, chipped my favorite tooth, and left me sprawled in the dirt. Like a fool, I'd gone down on one knee to comb the stiff hacked grass for the keys, my mind making connections in the most dragged-out, testudineous way, knowing that things had gone wrong, that I was in a lot of trouble, and that the lost ignition key was my grail and my salvation. The three or four succeeding blows were mainly absorbed by my right buttock and the tough piece of bone at the base of my spine.

Meanwhile, Digby vaulted the kissing bumpers and delivered a savage kung-fu blow to the greasy character's collarbone. Digby had just finished a course in martial arts for phys-ed credit and had spent the better part of the past two nights telling us apocryphal tales of Bruce Lee types and of the raw power invested in lightning blows shot from coiled wrists, ankles, and elbows. The greasy character was unimpressed. He merely backed off a step, his face like a Toltec mask, and laid Digby out with a single whistling roundhouse blow . . . but by now Jeff had got into the act, and I was beginning to extricate myself from the dirt, a tinny compound of shock, rage, and impotence wadded in my throat.

Jeff was on the guy's back, biting at his ear. Digby was on the ground, cursing. I went for the tire iron I kept under the driver's seat. I kept it there because bad characters always keep tire irons under the driver's seat, for just such an occasion as this. Never mind that I hadn't been involved in a fight since sixth grade, when a kid with a sleepy eye and two streams of mucus depending from his nostrils hit me in the knee with a Louisville slugger; never mind that I'd touched the tire iron exactly twice before, to change tires: it was there. And I went for it.

I was terrified. Blood was beating in my ears, my hands were shaking, my heart turning over like a dirtbike in the wrong gear.

My antagonist was shirtless, and a single cord of muscle flashed across his chest as he bent forward to peel Jeff from his back like a wet overcoat. "Motherfucker," he spat, over and over, and I was aware in that instant that all four of us—Digby, Jeff, and myself included—were chanting "motherfucker, motherfucker," as if it were a battle cry. (What happened next? the detective asks the murderer from beneath the turned-down brim of his porkpie hat. I don't know, the murderer says, something came over me. Exactly.)

Digby poked the flat of his hand in the bad character's face and I came at him like a kamikaze, mindless, raging, stung with humiliation—the whole thing, from the initial boot in the chin to this murderous primal instant involving no more than sixty hyperventilating, gland-flooding seconds—I came at him and brought the tire iron down across his ear. The effect was instantaneous, astonishing. He was a stunt man and this was Hollywood, he was a big grimacing toothy balloon and I was a man with a straight pin. He collapsed. Wet his pants. Went loose in his boots.

A single second, big as a zeppelin, floated by. We were standing over him in a circle, gritting our teeth, jerking our necks, our limbs and hands and feet twitching with glandular discharges. No one said anything. We just stared down at the guy, the car freak, the lover, the bad greasy character laid low. Digby looked at me; so did Jeff. I was still holding the tire iron, a tuft of hair clinging to the crook like dandelion fluff, like down. Rattled, I dropped it in the dirt, already envisioning the headlines, the pitted faces of the police inquisitors, the gleam of handcuffs, clank of bars, the big black shadows rising from the back of the cell . . . when suddenly a raw torn shriek cut through me like all the juice in all the electric chairs in the country.

It was the fox. She was short, barefoot, dressed in panties and a man's shirt. "Animals!" she screamed, running at us with her fists clenched and wisps of blow-dried hair in her face. There was a silver chain round her ankle, and her toenails flashed in the glare of the headlights. I think it was the toenails that did it. Sure, the gin and the cannabis and even the Kentucky Fried may have had a hand in it, but it was the sight of those flaming toes that set us off—the toad emerging from the loaf in *Virgin Spring*, lipstick smeared on a child: she was already tainted. We were on her like Bergman's deranged brothers—see no evil, hear none, speak none—panting, wheezing, tearing at her clothes, grabbing for flesh. We were bad characters, and we were scared and hot and three steps over the line—anything could have happened.

It didn't.

Before we could pin her to the hood of the car, our eyes masked with lust and greed and the purest primal badness, a pair of head-lights swung into the lot. There we were, dirty, bloody, guilty, dissociated from humanity and civilization, the first of the Ur-crimes behind us, the second in progress, shreds of nylon panty and spandex brassiere dangling from our fingers, our flies open, lips licked—there we were, caught in the spotlight. Nailed.

We bolted. First for the car, and then, realizing we had no way of starting it, for the woods. I thought nothing. I thought escape. The headlights came at me like accusing fingers. I was gone.

Ram-bam-bam, across the parking lot, past the chopper and into the feculent undergrowth at the lake's edge, insects flying up in my face, weeds whipping, frogs and snakes and red-eyed turtles splashing off into the night: I was already ankle-deep in muck and tepid water and still going strong. Behind me, the girl's screams rose in intensity, disconsolate, incriminating, the screams of the Sabine women, the Christian martyrs, Anne Frank dragged from the garret. I kept going, pursued by those cries, imagining cops and bloodhounds. The water was up to my knees when I realized what I was doing: I was going to swim for it. Swim the breadth of Greasy Lake and hide myself in the thick clot of woods on the far side. They'd never find me there.

I was breathing in sobs, in gasps. The water lapped at my waist as I looked out over the moon-burnished ripples, the mats of algae that clung to the surface like scabs. Digby and Jeff had vanished. I paused. Listened. The girl was quieter now, screams tapering to sobs, but there were male voices, angry, excited, and the high-pitched ticking of the second car's engine. I waded deeper, steal-thy, hunted, the ooze sucking at my sneakers. As I was about to take the plunge—at the very instant I dropped my shoulder for the first slashing stroke—I blundered into something. Something unspeakable, obscene, something soft, wet, moss-grown. A patch of weed? A log? When I reached out to touch it, it gave like a rubber duck, it gave like flesh.

In one of those nasty little epiphanies for which we are prepared by films and TV and childhood visits to the funeral home to ponder the shrunken painted forms of dead grandparents, I understood what it was that bobbed there so inadmissibly in the dark. Understood, and stumbled back in horror and revulsion, my mind yanked in six different directions (I was nineteen, a mere child, an infant, and here in the space of five minutes I'd struck down one greasy character and blundered into the waterlogged carcass of a second), thinking, The keys, the keys, why did I have to go and lose the keys? I stumbled back, but the muck took hold of my feet—a sneaker snagged, balance lost—and suddenly I was pitching face forward into the buoyant black mass, throwing out my hands in desperation while simultaneously conjuring the image of reeking frogs and muskrats revolving in slicks of their own deliquescing juices. AAAAArrrgh! I shot from the water like a torpedo, the dead man rotating to expose a mossy beard and eyes cold as the moon. I must have shouted out, thrashing around in the weeds, because the voices behind me suddenly became animated.

"What was that?"

"It's them, it's them: they tried to, tried to . . . *rape* me!" Sobs.

A man's voice, flat Midwestern accent. "You sons a bitches, we'll kill you!"

Frogs, crickets.

Then another voice, harsh, *r*-less, Lower East Side: "Motherfucker!" I recognized the verbal virtuosity of the bad greasy character in the engineer boots. Tooth chipped, sneakers gone, coated in mud and slime and worse, crouching breathless in the weeds waiting to have my ass thoroughly and definitively kicked and fresh from the hideous stinking embrace of a three-days-dead-corpse, I suddenly felt a rush of joy and vindication: the son of a bitch was alive! Just as quickly, my bowels turned to ice. "Come on out of there, you pansy motherfuckers!" the bad greasy character was screaming. He shouted curses till he was out of breath.

The crickets started up again, then the frogs. I held my breath. All at once there was a sound in the reeds, a swishing, a splash: thunk-a-thunk. They were throwing rocks. The frogs fell silent. I cradled my head. Swish, swish, thunk-a-thunk. A wedge of feldspar the size of a cue ball glanced off my knee. I bit my finger.

It was then that they turned to the car. I heard a door slam, a curse, and then the sound of the headlights shattering—almost a good-natured sound, celebratory, like corks popping from the necks of bottles. This was succeeded by the dull booming of the fenders, metal on metal, and then the icy crash of the windshield. I inched forward, elbows and knees, my belly pressed to the muck, thinking of guerrillas and commandos and *The Naked and the Dead.* I parted the weeds and squinted the length of the parking lot.

The second car—it was a Trans-Am—was still running, its high beams washing the scene in a lurid stagy light. Tire iron flailing, the greasy bad character was laying into the side of my mother's Bel Air like an avenging demon, his shadow riding up the trunks of the trees. Whomp. Whomp. Whomp-whomp. The other two guys—blond types, in fraternity jackets—were helping out with tree branches and skull-sized boulders. One of them was gathering up bottles, rocks, muck, candy wrappers, used condoms, poptops, and other refuse and pitching it through the window on the driver's side. I could see the fox, a white bulb behind the windshield of the '57 Chevy. "Bobbie," she whined over the thumping, "come *on.*" The greasy character paused a moment, took one good swipe at the left taillight, and then heaved the tire iron halfway across the lake. Then he fired up the '57 and was gone.

Blond head nodded at blond head. One said something to the other, too low for me to catch. They were no doubt thinking that in helping to annihilate my mother's car they'd committed a fairly rash act, and thinking too that there were three bad characters connected with that very car watching them from the woods. Perhaps other possibilities occurred to them as well—police, jail cells, justices of the peace, reparations, lawyers, irate parents, fraternal censure. Whatever they were thinking, they suddenly dropped branches, bottles, and rocks and sprang for their car in unison, as if they'd choreographed it. Five seconds. That's all it took. The engine shrieked, the tires squealed, a cloud of dust rose from the rutted lot and then settled back on darkness.

I don't know how long I lay there, the bad breath of decay all around me, my jacket heavy as a bear, the primordial ooze subtly reconstituting itself to accommodate my upper thighs and testicles. My jaws ached, my knee throbbed, my coccyx was on fire. I contemplated suicide, wondered if I'd need bridgework, scraped the recesses of my brain for some sort of excuse to give my parents—a tree had fallen on the car, I was blindsided by a bread truck, hit and run, vandals had got to it while we were playing chess at Digby's. Then I thought of the dead man. He was probably the only person on the planet worse off than I was. I thought about him, fog on the lake, insects chirring eerily, and felt the tug of fear, felt the darkness opening up inside me like a set of jaws. Who was he, I wondered, this victim of time and circumstance bobbing sorrowfully in the lake at my back. The owner of the chopper, no doubt, a bad older character come to this. Shot during a murky drug deal, drowned while drunkenly frolicking in the lake. Another headline. My car was wrecked; he was dead.

When the eastern half of the sky went from black to cobalt and the trees began to separate themselves from the shadows, I pushed myself up from the mud and stepped out into the open. By now the birds had begun to take over for the crickets, and dew lay slick on the leaves. There was a smell in the air, raw and sweet at the same time, the smell of the sun firing buds and opening blossoms. I contemplated the car. It lay there like a wreck along the highway, like a steel sculpture left over from a vanished civilization. Everything was still. This was nature.

I was circling the car, as dazed and bedraggled as the sole survivor of an air blitz, when Digby and Jeff emerged from the trees behind me. Digby's face was crosshatched with smears of dirt; Jeff's jacket was gone and his shirt was torn across the shoulder. They slouched across the lot, looking sheepish, and silently came up beside me to gape at the ravaged automobile. No one said a

word. After a while Jeff swung open the driver's door and began to
scoop the broken glass and garbage off the seat. I looked at Digby.
He shrugged. "At least they didn't slash the tires," he said.

It was true: the tires were intact. There was no windshield, the
headlights were staved in, and the body looked as if it had been
sledge-hammered for a quarter a shot at the county fair, but the
tires were inflated to regulation pressure. The car was drivable. In
silence, all three of us bent to scrape the mud and shattered glass
from the interior. I said nothing about the biker. When we were
finished, I reached in my pocket for the keys, experienced a nasty
stab of recollection, cursed myself, and turned to search the grass.
I spotted them almost immediately, no more than five feet from
the open door, glinting like jewels in the first tapering shaft of
sunlight. There was no reason to get philosophical about it: I
eased into the seat and turned the engine over.

It was at that precise moment that the silver Mustang with the
flame decals rumbled into the lot. All three of us froze; then
Digby and Jeff slid into the car and slammed the door. We
watched as the Mustang rocked and bobbed across the ruts and
finally jerked to a halt beside the forlorn chopper at the far end of
the lot. "Let's go," Digby said. I hesitated, the Bel Air wheezing
beneath me.

Two girls emerged from the Mustang. Tight jeans, stiletto
heels, hair like frozen fur. They bent over the motorcycle, paced
back and forth aimlessly, glanced once or twice at us, and then
ambled over to where the reeds sprang up in a green fence round
the perimeter of the lake. One of them cupped her hands to her
mouth. "Al," she called. "Hey, Al!"

"Come on," Digby hissed. "Let's get out of here."

But it was too late. The second girl was picking her way across
the lot, unsteady on her heels, looking up at us and then away.
She was older—twenty-five or -six—and as she came closer we
could see there was something wrong with her: she was stoned or
drunk, lurching now and waving her arms for balance. I gripped
the steering wheel as if it were the ejection lever of a flaming jet,
and Digby spat out my name, twice, terse and impatient.

"Hi," the girl said.

We looked at her like zombies, like war veterans, like deaf-and-dumb pencil peddlers.

She smiled, her lips cracked and dry. "Listen," she said, bending from the waist to look in the window, "you guys seen Al?" Her pupils were pinpoints, her eyes glass. She jerked her neck. "That's his bike over there—Al's. You seen him?"

Al. I didn't know what to say. I wanted to get out of the car and retch, I wanted to go home to my parents' house and crawl into bed. Digby poked me in the ribs. "We haven't seen anybody," I said.

The girl seemed to consider this, reaching out a slim veiny arm to brace herself against the car. "No matter," she said, slurring the *t*'s, "he'll turn up." And then, as if she'd just taken stock of the whole scene—the ravaged car and our battered faces, the desolation of the place—she said: "Hey, you guys look like some pretty bad characters—been fightin', huh?" We stared straight ahead, rigid as catatonics. She was fumbling in her pocket and muttering something. Finally she held out a handful of tablets in glassine wrappers: "Hey, you want to party, you want to do some of these with me and Sarah?"

I just looked at her. I thought I was going to cry. Digby broke the silence. "No, thanks," he said, leaning over me. "Some other time."

I put the car in gear and it inched forward with a groan, shaking off pellets of glass like an old dog shedding water after a bath, heaving over the ruts on its worn springs, creeping toward the highway. There was a sheen of sun on the lake. I looked back. The girl was still standing there, watching us, her shoulders slumped, hand outstretched.

Caviar

I ought to tell you right off I didn't go to college. I was on the wrong rung of the socioeconomic ladder, if you know what I mean. My father was a commercial fisherman on the Hudson, till the PCBs got to him, my mother did typing and filing down at the lumberyard, and my grandmother crocheted doilies and comforters for sale to rich people. Me, I took over my father's trade. I inherited the shack at the end of the pier, the leaky fourteen-foot runabout with the thirty-five-horse Evinrude motor and the seine that's been in the family for three generations. Also, I got to move into the old man's house when he passed on, and he left me his stamp collection and the keys to his '62 Rambler, rusted through till it looked like a gill net hung out to dry.

Anyway, it's a living. Almost. And if I didn't go to college I do read a lot, magazines mostly, but books on ecology and science

too. Maybe it was the science part that did me in. You see, I'm the
first one around here—I mean, me and Marie are the first ones—
to have a baby this new way, where you can't have it on your own.
Dr. Ziss said not to worry about it, a little experiment, think of it
as a gift from heaven.

Some gift.

But don't get me wrong, I'm not complaining. What happens
happens, and I'm as guilty as anybody, I admit it. It's just that
when the guys at the Flounder Inn are sniggering in their beer
and Marie starts looking at me like I'm a toad or something,
you've got to put things in perspective, you've got to realize that it
was her all along, she's the one that started it.

"I want a baby," was how she put it.

It was April, raw and wet. Crocuses and dead man's fingers
were poking through the dirt along the walk, and the stripers
were running. I'd just stepped in the door, beat, chilled to the
teeth, when she made her announcement. I went straight for the
coffeepot. "Can't afford it," I said.

She didn't plead or try to reason with me. All she did was repeat
herself in a matter-of-fact tone, as if she were telling me about
some new drapes or a yard sale, and then she marched through
the kitchen and out the back door. I sipped at my coffee and
watched her through the window. She had a shovel. She was
burying something. Deep. When she came back in, her nose was
running a bit and her eyes were crosshatched with tiny red lines.

"What were you doing out there?" I asked.

Her chin was crumpled, her hair was wild. "Burying something."

I waited while she fussed with the teapot, my eyebrows arched
like question marks. Ten seconds ticked by. "Well, what?"

"My diaphragm."

I've known Marie since high school. We were engaged for five
years while she worked for *Reader's Digest* and we'd been married for three and a half when she decided she wanted some off-
spring. At first I wasn't too keen on the idea, but then I had to
admit she was right: the time had come. Our lovemaking had al-

ways been lusty and joyful, but after she buried the diaphragm it
became tender, intense, purposeful. We tried. For months we
tried. I'd come in off the river, reeking of the creamy milt and
silver roe that floated two inches deep in the bottom of the boat
while fifty- and sixty-pound stripers gasped their last, come in like
a wild bull or something, and Marie would be waiting for me upstairs in her nightie and we'd do it before dinner, and then again
after. Nothing happened.

Somewhere around July or August, the sweet blueclaw crabs
crawling up the riverbed like an army on maneuvers and the
humid heat lying over the valley like a cupped hand, Marie went
to Sister Eleazar of the Coptic Brotherhood of Ethiop. Sister Eleazar was a black woman, six feet tall at least, in a professor's gown
and a fez with a red tassel. Leroy Lent's wife swore by her. Six
years Leroy and his wife had been going at it, and then they went
to Sister Eleazar and had a pair of twins. Marie thought it was
worth a try, so I drove her down there.

The Coptic Brotherhood of Ethiop occupied a lime-green building the size of a two-car garage with a steeple and cross pinned to
the roof. Sister Eleazar answered our knock scowling, a little crescent of egg yolk on her chin. "What you want?" she said.

Standing there in the street, a runny-eyed Chihuahua sniffing
at my heels, I listened to Marie explain our problem and watched
the crescent of egg on Sister Eleazar's face fracture with her smile.
"Ohhh," she said, "well, why didn't you say so? Come own in,
come own in."

There was one big room inside, poorly lit. Old bottom-bur-
nished pews stretched along three of the four walls and there was
a big shiny green table in the center of the floor. The table was
heaped with religious paraphernalia—silver salvers and chalices
and tinted miniatures of a black man with a crown dwarfing his
head. A cot and an icebox huddled against the back wall, which
was decorated with magazine clippings of Africa. "Right here,
sugar," Sister Eleazar said, leading Marie up to the table. "Now,
you take off your coat and your dress, and less ex-amine them
wombs."

Marie handed me her coat, and then her tight blue dress with the little white clocks on it, while Sister Eleazar cleared the chalices and whatnot off the table. The Chihuahua had followed us in, and now it sprang up onto the cot with a sigh and buried its nose in its paws. The room stank of dog.

"All right," Sister Eleazar said, turning back to Marie, "you climb up own the table now and stretch yourself out so Sister 'Leazar can listen to your insides and say a prayer over them barren wombs." Marie complied with a nervous smile, and the black woman leaned forward to press an ear to her abdomen. I watched the tassel of Sister Eleazar's fez splay out over Marie's rib cage and I began to get excited: the place dark and exotic, Marie in brassiere and panties, laid out on the table like a sacrificial virgin. Then the sister was mumbling something—a prayer, I guess—in a language I'd never heard before. Marie looked embarrassed. "Don't you worry about nothin'," Sister Eleazar said, looking up at me and winking. "I got just the thing."

She fumbled around underneath the cot for a minute, then came back to the table with a piece of blue chalk—the same as they use in geography class to draw rivers and lakes on the blackboard—and a big yellow can of Colman's dry mustard. She bent over Marie like a heart surgeon, and then, after a few seconds of deliberation, made a blue X on Marie's lower abdomen and said, "Okay, honey, you can get up now."

I watched Marie shrug into her dress, thinking the whole thing was just a lot of superstitious mumbo jumbo and pisantry, when I felt Sister Eleazar's fingers on my arm; she dipped her head and led me out the front door. The sky was overcast. I could smell rain in the air. "Listen," the black woman whispered, handing me the can of mustard, "the problem ain't with her, it's with you. Must be you ain't penetratin' deep enough." I looked into her eyes, trying to keep my face expressionless. Her voice dropped. "What you do is this: make a plaster of this here mustard and rub it on your parts before you go into her, and it'll force out that 'jaculation like a torpedo coming out a submarine—know what I mean?" Then she winked. Marie was at the door. A man with a hoe was digging at his garden in the next yard over. "Oh yeah," the sister said, hold-

ing out her hand, "you want to make a donation to the Brotherhood, that'll be eleven dollars and fifty cent."

I never told Marie about the mustard—it was too crazy. All I
said was that the sister had told me to give her a mustard plaster
on the stomach an hour after we had intercourse—to help the
seeds take. It didn't work, of course. Nothing worked. But the
years at *Reader's Digest* had made Marie a superstitious woman,
and I was willing to go along with just about anything as long as it
made her feel better. One night I came to bed and she was
perched naked on the edge of the footstool, wound round three
times with a string of garlic. "I thought that was for vampires?" I
said. She just parted her lips and held out her arms.
      In the next few weeks she must have tried every quack remedy
in the book. She kept a toad in a clay pot under the bed, ate soup
composed of fish eyes and roe, drank goat's milk and cod-liver oil,
and filled the medicine chest with elixirs made from nimble weed
and rhinoceros horn. Once I caught her down in the basement,
dancing in the nude round a live rooster. I was eating meat three
meals a day to keep my strength up. Then one night I came across
an article about test-tube babies in *Science Digest.* I studied the
pictures for a long while, especially the one at the end of the
article that showed this English couple, him with a bald dome and
her fat as a sow, with their little test-tube son. Then I called
Marie.

Dr. Ziss took us right away. He sympathized with our plight, he
said, and would do all he could to help us. First he would have to
run some tests to see just what the problem was and whether it
could be corrected surgically. He led us into the examining room
and looked into our eyes and ears, tapped our knees, measured
our blood pressure. He drew blood, squinted at my sperm under
a microscope, took X rays, did a complete pelvic exam on Marie.
His nurse was Irene Goddard, lived up the street from us. She
was a sour, square-headed woman in her fifties with little vertical
lines etched around her lips. She prodded and poked and pricked
us and then had us fill out twenty or thirty pages of forms that

asked about everything from bowel movements to whether my grandmother had any facial hair. Two weeks later I got a phone call. The doctor wanted to see us.

We'd hardly got our jackets off when Mrs. Goddard, with a look on her face like she was about to pull the switch at Sing Sing, showed us into the doctor's office. I should tell you that Dr. Ziss is a young man—about my age, I guess—with narrow shoulders, a little clipped mustache, and a woman's head of hair that he keeps brushing back with his hand. Anyway, he was sitting behind his desk sifting through a pile of charts and lab reports when we walked in. "Sit down," he said. "I'm afraid I have some bad news for you." Marie went pale, like she did the time the state troopers called about her mother's accident; her ankles swayed over her high heels and she fell back into the chair as if she'd been shoved. I thought she was going to cry, but the doctor forestalled her. He smiled, showing off all those flossed and fluoridated teeth: "I've got some good news too."

The bad news was that Marie's ovaries were shot. She was suffering from the Stein-Leventhal syndrome, he said, and was unable to produce viable ova. He put it to us straight: "She's infertile, and there's nothing we can do about it. Even if we had the facilities and the know-how, test-tube reproduction would be out of the question."

Marie was stunned. I stared down at the linoleum for a second and listened to her sniffling, then took her hand.

Dr. Ziss leaned across the desk and pushed back a stray lock of hair. "But there is an alternative."

We both looked at him.

"Have you considered a surrogate mother? A young woman who'd be willing to impregnate herself artificially with the husband's semen—for a fee, of course—and then deliver the baby to the wife at the end of the term." He was smoothing his mustache. "It's being done all over the country. And if Mrs. Trimpie pads herself during her 'pregnancy' and 'delivers' in the city, none of your neighbors need ever know that the child isn't wholly and naturally yours."

My mind was racing. I was bombarded with selfish and acquisitive thoughts, seething with scorn for Marie—*she* was the one, *she* was defective, not me—bursting to exercise my God-given right to a child and heir. It's true, it really is—you never want something so much as when somebody tells you you can't have it. I found myself thinking aloud: "So it would really be half ours, and . . . and half—"

"That's right, Mr. Trimpie. And I have already contacted a young woman on your behalf, should you be interested."

I looked at Marie. Her eyes were watering. She gave me a weak smile and pressed my hand.

"She's Caucasian, of course, attractive, fit, very bright: a first-year medical student in need of funds to continue her education."

"Um, uh," I fumbled for the words, "how much; I mean, if we decide to go along with it, how much would it cost?"

The doctor was ready for this one. "Ten thousand dollars," he said without hesitation, "plus hospital costs."

Two days later there was a knock at the door. A girl in peacoat and blue jeans stood there, flanked by a pair of scuffed aquamarine suitcases held shut with masking tape. She looked to be about sixteen, stunted and bony and pale, cheap mother-of-pearl stars for earrings, her red hair short and spiky, as if she were letting a crewcut grow out. I couldn't help thinking of those World War II movies where they shave the actresses' heads for consorting with the Germans; I couldn't help thinking of waifs and wanderers and runaway teen-agers. Dr. Ziss's gunmetal Mercedes sat at the curb, clouds of exhaust tugging at the tailpipe in the chill morning air; he waved, and then ground away with a crunch of gravel. "Hi," the girl said, extending her hand, "I'm Wendy."

It had all been arranged. Dr. Ziss thought it would be a good idea if the mother-to-be came to stay with us two weeks or so before the "procedure," to give us a chance to get to know one another, and then maybe stay on with us through the first couple of months so we could experience the pregnancy firsthand; when she began to show she'd move into an apartment on the other side of town, so as not to arouse any suspicion among the neighbors. He was delicate about the question of money, figuring a commercial fisherman and a part-time secretary, with no college and driving a beat-up Rambler, might not exactly be rolling in surplus capital. But the money wasn't a problem really. There was the insurance payoff from Marie's mother—she'd been blindsided by a semi coming off the ramp on the thruway—and the thirty-five hundred I'd got for delivering spawning stripers to Con Ed so they could hatch fish to replace the ones sucked into the screens at the nuclear plant. It was sitting in the County Trust, collecting five and a quarter percent, against the day some emergency came up. Well, this was it. I closed out the account.

The doctor took his fee and explained that the girl would get five thousand dollars on confirmation of pregnancy, and the balance when she delivered. Hospital costs would run about fifteen hundred dollars, barring complications. We shook hands on it, and Marie and I signed a form. I figured I could work nights at the bottling plant if I was strapped.

Now, with the girl standing there before me, I couldn't help feeling a stab of disappointment—she was pretty enough, I guess, but I'd expected something a little more, well, substantial. And red hair. It was a letdown. Deep down I'd been hoping for a blonde, one of those Scandinavian types you see in the cigarette ads. Anyway, I told her I was glad to meet her, and then showed her up to the spare room, which I'd cleaned up and outfitted with a chest of drawers, a bed and a Salvation Army desk, and some cheery knickknacks. I asked her if I could get her a bite to eat, Marie being at work and me waiting around for the tide to go out. She was sitting on the bed, looking tired; she hadn't even bothered to glance out the window at the view of Croton Bay. "Oh yeah," she said after a minute, as if she'd been asleep or daydreaming, "Yeah, that would be nice." Her eyes were gray, the color of drift ice on the river. She called me Nathaniel, soft and formal, like a breathless young schoolteacher taking attendance. Marie never called me anything but Nat, and the guys at the marina settled for Ace. "Have you got a sandwich, maybe? And a cup of hot Nestlé's? I'd really like that, Nathaniel."

I went down and fixed her a BLT, her soft syllables tingling in my ears like a kiss. Dr. Ziss had called her an "oh pear" girl, which

I guess referred to her shape. When she'd slipped out of her coat I saw that there was more to her than I'd thought—not much across the top, maybe, but sturdy in the hips and thighs. I couldn't help thinking it was a good sign, but then I had to check myself: I was looking at her like a horse breeder or something.

She was asleep when I stepped in with the sandwich and hot chocolate. I shook her gently and she started up with a gasp, her eyes darting round the room as if she'd forgotten where she was. "Oh yes, yes, thanks," she said, in that maddening, out-of-breath, little girl's voice. I sat on the edge of the desk and watched her eat, gratified to see that her teeth were strong and even, and her nose just about right. "So you're a medical student, Dr. Ziss tells me."

"Hm-hmm," she murmured, chewing. "First-year. I'm going to take the spring semester off, I mean for the baby and all—"

This was the first mention of our contract, and it fell over the conversation like a lead balloon. She hesitated, and I turned red. Here I was, alone in the house with a stranger, a pretty girl, and she was going to have my baby.

She went on, skirting the embarrassment, trying to brighten her voice. "I mean, I love it and all—med school—but it's a grind already and I really don't see how I can afford the tuition, without, without"—she looked up at me—"without your help."

I didn't know what to say. I stared into her eyes for a minute and felt strangely excited, powerful, like a pasha interviewing a new candidate for the harem. Then I picked up the china sturgeon on the desk and turned it over in my hands. "I didn't go to college," I said. And then, as if I were apologizing, "I'm a fisherman."

A cold rain was falling the day the three of us drove down to Dr. Ziss's for the "procedure." The maples were turning, the streets splashed with red and gold, slick, glistening, the whole world a cathedral. I felt humbled somehow, respectful in the face of life and the progress of the generations of man: *My seed is going to take hold,* I kept thinking. *In half an hour I'll be a father.* Marie and Wendy, on the other hand, seemed oblivious to the whole thing, chattering away like a sewing circle, talking about shoes and needlepoint and some actor's divorce. They'd hit it off pretty well, the two of them, sitting in the kitchen over coffee at night, going to movies and thrift shops together, trading gossip, looking up at me and giggling when I stepped into the room. Though Wendy didn't do much around the house—didn't do much more than lie in bed and stare at textbooks—I don't think Marie really minded. She was glad for the company, and there was something more too, of course: Wendy was making a big sacrifice for us. Both of us were deeply grateful.

Dr. Ziss was all smiles that afternoon, pumping my hand, kissing the girls, ushering us into his office like an impresario on opening night. Mrs. Goddard was more restrained. She shot me an icy look, as if I was conspiring to overthrow the Pope or corrupt Girl Scouts or something. Meanwhile, the doctor leaned toward Marie and Wendy and said something I didn't quite catch, and suddenly they were all three of them laughing like Canada geese. Were they laughing at me, I wondered, all at once feeling self-conscious and vulnerable, the odd man out. Dr. Ziss, I noticed, had his arm around Wendy's waist.

If I felt left out, I didn't have time to brood over it. Because Mrs. Goddard had me by the elbow and she was marching me down the hallway to the men's room, where she handed me a condom sealed in tinfoil and a couple of tattered girlie magazines. I didn't need the magazines. Just the thought of what was going to happen in the next room—Marie had asked the doctor if she could do the insemination herself—gave me an erection like a tire iron. I pictured Wendy leaning back on the examining table in a little white smock, nothing underneath, and Marie, my big loving wife, with this syringelike thing . . . that's all it took. I was out of the bathroom in sixty seconds, the wet condom tucked safely away in a sterilized jar.

Afterward, we shared a bottle of pink champagne and a lasagna dinner at Mama's Pasta House. My treat.

One morning, about a month later, I was lying in bed next to Marie and I heard Wendy pad down the hallway to the bathroom.

The house was still, and a soft gray light clung to the window sill like a blanket. I was thinking of nothing, or maybe I was thinking of striped bass, sleek and silver, how they ride up out of the deep like pieces of a dream. Next thing I heard was the sound of gagging. Morning sickness, I thought, picking up on a phrase from one of the countless baby books scattered round the house, and suddenly, inexplicably, I was doubled over myself. "Aaaaargh," Wendy gasped, the sound echoing through the house, "aaaargh," and it felt like somebody was pulling my stomach inside out.

At breakfast, she was pale and haggard, her hair greasy and her eyes puffed out. She tried to eat a piece of dry toast, but wound up spitting it into her hand. I couldn't eat, either. Same thing the next day, and the next: she was sick, I was sick. I'd pull the cord on the outboard and the first whiff of exhaust would turn my stomach and I'd have to lean over and puke in the river. Or I'd haul the gill nets up off the bottom and the exertion would nearly kill me. I called the doctor.

"Sympathetic pregnancy," he said, his voice cracking at the far end of a bad connection. "Perfectly normal. The husband identifies with the wife's symptoms."

"But I'm not her husband."

"Husband, father: what difference does it make. You're it."

I thought about that. Thought about it when Wendy and I began to eat like the New York Jets at the training table, thought about it nights at the bottling plant, thought about it when Wendy came into the living room in her underwear one evening and showed us the hard white bulge that was already beginning to open her navel up like a flower. Marie was watching some soppy hospital show on TV; I was reading about the dead water between Manhattan and Staten Island—nothing living there, not even eels. "Look," Wendy said, an angels-in-heaven smile on her face, "it's starting to show." Marie got up and embraced her. I grinned like an idiot, thrilled at the way the panties grabbed her thighs— white nylon with dancing pink flowers—and how her little pointed breasts were beginning to strain at the brassiere. I wanted to put my tongue in her navel.

Next day, while Marie was at work, I tapped on Wendy's door.

"Come on in," she said. She was wearing a housecoat, Japanese-y, with dragons and pagodas on it, propped up against the pillows reading an anatomy text. I told her I didn't feel like going down to the river and wondered if she wanted anything. She put the book down and looked at me like a pat of butter sinking into a halibut steak. "Yes," she said, stretching it to two syllables, "as a matter of fact I do." Then she unbuttoned the robe. Later she smiled at me and said: "So what did we need the doctor for, anyway?"

If Marie suspected anything, she didn't show it. I think she was too caught up in the whole thing to have an evil thought about either one of us. I mean, she doted on Wendy, hung on her every word, came home from work each night and shut herself up in Wendy's room for an hour or more. I could hear them giggling. When I asked her what the deal was, Marie just shrugged. "You know," she said, "the usual—girls' talk and such." The shared experience had made them close, closer than sisters, and sometimes I would think of us as one big happy family. But I stopped short of telling Marie what was going on when she was out of the house. Once, years ago, I'd had a fling with a girl we'd known in high school—an arrow-faced little fox with starched hair and raccoon eyes. It had been brief and strictly biological, and then the girl had moved to Ohio. Marie never forgot it. Just the mention of Ohio—even so small a thing as the TV weatherman describing a storm over the Midwest—would set her off.

I'd like to say I was torn, but I wasn't. I didn't want to hurt Marie—she was my wife, my best friend, I loved and respected her—and yet there was Wendy, with her breathy voice and gray eyes, bearing my child. The thought of it, of my son floating around in his own little sea just behind the sweet bulge of her belly . . . well, it inflamed me, got me mad with lust and passion and spiritual love too. Wasn't Wendy as much my wife as Marie? Wasn't marriage, at bottom, simply a tool for procreating the species? Hadn't Sarah told Abraham to go in unto Hagar? Looking back on it, I guess Wendy let me make love to her because maybe she was bored and a little horny, lying around in a negligee day and night and studying all that anatomy. She sure didn't feel the

way I did—if I know anything, I know that now. But at the time I
didn't think of it that way, I didn't think at all. Surrogate mother,
surrogate wife. I couldn't get enough of her.

Everything changed when Marie taped a feather bolster around
her waist and our "boarder" had to move over to Depew Street.
("Don't know what happened," I told the guys down at the Flounder, "she just up and moved out. Low on bucks, I guess." Nobody
so much as looked up from their beer until one of the guys mentioned the Knicks game and Alex DeFazio turned to me and said,
"So you got a bun in the oven, is what I hear.") I was at a loss.
What with Marie working full-time now, I found myself stuck in
the house, alone, with nothing much to do except wear a path in
the carpet and eat my heart out. I could walk down to the river,
but it was February and nothing was happening, so I'd wind up at
the Flounder Inn with my elbows on the bar, watching the mollies
and swordtails bump into the sides of the aquarium, hoping somebody would give me a lift across town. Of course Marie and I
would drive over to Wendy's after dinner every couple of days or
so, and I could talk to her on the telephone till my throat went
dry—but it wasn't the same. Even the few times I did get over
there in the day, I could feel it. We'd make love, but she seemed
shy and reluctant, as if she were performing a duty or something.
"What's wrong?" I asked her. "Nothing," she said. It was as if
someone had cut a neat little hole in the center of my life.

One time, a stiff windy day in early March, I couldn't stand the
sight of four walls any more and I walked the six miles across town
and all the way out Depew Street. It was an ugly day. Clouds like
steel wool, a dirty crust of ice underfoot, dog turds preserved like
icons in the receding snowbanks. The whole way over there I kept
thinking up various scenarios: Wendy and I would take the bus for
California, then write Marie to come join us; we'd fly to the Virgin
Islands and raise the kid on the beach; Marie would have an accident. When I got there, Dr. Ziss's Mercedes was parked out
front. I thought that was pretty funny, him being there in the
middle of the day, but then I told myself he was her doctor after
all. I turned around and walked home.

Nathaniel Jr. was born in New York City at the end of June, nine pounds, one ounce, with a fluff of orange hair and milky gray eyes. Wendy never looked so beautiful. The hospital bed was cranked up, her hair, grown out now, was fresh-washed and brushed, she was wearing the turquoise earrings I'd given her. Marie, meanwhile, was experiencing the raptures of the saints. She gave me a look of pride and fulfillment, rocking the baby in her arms, cooing and beaming. I stole a glance at Wendy. There were two wet circles where her nipples touched the front of her gown. When she put Nathaniel to her breast I thought I was going to faint from the beauty of it, and from something else too: jealousy. I wanted her, then and there.

Dr. Ziss was on the scene, of course, all smiles, as if he'd been responsible for the whole thing. He pecked Marie's cheek, patted the baby's head, shook my hand, and bent low to kiss Wendy on the lips. I handed him a cigar. Three days later Wendy had her five thousand dollars, the doctor and the hospital had been paid off, and Marie and I were back in Westchester with our son. Wendy had been dressed in a loose summer gown and sandals when I gave her the check. I remember she was sitting there on a lacquered bench, cradling the baby, the hospital corridor lit up like a clerestory with sunbeams. There were tears—mainly Marie's—and promises to keep in touch. She handed over Nathaniel as if he was a piece of meat or a sack of potatoes, no regrets. She and Marie embraced, she rubbed her cheek against mine and made a perfunctory little kissing noise, and then she was gone.

I held out for a week. Changing diapers, heating formula, snuggling up with Marie and little Nathaniel, trying to feel whole again. But I couldn't. Every time I looked at my son I saw Wendy, the curl of the lips, the hair, the eyes, the pout—in my distraction, I even thought I heard something of her voice in his gasping howls. Marie was asleep, the baby in her arms. I backed the car out and headed for Depew Street.

The first thing I saw when I rounded the corner onto Depew was the doctor's Mercedes, unmistakable, gunmetal gray, gleaming at the curb like a slap in the face. I was so startled to see it there I almost ran into it. What was this, some kind of postpartum emergency or something? It was 10:00 A.M. Wendy's curtains were drawn. As I stamped across the lawn my fingers began to tremble like they do when I'm tugging at the net and I can feel something tugging back.

The door was open. Ziss was sitting there in T-shirt and jeans, watching cartoons on TV and sipping at a glass of milk. He pushed the hair back from his brow and gave me a sheepish grin. "David?" Wendy called from the back room. "David? Are you going out?" I must have looked like the big loser on a quiz show or something, because Ziss, for once, didn't have anything to say. He just shrugged his shoulders. Wendy's voice, breathy as a flute, came at us again: "Because if you are, get me some sweetcakes and yogurt, and maybe a couple of corn muffins, okay? I'm hungry as a bear."

Ziss got up and walked to the bedroom door, mumbled something I couldn't hear, strode past me without a glance and went on out the back door. I watched him bend for a basketball, dribble around in the dirt, and then cock his arm for a shot at an imaginary basket. On the TV, Sylvester the cat reached into a trash can and pulled out a fish stripped to the bones. Wendy was standing in the doorway. She had nothing to say.

"Look, Wendy," I began. I felt betrayed, cheated, felt as if I was the brunt of a joke between this girl in the housecoat and the curly-headed hotshot fooling around on the lawn. What was his angle, I wondered, heart pounding at my chest, what was hers? "I suppose you two had a good laugh over me, huh?"

She was pouting, the spoiled child. "I fulfilled my part of the bargain."

She had. I got what I'd paid for. But all that had changed, couldn't she see that? I didn't want a son, I didn't want Marie; I wanted her. I told her so. She said nothing. "You've got something going with Ziss, right?" I said, my voice rising. "All along, right?"

She looked tired, looked as if she'd been up for a hundred nights running. I watched her shuffle across the room into the kitchenette, glance into the refrigerator, and come up with a jar of

jam. She made herself a sandwich, licking the goo from her fingers, and then she told me I stank of fish. She said she couldn't
have a lasting relationship with me because of Marie.

"That's a lot of crap, and you know it." I was shouting. Ziss, fifty
feet away, turned to look through the open door.

"All right. It's because we're—" She put the sandwich down,
wiped a smear of jelly from her lip. "Because we move in different
circles."

"You mean because I'm not some fancy-ass doctor, because I
didn't go to college."

She nodded. Slow and deliberate, no room for argument, she
held my eyes and nodded.

I couldn't help it. Something just came loose in my head, and
the next second I was out the door, knocking Ziss into the dirt. He
kicked and scratched, tried to bite me on the wrist, but I just took
hold of his hair and laid into his face while Wendy ran around in
her Japanese housecoat, screeching like a cat in heat. By the time
the police got there I'd pretty well closed up both his eyes and
rearranged his dental work. Wendy was bending over him with a
bottle of rubbing alcohol when they put the cuffs on me.

Next morning there was a story in the paper. Marie sent Alex
DeFazio down with the bail money, and then she wouldn't let me
in the house. I banged on the door halfheartedly, then tried one of
the windows, only to find she'd nailed it shut. When I saw that, I
was just about ready to explode, but then I figured what the hell
and fired up the Rambler in a cloud of blue smoke. Cops, dogs,
kids, and pedestrians be damned, I ran it like a stock car eight
blocks down to the dock and left it steaming in the parking lot.
Five minutes later I was planing across the river, a wide brown
furrow fanning out behind me.

This was my element, sun, wind, water, life pared down to the
basics. Gulls hung in the air like puppets on a wire, spray flew up
in my face, the shore sank back into my wake until docks and
pleasure boats and clapboard houses were swallowed up and I was
alone on the broad gray back of the river. After a while I eased up
on the throttle and began scanning the surface for the buoys that

marked my gill nets, working by rote, the tight-wound spool in my chest finally beginning to pay out. Then I spotted them, white and red, jogged by the waves. I cut the engine, coasted in and caught hold of the nearest float.

Wendy, I thought, as I hauled at the ropes, ten years, twenty-five, a lifetime: every time I look at my son I'll see your face. Hand over hand, Wendy, Wendy, Wendy, the net heaving up out of the swirling brown depths with its pounds of flesh. But then I wasn't thinking about Wendy any more, or Marie or Nathaniel Jr.—I was thinking about the bottom of the river, I was thinking about fins and scales and cold lidless eyes. The instant I touched the lead rope I knew I was on to something. This time of year it would be sturgeon, big as logs, long-nosed and barbeled, coasting up the riverbed out of some dim watery past, anadromous, prepro-grammed, homing in on their spawning grounds like guided mis-siles. Just then I felt a pulsing in the soles of my sneakers and turned to glance up at the Day Liner, steaming by on its way to Bear Mountain, hundreds of people with picnic baskets and coolers, waving. I jerked at the net like a penitent.

There was a single sturgeon in the net, tangled up like a ball of string. It was dead. I strained to haul the thing aboard, six feet long, two hundred pounds. Cold from the depths, still supple, it hadn't been dead more than an hour—while I banged at my own front door, locked out, it had been thrashing in the dark, locked in. The gulls swooped low, mocking me. I had to cut it out of the net.

Back at the dock I got one of the beer drinkers to give me a hand and we dragged the fish over to the skinning pole. With sturgeon, we hang them by the gills from the top of a ten-foot pole, and then we peel back the scutes like you'd peel a banana. Four or five of the guys stood there watching me, nobody saying anything. I cut all the way round the skin just below the big stiff gill plates and then made five vertical slits the length of the fish. Flies settled on the blade of the knife. The sun beat at the back of my head. I remember there was a guy standing there, somebody I'd never seen before, a guy in a white shirt with a kid about eight or so. The kid was holding a fishing pole. They stepped back, both of them, when I tore the first strip of skin from the fish.

Sturgeon peels back with a raspy, nails-on-the-blackboard sort of sound, reminds me of tearing up sheets or ripping bark from a tree. I tossed the curling strips of leather in a pile, flies sawing away at the air, the big glistening pink carcass hanging there like a skinned deer, blood and flesh. Somebody handed me a beer: it stuck to my hand and I drained it in a gulp. Then I turned to gut the fish, me a doctor, the knife a scalpel, and suddenly I was digging into the vent like Jack the Ripper, slitting it all the way up to the gills in a single violent motion.

"How do you like that?" the man in the white shirt said. "She's got eggs in her."

I glanced down. There they were, wet, beaded, and gray, millions of them, the big clusters tearing free and dropping to the ground like ripe fruit. I cupped my hands and held the trembling mass of it there against the gashed belly, fifty or sixty pounds of the stuff, slippery roe running through my fingers like the silver coins from a slot machine, like a jackpot.

Ike and Nina

The years have put a lid on it, the principals passed into oblivion. I think I can now, in good conscience, reveal the facts surrounding one of the most secretive and spectacular love affairs of our time: the *affaire de coeur* that linked the thirty-fourth president of the United States and the then first lady of the Soviet Union. Yes: the eagle and the bear, defrosting the Cold War with the heat of their passion, Dwight D. Eisenhower—Ike—virile, dashing, athletic, in the arms of Madame Nina Khrushcheva, the svelte and seductive schoolmistress from the Ukraine. Behind closed doors, in embassy restrooms and hotel corridors, they gave themselves over to the urgency of their illicit love, while the peace and stability of the civilized world hung in the balance.

Because of the sensitive—indeed sensational—nature of what follows, I have endeavored to tell my story as dispassionately as possible, and must say in my own defense that my sole interest in coming forward at this late date is to provide succeeding genera-tions with a keener insight into the events of those tumultuous times. Some of you will be shocked by what I report here, others moved. Still others—the inevitable naysayers and skeptics—may find it difficult to believe. But before you turn a deaf ear, let me remind you how unthinkable it once seemed to credit reports of Errol Flynn's flirtation with Nazis and homosexuals, FDR's thirty-year obsession with Lucy Mercer, or Ted Kennedy's over-mastering desire for an ingenuous campaign worker eleven years his junior. The truth is often hard to swallow. But no historian worth his salt, no self-respecting journalist, no faithful eyewitness to the earth-shaking and epoch-making events of human history has ever blanched at it.

Here then, is the story of Ike and Nina.

In September of 1959, I was assistant to one of Ike's junior staffers, thirty-one years old, schooled in international law, and a consultant to the Slavic-languages program at one of our major universities.* I'd had very little contact with the president, had in fact laid eyes on him but twice in the eighteen months I'd worked for the White House (the first time, I was looking for a drinking fountain when I caught a glimpse of him—a single flash of his radiant brow—huddled in a back room with Foster Dulles and Andy Goodpaster; a week later, as I was hurrying down a corridor with a stack of reports for shredding, I spotted him slipping out a service entrance with his golf clubs). Like dozens of bright, ambi-tious young men apprenticed to the mighty, I was at this stage of my career a mere functionary, a paper shuffler, so deeply buried in the power structure I must actually have ranked below the pastry chef's croissant twister. I was good—I had no doubt of it— but I was as yet untried, and for all I knew unnoticed. You can imagine my surprise when early one morning I was summoned to the Oval Office.

*I choose not to name it, just as I decline to reveal my actual identity here, for obvious reasons.

It was muggy, and though the corridors hummed with the gentle ministrations of the air conditioners, my shirt was soaked through by the time I reached the door of the president's inner sanctum. A crewcut ramrod in uniform swung open the door, barked out my name, and ushered me into the room. I was puzzled, apprehensive, awed; the door closed behind me with a soft click and I found myself in the Oval Office, alone with the president of the United States. Ike was standing at the window, gazing out at the trees, whistling "The Flirtation Waltz," and turning a book of crossword puzzles over in his hands. "Well," he said, turning to me and extending his hand, "Mr. Paderewski, is that right?"

"Yes sir," I said. He pronounced it "Paderooski."*

"Well," he repeated, taking me in with those steely blue eyes of his as he sauntered across the room and tossed the book on his desk like a slugger casually dropping his bat after knocking the ball out of the park. He looked like a golf pro, a gymnast, a competitor, a man who could come at you with both hands and a nine iron to boot. Don't be taken in by all those accounts of his declining health—I saw him there that September morning in the Oval Office, broad-shouldered and trim-waisted, lithe and commanding. Successive heart attacks and a bout with ileitis hadn't slowed the old warrior a bit. A couple of weeks short of his sixty-ninth birthday, and he was jaunty as a high-schooler on prom night. Which brings me back to the reason for my summons.

"You're a good egg, aren't you, Paderewski?" Ike asked.

I replied in the affirmative.

"And you speak Russian, is that right?"

"Yes, sir, Mr. President—and Polish, Sorbian, Serbo-Croatian, and Slovene as well."

He grunted, and eased his haunch down on the corner of the desk. The light from the window played off his head till it glowed like a second sun. "You're aware of the upcoming visit of the Soviet premier and his, uh, wife?"

---

*This is a pseudonym I've adopted as a concession to dramatic necessity in regard to the present narrative.

I nodded.

"Good, that's very good, Paderewski, because as of this moment I'm appointing you my special aide for the duration of that visit." He looked at me as if I were some odd and insignificant form of life that might bear further study under the microscope, looked at me like the man who had driven armies across Europe and laid Hitler in his grave. "Everything that happens, every order I give you, is to be held strictly confidential—top secret—is that understood?"

I was filled with a sense of mission, importance, dignity. Here I was, elevated from the ranks to lend my modest talents to the service of the first citizen of the nation, the commander-in-chief himself. "Understood, Mr. President," I said, fighting the impulse to salute.

This seemed to relax him, and he leaned back on the desk and told me a long, involved story about an article he'd come across in the *National Geographic*, something about Egyptian pyramids and how the members of a pharaoh's funeral procession were either blinded on the spot or entombed with their leaders—something along those lines. I didn't know what to make of it. So I put on my meditative look, and when he finished I flashed him a smile that would have melted ice.

Ike smiled back.

By now, of course, I'm sure you've guessed just what my special duties were to consist of—I was to be the president's liaison with Mrs. Khrushchev, a go-between, a pillow smoother and excuse maker: I was to be Ike's panderer. Looking back on it, I can say in all honesty that I did not then, nor do I now, feel any qualms whatever regarding my role in the affair. No, I feel privileged to have witnessed one of the grand passions of our time, a love both tender and profane, a love that smoldered beneath the watchful eyes of two embattled nations and erupted in an explosion of passionate embraces and hungry kisses.

Ike, as I was later to learn, had first fallen under the spell of Madame K. in 1945, during his triumphal visit to Moscow after the fall of the Third Reich. It was the final day of his visit, a mo-

mentous day, the day Japan had thrown in the towel and the great
war was at long last ended. Ambassador Harriman arranged a reception and buffet supper at the U.S. embassy by way of celebra-
tion, and to honor Ike and his comrade-in-arms, Marshal Zhukov.
In addition to Ike's small party, a number of high-ranking Russian
military men and politicos turned out for what evolved into an
uproarious evening of singing, dancing, and congratulatory back-
slapping. Corks popped, vodka flowed, the exuberant clamor of
voices filled the room. And then Nina Khrushcheva stepped
through the door.

Ike was stunned. Suddenly nothing existed for him—not
Zhukov, not Moscow, not Harriman, the armistice, or "The Song
of the Volga Boatmen," which an instant before had been ringing
in his ears—there was only this vision in the doorway, simple,
unadorned, elegant, this true princess of the earth. He didn't
know what to say, didn't know who she was; the only words of
Russian he could command—*zdrav'st* and *spasibo**—flew to his
lips like an unanswered prayer. He begged Harriman for an introduction, and then spent the rest of the evening at her side, the
affable Ike, gazing into the quiet depths of her rich mud-brown
eyes, entranced. He didn't need an interpreter.

It would be ten long years before their next meeting, years that
would see the death of Stalin, the ascendancy of Khrushchev, and
Ike's own meteoric rise to political prominence as the thirty-fourth
president of the United States. Through all that time, through all
the growing enmity between their countries, Ike and Nina cher-
ished that briefest memory of one another. For his part, Ike felt
he had seen a vision, sipped from the cup of perfection, and that
no other woman could hope to match it—not Mamie, not Ann
Whitman, not even his old flame, the lovely and adept Kay Sum-
mersby. He plowed through CIA dossiers on this captivating
spirit, Nina Petrovna, wife of the Soviet premier, maintained a
scrapbook crammed with photos of her and news clippings detail-
ing her husband's movements; twice, at the risk of everything, he
was able to communicate with her through the offices of a discreet

---

*"Hello" and "thank you."

and devoted agent of the CIA. In July of 1955, he flew to Geneva, hungering for peaceful coexistence.

At the Geneva Conference, the two came together once again, and what had begun ten years earlier as a riveting infatuation blossomed into the mature and passionate love that would haunt them the rest of their days. Ike was sixty-five, in his prime, the erect warrior, the canny leader, a man who could shake off a stroke as if it were a head cold; Nina, ten years his junior, was in the flush of womanly maturity, lovely, solid, a soft inscrutable smile playing on her elfin lips. With a subterfuge that would have tied the intelligence networks of their respective countries in knots, the two managed to steal ten minutes here, half an hour there—they managed, despite the talks, the dinners, the receptions, and the interminable, stultifying rounds of speechmaking, to appease their desire and sanctify their love forever. "Without personal contact," Ike said at a dinner for the Russian delegation, his boyish blue eyes fixed on Mrs. Khrushchev, "you might imagine someone was fourteen feet high, with horns and a tail." Russians and Americans alike burst into spontaneous laughter and applause. Nina Petrovna, first lady of the Soviet Union, stared down at her chicken Kiev and blushed.

And so, when the gargantuan Soviet TU 114 shrieked into Andrews Air Force Base in September of 1959, I stood by my president with a lump in my throat: I alone knew just how much the Soviet visit meant to him, I alone knew by how tenuous a thread hung the balance of world peace. What could the president have been thinking as the great sleek jet touched down? I can only conjecture. Perhaps he was thinking that she'd forgotten him, or that the scrutiny of the press would make it impossible for them to steal their precious few moments together, or that her husband— that torpedo-headed bully boy—would discover them and tear the world to pieces with his rage. Consider Ike at that moment, consider the all-but-insurmountable barriers thrown in his way, and you can appreciate my calling him one of the truly impassioned lovers of all time. Romeo had nothing on him, nor Douglas Fairbanks either—even the starry-eyed Edward Windsor pales by comparison. At any rate, he leaped at his opportunity like a desert nomad delivered to the oasis: there would be an assignation that very night, and I was to be instrumental in arranging it.

After the greeting ceremonies at Andrews, during which Ike could do no more than exchange smiles and handshakes with the premier and premiersha, there was a formal state dinner at the White House. Ambassador Menshikov was there, Khrushchev and his party, Ike and Mamie, Christian Herter, Dick Nixon, and others; afterward, the ladies retired to the Red Room for coffee. I sat at Ike's side throughout dinner, and lingered in the hallway outside the Red Room directly thereafter. At dinner, Ike had kissed Madame K.'s hand and chatted animatedly with her for a few minutes, but they covered their emotions so well that no one would have guessed they were anything other than amenable strangers wearing their social faces. Only I knew better.

I caught the premiersha as she and Mamie emerged from the Red Room in a burst of photographers' flashbulbs. As instructed, I took her arm and escorted her to the East Room, for the program of American songs that would highlight the evening. I spoke to her in Russian, though to my surprise she seemed to have a rudimentary grasp of conversational English (did she recall it from her schoolteaching days, or had she boned up for Ike?). Like a Cyrano, I told her that the president yearned for her tragically, that he'd thought of nothing else in the four years since Geneva, and then I recited a love poem he'd written her in English—I can't recall the sense of it now, but it boiled with Elizabethan conceits and the imagery of war, with torn hearts, manned bastions, and references to heavy ordnance, pillboxes, and scaling the heights of love. Finally, just before we entered the East Room, I pressed a slip of paper into her hand. It read, simply: *3:00 A.M., back door, Blair House.*

At five of three, in a rented, unmarked limousine, the president and I pulled up at the curb just down the street from Blair House, where the Khrushchev party had been installed for the night. I was driving. The rear panel slid back and the president's voice leaped at me out of the darkness: "Okay, Paderewski, do your stuff—and good luck."

I eased out of the car and started up the walk. The night was warm and damp, the darkness a cloak, street lights dulled as if they'd been shaded for the occasion. Every shadow was of course teeming with Secret Service agents—there were enough of them ringing the house to fill Memorial Stadium twice over—but they gave way for me. (Ike had arranged it thus: one person was to be allowed to enter the rear of Blair House at the stroke of three; two would be leaving an instant thereafter.)

She was waiting for me at the back door, dressed in pants and a man's overcoat and hat. "Madame Khrushcheva?" I whispered. "*Da*," came the reply, soft as a kiss. We hurried across the yard and I handed her into the car, admiring Ike's cleverness: if anyone—including the legion of Secret Service, CIA, and FBI men—had seen us, they would have mistaken the madame for her husband and concluded that Ike had set up a private, ultrasecret conference. I slid into the driver's seat and Ike's voice, shaken with emotion, came at me again: "Drive, Paderewski," he said. "Drive us to the stars." And then the panel shot to with a passionate click.

For two hours I circled the capitol, and then, as prearranged, I returned to Blair House and parked just down the street. I could hear them—Ike and Nina, whispering, embracing, rustling clothing—as I cut the engine. She giggled. Ike was whistling. She giggled again, a lovely windchime of a sound, musical and coltish—if I hadn't known better I would have thought Ike was back there with a coed. I was thinking with some satisfaction that we'd just about pulled it off when the panel slid back and Ike said: "Okay, Paderewski—let's hit it." There was the sound of a protracted kiss, a sound we all recognize not so much through experience—who's listening, after all?—but thanks to the attention Hollywood sound men have given it. Then Ike's final words to her, delivered in a passionate susurrus, words etched in my memory as if in stone: "Till we meet again," he whispered.

Something odd happened just then, just as I swung back the door for Mrs. Khrushchev: a car was moving along the street in the opposite direction, a foreign car, and it slowed as she stepped from the limousine. Just that—it slowed—and nothing more. I hardly remarked it at the time, but that instant was to reverberate in history. The engine ticked up the street, crickets chirruped. With all dispatch, I got Mrs. Khrushchev round back of Blair House, saw her in the door, and returned to the limousine.

"Well done, Paderewski, well done," Ike said as I put the car in drive and headed up the street, and then he did something he hadn't done in years—lit a cigarette. I watched the glow of the match in the rearview mirror, and then he was exhaling with rich satisfaction, as if he'd just come back from swimming the Potomac or taming a mustang in one of those televised cigarette ads. "The White House," he said. "Chop-chop."

Six hours later, Madame K. appeared with her husband on the front steps of Blair House and fielded questions from reporters. She wore a modest gray silk chemise and a splash of lipstick. One of the reporters asked her what she was most interested in seeing while touring the U.S., and she glanced over at her husband before replying (he was grinning to show off his pointed teeth, as impervious to English as he might have been to Venusian). "Whatever is of biggest interest to Mr. Khrushchev," she said. The reporters lapped it up: flashbulbs popped, a flurry of stories went out over the wire. Who would have guessed?

From there, the Khrushchevs took a special VIP train to New York, where Madame K. attended a luncheon at the Waldorf and her husband harangued a group of business magnates in Averell Harriman's living room. "The Moscow Cha-Cha" and Jimmy Driftwood's "The Bear Flew over the Ocean" blared from every radio in town, and a special squad of NYPD's finest—six-footers, expert in jujitsu and marksmanship—formed a human wall around the premier and his wife as they took in the sights of the Big Apple. New York rolled out the red carpet, and the Khrushchevs trod it with a stately satisfaction that rapidly gave way to finger-snapping, heel-kicking glee. As the premier boarded the plane for Los Angeles, Nina at his side, he mugged for cameras, kissed babies, and shook hands so assiduously he might have been running for office.

And then the bottom fell out.

In Los Angeles, ostensibly because he was nettled at Mayor Paulson's hardline speech and because he discovered that Disneyland would not be on his itinerary, the raging, tabletop-pounding, Magyar-cowing Khrushchev came to the fore: he threw a tantrum. The people of the United States were inhospitable boors—they'd invited him to fly halfway round the world simply to abuse him. He'd had enough. He was curtailing the trip and heading back to Moscow.

I was with Ike when the first reports of the premier's explosion flashed across the TV screen. Big-bellied and truculent, Khrushchev was lecturing the nation on points of etiquette, jowls atremble, fists beating the air, while Nina, her head bowed, stood meekly at his side. Ike's voice was so pinched it could have come from a ventriloquist's dummy: "My God," he whispered, "he knows." (I suddenly remembered the car slowing, the flash of a pale face behind the darkened glass, and thought of Alger Hiss, the Rosenbergs, the vast network of Soviet spies operating unchecked in the land of the free: they'd seen her after all.) Shaking his head, Ike got up, crossed the room, and lit another verboten cigarette. He looked weary, immeasurably old, Rip Van Winkle waking beside his rusted gun. "Well, Paderewski," he sighed, a blue haze playing round the wisps of silver hair at his temples, "I guess now the shit's really going to hit the fan."

He was right, but only partially. To his credit, Khrushchev covered himself like a trouper—after all, how could he reveal so shocking and outrageous a business as this without losing face himself, without transforming himself in that instant from the virile, bellicose, iron-fisted ruler of the Soviet masses to a pudgy, pathetic cuckold? He allowed himself to be mollified by apologies from Paulson and Cabot Lodge over the supposed insult, posed for a photograph with Shirley MacLaine at Twentieth Century–Fox, and then flew on to San Francisco for a tense visit. He made a dilatory stop in Iowa on his way back to Washington and the inevitable confrontation with the man who had suddenly emerged as his rival in love as well as ideology. (I'm sure you recall the celebrated photographs in *Life*, *Look*, and *Newsweek*—Khrushchev leering at a phallic ear of corn, patting the belly of a crewcut interloper at the Garst farm in Iowa, hefting a piglet by the scruff of its neck. Study them today—especially in contrast to the pre–Los Angeles photos—and you'll be struck by the mixture of jealous rage and incomprehension playing across the premier's features, and the soft, tragic, downcast look in his wife's eyes.)

I sat beside the president on the way out to Camp David for the talks that would culminate the Khrushchev visit. He was subdued, desolated, the animation gone out of his voice. He'd planned for these talks as he'd planned for the European Campaign, devising stratagems and feints, studying floorplans, mapping the territory, confident he could spirit away his inamorata for an idyllic hour or two beneath the pines. Now there was no chance of it. No chance, in fact, that he'd ever see her again. He was slumped in his seat, his head thrown back against the bullet-proof glass as if he no longer had the will to hold it up. And then— I've never seen anything so moving, so emotionally ravaging in my life—he began to cry. I offered him my handkerchief but he motioned me away, great wet heaving sobs tearing at his lungs, the riveting blue eyes that had gazed with equanimity on the most heinous scenes of devastation known to civilized man reddened with a sorrow beyond despair. "Nina," he choked, and buried his face in his hands.

You know the rest. The "tough" talks at Camp David (ostensibly over the question of the Berlin Wall), the Soviet premier's postponement of Ike's reciprocal visit till the spring, "when things are in bloom," the eventual rescinding of the invitation altogether, and the virulent anti-Eisenhower speech Khrushchev delivered in the wake of the U-2 incident. Then there was Ike's final year in office, his loss of animation, his heart troubles (*heart troubles*— could anything be more ironic?), the way in which he so rapidly and visibly aged, as if each moment of each day weighed on him like an eternity. And finally, our last picture of him: the affable, slightly foggy old duffer chasing a white ball across the links as if it were some part of himself he'd misplaced.

As for myself, I was rapidly demoted after the Khrushchev visit—it almost seemed as if I were an embarrassment to Ike, and in a way I guess I was, having seen him with his defenses down and his soul laid bare. I left the government a few months later and have pursued a rewarding academic career ever since, and am in fact looking forward to qualifying for tenure in the upcoming year. It has been a rich and satisfying life, one that has had its ups and downs, its years of quotidian existence and its few breathless moments at the summit of human history. Through it all, through all the myriad events I've witnessed, the loves I've known, the emotions stirred in my breast by the tragic events of our times, I can say with a sense of reverent gratitude and the deepest sincerity that nothing has so moved and tenderly astonished me as the joy, the sorrow, the epic sweep of the star-crossed love of Ike and Nina. I think of the Cold War, of nuclear proliferation, of Hungary, Korea, and the U-2 incident, and it all finally pales beside this: he loved her, and she loved him.

Rupert Beersley and the Beggar Master of Sivani-Hoota

It was on a dark, lowering day during one of the interstices of the monsoon that His Highness Yadavindra Singh, nawab of the remote Deccan state of Sivani-Hoota, began to miss his children. That is, the children began to turn up missing, and to an alarming degree. It began with little Gopal, who had been born with a mottled, pale birthmark in the shape of a half moon under the crease of his left buttock. Miss Elspeth Compton-Divot, the children's English governess, whose responsibility it was to instruct her wards in the dead language and living literature of Greece and to keep watch over them as a shepherd keeps watch over his flock (flock, indeed—there were twenty-five sibling Singhs under her care originally), was the first to discover little Gopal's absence. She bowed her way into the nawab's reception room immediately after lessons on that fateful afternoon, the sky so striped with cloud it might have been flayed, to find the nawab and his wife, the third begum, in attendance on several prominent local figures, including Mr. Bagwas the rubber-goods proprietor, and Mr. Patel the grain merchant. "Most High, Puissant, Royal, and Wise Hegemon Whose Duty It Is to Bring the Word of God and the Will of Just Government to the Peoples of Sivani-Hoota and Environs," she began, "I come before you on a matter of gravest import."

The nawab, a man in late middle age who had attended Oxford in the days of Pater and was given to ejaculations like "What ho!" and *"L'art pour l'art!,"* told her to stuff the formality and come to the point.

"It's your third youngest, sir—little Gopal."

"Yes?"

"He seems to have disappeared."

The nawab shifted his bulk uneasily in his chair—for he was a big man, fattened on ghee, sweet cream, and chapattis slathered with orange-blossom honey—glanced at his begum and then expelled a great exasperated puff of air. "What a damnable nuisance," he said. "I don't doubt the little beggar's up to some mischief, hiding himself in the servants' pantry or some such rot. Which one did you say it was?"

"Little Gopal, sir."

"Gopal?"

It was then that the begum spoke rapidly to her husband in Tamil and he began almost simultaneously to nod his head, muttering, "Yes, yes, a good boy that. A pity, a real pity."

The governess went on to explain the circumstances of the boy's disappearance—the testimony of the night nurse who'd put him to bed, his eldest-brother-but-six's assertion that they'd played together at cribbage before falling off to sleep, her own discovery of little Gopal's absence early that day, when she commenced morning lessons by comparing her seating chart with the nearly identical moon-shaped grinning brown faces of the nawab's brood.

Mr. Bagwas, who had been silently pulling at a clay pipe

through all of this, abruptly pronounced a single word: "Leopards."

But it was not leopards. Though the stealthy cats commonly carried off six or seven of the village's children a night, the occasional toothless grandmother, and innumerable goats, dogs, cows, fowl, royal turtles, and even the ornamental koi that graced the nawab's ponds, they were absolved of suspicion in the present case. After Abha, aged seven, and then the eleven-year-old Shanker vanished on successive nights, the nawab, becoming concerned, called in Mr. Hugh Tureen, game hunter, to put out baits and exterminate the spotted fiends. Though in the course of the ensuing week Mr. Tureen shot some seventy-three leopards, sixteen tigers, twelve wolves, and several hundred skunks, mongeese, badgers, and the like, the nawab continued to lose children. Santha, aged nine and with the mark of the dung beetle on the arches of both feet, vanished under the noses of three night nurses and half a dozen watchmen specially employed to stand guard over the nursery. This time, however, there was a clue. Bhupinder, aged six, claimed to have seen a mysterious shrouded figure hanging over his sister's bed, a figure rather like that of an ape on whom a tent has collapsed. Two days later, when the harsh Indian sun poked like a lance into the muslin-hung sanctuary of the children's quarters, Bhupinder's bed was empty.

The nawab and his begum, who two and a half weeks earlier had been rich in children, now had but twenty. They were distraught. Helpless. At their wits' end. Clearly, this was a case for Rupert Beersley.

We left Calcutta in a downpour, Beersley and I, huddled in our mackintoshes like a pair of dacoits. The train was three hours late, the tea was wretched, and the steward served up an unpalatable mess of curried rice that Beersley, in a fit of pique, overturned on the floor. Out of necessity—Beersley's summons had curtailed my supper at the club—I ate my own portion and took a cup of native beer with it. "Really," Beersley said, the flanges of his extraordinary nostrils drawn up in disgust, "how can you eat that slop?"

It was a sore point between us, this question of native food,

going all the way back to our first meeting at Cawnpore some
twenty years back, when he was a freshly commissioned young
leftenant in the Eleventh Light Dragoons, India Corps, and I a
seasoned sergeant-major. "I'll admit I've had better, old boy," I
said, "but one must adapt oneself to one's circumstances."

Beersley waved his hand in a gesture of dismissal and quoted
sourly from his favorite poem—indeed, the only poem from which
he ever quoted—Keats's "Lamia": "'Not three score old, yet of
sciential brain / To unperplex bliss from its neighbor pain.'"

An electric-green fly had settled itself on a congealed lump of
rice that lay on the table before us. I shrugged and lifted the fork
to my mouth.

We arrived at the Sivani-Hoota station in the same downpour
transposed a thousand miles, and were met by the nawab's silver-
plated Rolls, into the interior of which we ducked, wet as water
fowl, while the lackey stowed away our baggage. The road out to
the palace was black as the caverns of hell and strewn with enough
potholes to take the teeth out of one's head. Rain crashed down on
the roof as if it would cave it in, beasts roared from the wayside,
and various creatures of the night slunk, crept, and darted before
the headlights as if rehearsing for some weird menagerie. Nearly
an hour after leaving the station, we began to discern signs of
civilization along the dark roadway. First a number of thatch huts
began to flash by the smeared windows, then the more substantial
stone structures that indicated the approach to the palace, and
finally the white marble turrets and crenellated battlements of the
palace itself.

As we hurried into the entrance hall dripping like jellyfish, the
nawab, who had lost two more children in the interval between
his summons and our arrival, came out to meet us, a distraught
begum at his side. Servants sprang up like mushrooms after a rain,
turbaned Sikhs with appropriately somber faces, houseboys in
white, ladies in waiting with great dark, staring eyes. "Mr. Beersley, I presume," the nawab said, halting five paces from us and
darting his eyes distractedly between Rupert's puggree helmet
and my plaid tam-o'-shanter.

"The same," answered Beersley, bowing curtly from the waist

and stepping forward to seize the nawab's hand. "Pleased, I'm sure," he said, and then, before pausing either to introduce me or to pay his respects to the begum, he pointed to the wild-haired sadhu seated in the corner and praying over the yellowish flame of a dung fire. "And what precisely is the meaning of this?" he demanded.

I should say at this juncture that Beersley, though undeniably brilliant, tended also to be somewhat mercurial, and I could see that something had set him off. Perhaps it was the beastly weather or the long and poorly accommodated trip, or perhaps he was feeling the strain of overwork, called out on this case as he was so soon after the rigorous mental exercise he'd put into the baffling case of the Cornucopia Killer of Cooch Behar. Whatever it was, I saw to my embarrassment that he was in one of his dark India- and Indian-hating moods, in which he is as likely to refer to a Sikh as a "diaper head" as he is to answer "hello" on picking up the phone receiver.

"Beg pardon?" the nawab said, looking puzzled.

"This fellow over here in the corner, this muttering half-naked fakir—what precisely is his function?" Ignoring the shocked looks and dropped jaws of his auditors, Beersley rushed on, as if he were debating in a tavern. "What I mean to say, sir, is this: how can you expect me to take on a case of this nature when I find my very sensibilities affronted by this . . . this pandering to superstition and all the damnable mumbo jumbo that goes with it?"

The beards of the Sikhs bristled, their eyes flared. The nawab, to his credit, made an effort to control himself, and, with his welcoming smile reduced to a tight grim compression of the lips, he explained that the holy man in the corner was engaged in the Vedic rite of the sacred fire, energizer and destroyer, one of the three sacred elements of the Hindu trinity. Twice a day, he would also drink of the *pancha garia*, composed in equal parts of the five gifts of the sacred cow: milk, curds, ghee, urine, and dung. The nawab had felt that the performance of these sacred rites might help cleanse and purify his house against the plague that had assailed it.

Beersley listened to all this with his lip curled in a sneer, then muttered "humbug" under his breath. The room was silent. I shuffled my feet uneasily. The begum fastened me with the sort of look reserved for the deviates one encounters in the Bois de Boulogne, and the nawab's expression arranged itself in an unmistakable scowl.

"'Do not all charms fly / At the mere touch of cold philosophy?'" Beersley said, and then turned abruptly on his heel and strode off in the direction the lackey had taken with our baggage.

In the morning, Beersley (who had refused the previous evening to attend the dinner the nawab had arranged in his honor, complaining of fatigue and wishing only that a bit of yoghurt and a bowl of opium be sent up to his room) assembled all the principals outside the heavy mahogany door to the nawab's library. The eighteen remaining children were queued up to be interviewed separately, the nawab and begum were grilled in my presence as if they were pickpockets apprehended on the docks at Leeds, the night nurses, watchmen, chauffeurs, Sikhs, gardeners, cooks, and bottle washers were subjected to a battery of questions on subjects ranging from their sexual habits, through recurring dreams and feelings about their mothers, to their recollections of Edward's coronation and their perceptions as to the proper use of the nine iron. Finally, toward the end of the day, as the air rose from the gutters in a steaming miasma and the punkah wallah fell asleep over his task, Miss Compton-Divot was ushered into the room.

Immediately a change came over Beersley. Where he'd been officious, domineering, as devious, threatening, and assured as one of the czar's secret police, he now flushed to his very ears, groped after his words, and seemed confused. I'd never seen anything like it. Beersley was known for his composure, his stoicism, his relentless pursuit of the evidence under even the most distracting circumstances. Even during the bloody and harrowing case of the Tiger's Paw (in which Beersley ultimately deduced that the killer was dispatching his victims with the detached and taxidermically preserved paw of the rare golden tiger of Hyderabad), while the victims howled their death agony from the courtyard and whole families ran about in terror and confusion, he never flinched from his strenuous examination of the chief suspects. And now, here he was, in the presence of a comely russet-haired lass from Hertfordshire, as tongue-tied as a schoolboy.

"'Miss Compton-Divot,'" I said, to break the awkward silence. "May I present the celebrated Mr. Rupert Beersley?"

She curtsied and smiled like a plate of buttered scones.

"And may I take this opportunity to introduce myself as well?" I continued, taking her hand. "Sergeant-Major Plantagenet Randolph, retired, at your service. Please have a seat."

I waited for Beersley to begin, but he said nothing, merely sitting there and fixing the governess with a vacuous, slack-jawed gaze. She blushed prettily and looked down to smooth her dress and arrange her petticoats. After an interval, Beersley murmured, "'And soon his eyes had drunk her beauty up, / Leaving no drop in the bewildering cup, / And still the cup was full.'"

And that was it; he had no more to say. I prompted him, but he wouldn't be moved. Miss Compton-Divot, feeling, I think, the meaning of his stare, began to titter and twist the fabric of the dress in her hands. Finally, heaving an exhausted sigh and thinking ahead to dinner and the nawab's fine Lisbon port, which I'd been pleased to sample the previous evening, I showed her out of the room.

That night, little Govind, aged three and a half, disappeared without a trace.

I found Beersley in the garden the following morning, bending close over a spray of blood-red orchids. Had he found something? I hurried up to him, certain he'd uncovered the minute but crucial bit of evidence from which the entire case would unravel like a skein of yarn, as when he'd determined the identity of the guilty party in the Srinagar Strangler case from a single strand of hair found among countless thousands of others in a barber's refuse bin. Or when an improperly canceled stamp led him to the Benares Blackmailer. Or when half a gram's worth of flaked skin painstakingly sifted from the faded homespun loincloth of a murdered *harijan* put him on the trail of the Leaping Leper of Mangalore. "Beersley," I spurted in a barely suppressed yelp of excitement, "are you on to something, old boy?"

I was in for a shock. When he turned to me, I saw that the lucid reptilian sheen of his eyes had been replaced by a dull glaze: I might have been staring into the face of some old duffer in St. James' Park rather than that of the most brilliant detective in all of Anglo-India. He merely lifted the corners of his mouth in a vapid smile and then turned back to the orchids, snuffing them with his great glorious nostrils like a cow up to his hocks in clover. It was the sun, I was sure of it. Or a touch of the malaria he'd picked up in Burma in ought-two.

"Rupert!" I snapped. "Come out of it, old boy!" And then— rather roughly, I must admit—I led him to a bench in the shade of a banyan tree. The sun slammed through the leaves like a mallet. From the near distance came the anguished stentorian cries of the nawab's prize pachyderms calling out for water. "Beersley," I said, turning him toward me, "is it the fever? Can I get you a glass of water?"

His eyes remained fixed on a point over my left shoulder, his lips barely moved. "'Some demon's mistress,'" he murmured, "'or the demon's self.'"

"Talk sense!" I shouted, becoming ever more alarmed and annoyed. Here we'd been in Sivani-Hoota for some two days and we'd advanced not a step in solving the case, while children continued to disappear under our very noses. I was about to remonstrate further when I noted the clay pipe protruding from his breast pocket—and then the unmistakable odor of incinerated opium. It all became clear in that instant: he'd been up through the night, numbing his perceptions with bowl after bowl of the narcotizing drug. Something had disturbed him deeply, there was no doubt about it.

I led him straightaway to his suite of rooms in the palace's east end and called for quinine water and hot tea. For hours, through that long, dreadful, heat-prostrated afternoon, I walked him up and down the floor, forcing the blood to wash through his veins, clear his perceptions, and resharpen his wits. By teatime he was able to sit back in an easy chair, cross his legs in the characteristic

brisk manner, and unburden himself. "It's the governess," he
croaked, "that damnable little temptress, that hussy: she's be-
witched me."

I was thunderstruck. He might as easily have confessed that he
was a homosexual or the Prince of Wales in disguise. "You don't
mean to say that some . . . some trifling sexual dalliance is going to
come between Rupert Beersley and the pursuit of a criminal
case?" My color was high, I'm sure, and my voice hot with outrage.

"No, no, no—you don't understand," he said, fixing me as of
old with that keen insolent gaze. "Think back, Planty," he said,
lifting the teacup to his lips. "Don't you remember the state I was
in when I first came to you?"

Could I ever forget? Twenty-two or -three, straight as a ramrod,
thin as a whippet, the pointed nose and outsized ears accentuated
by a face wasted with rigor, he'd been so silent those first months
he might as well have entered the Carthusian monastery in Gre-
noble as the India Corps. There'd been something eating at him
then, some deep canker of the soul or heart that had driven him
into exile on the subcontinent he so detested. Later, much later,
he'd told me. It had been a woman, daughter of a Hertford squire:
on the eve of their wedding she'd thrown him over for another
man. "Yes," I said, "of course I remember."

He uncoiled himself from the chair, set down the teacup, and
strode to the window. Below, on the polo maidan, the nawab and
half a dozen of his retainers glided to and fro on pampered Ara-
bians while the westering sun fell into the grip of a band of monsoon clouds. Beersley gazed out on the scene for half a moment,
then turned to me with an emotion twenty years dead quivering
in those magnificent nostrils. "Elspeth," he said, his voice catching. "She's her daughter."

That evening the nawab threw a sumptuous entertainment.
There was music, dancing, a display of moving lights. Turbaned
Sikhs poured French wines, jugglers juggled, the begum beamed,
and platter after platter of fine, toothsome morsels was set before
us. I'd convinced Beersley to overcome his antipathy to native

culture and accept the invitation, as a means both of drawing him out of his funk and of placating the nawab. As we were making our way into the banquet room, however, Beersley had suddenly stopped short and seized my arm. Mr. Bagwas and Mr. Patel were following close on our heels and nearly collided with us, so abruptly did we stop; Beersley waited for them to pass, then indicated a marble bench in the courtyard to our left. When we were alone he asked if I'd seen Miss Compton-Divot as we'd crossed the foyer on our way in.

"Why, yes," I said. She'd been dressed in native costume—a saffron-colored sari and hemp sandals—and had pulled the ginger hair back from her forehead in the way of the Brahman women.

"Did you notice anything peculiar?"

"No, not a bit," I said. "A charming girl really, nothing more."

"Tell me," he demanded, the old cutting edge restored to his voice, "if you didn't see her bent over the fakir for a moment— just the hair of a moment—as we stepped through the door."

"Well, yes, yes, old boy, I suppose I did. What of it?"

"Nothing, perhaps. But—"

At that moment we were interrupted by Mr. Bagwas, who stood grinning before us. "Most reverend gentlemen," he said, drawing back his lips in an idiotic grin that showed off the reddened stumps of teeth ravaged over the years by the filthy habit of betel-nut chewing, "the nawab awaits."

We were ushered to the nawab's table and given the place of honor beside the nawab and his begum, several of the older children, Messrs. Bagwas and Patel, the nawab's two former wives, six of his current concubines, and the keeper of the sacred monkeys. Miss Compton-Divot, I quickly ascertained, was not present. I thought it odd, but soon forgot all about her, as we applauded the jugglers, acrobats, musicians, temple dancers, and trained bears until the night began to grow old. It was then that the nawab rose heavily to his feet, waved his hands for silence, and haw-hawed a bit before making a brief speech. "Even in the darkest hour shines a light," he said, the customary fat pout of his lips giving way to a wistful grin. "What I mean to say, damn it, is that the begum here is pregnant, gravid, heavy with child, that even when we find ourselves swallowed up in grief over our lost lambs we discover that here is a bun in the oven after all."

Beersley gave a snort of withering contempt and was about, I'm sure, to expatiate on the fatuity of the native mind and its lack of proportion and balance—not to mention rigor, discipline, and concentration—when the whole party was thrown into an uproar by a sudden ululating shriek emanating from the direction of the nursery. My companion was up like a hound and out the door before anyone else in the room could so much as set down a water glass. Though I tend to stoutness myself and am rather shorter of breath than I was in my military days, I was nevertheless the fourth or fifth man out the doorway, down the corridor, across the courtyard, and up the jade steps to the children's quarters.

When I got there, heaving for breath and with the sweat standing out on my forehead, I found Beersley kneeling over the prostrate form of one of the watchmen, from between whose scapulae protruded the hilt of a cheap ten-penny nail file. The children had retreated screaming to the far end of the dormitory, where they clutched one another's nightgowns in terror. "Poison," Beersley said with a profound disgust at the crudity of the killer's method as he slipped the nail file from its fatal groove. A single sniff of its bloody, sharpened point bore him out. He carefully wrapped the thing in his handkerchief, stowed it away in his breast pocket, and then leaped to his feet. "The children!" he cried. "Quickly now, line them up and count them!"

The nawab stood bewildered in the doorway; the begum went pale and fell to her knees while her retainers wrung their hands in distress and the children shuffled about confusedly, their faces tear-stained, their nightgowns a collision of sad airy clouds. And then all at once Miss Compton-Divot appeared, striding the length of the room to gather up two of her smaller wards in her lovely arms. "One," she began, "two, three, four . . ." It wasn't until several hours later that we understood what had happened. The murder in the dormitory had been a ruse. A diversion. Vallabhbhi Shiva, aged sixteen, a plump, oleaginous boy who'd sat directly across from Beersley and me during the entertainment, was nowhere to be found.

"A concentrate of the venom of the banded krait," Beersley said, holding a test tube up to the light. It was early, not yet 9:00 A.M., and the room reeked of opium fumes. "Nasty stuff, Planty— works on the central nervous system. I calculate there was enough of it smeared on the nether end of that nail file to dispatch half the unwashables in Delhi and give the nawab's prize pachyderms the runs for a week."

I fell into an armchair draped with one of my companion's Oriental dressing gowns. "Monstrous," was all I could say.

Beersley's eyes were lidded with the weight of the opium. His speech was slow; and yet even that powerful soporific couldn't suppress the excitement in his voice. "Don't you see, old boy— she's solved the case for us."

"Who?"

"The Lamia. It's a little lesson in appearance and reality. Serpent's venom indeed, the little vixen." And then he was quoting: "'She was a gordian shape of dazzling hue, / Vermilion-spotted, golden, green, and blue . . .' Don't you see?"

"No, Beersley," I said, rising to my feet rather angrily and crossing the room to where the clay pipe lay on the dressing table, "no, I'm afraid I don't."

"It's the motive that puzzles me," he said, musing over the vial in his hand as I snatched the clay pipe from the table and stoutly snapped it in two. He barely noticed. All at once he was holding the nail file up before my face, cradling it carefully in its linen nest. "Do you have any idea where this was manufactured, old boy?"

I'd been about to turn on him and tell him he was off his head, about to curse his narcotizing, his *non sequiturs*, and the incessant bloody poetry quoting that had me at my wits' end, but he caught me up short. "What?"

"The nail file, old fellow."

"Well, er, no. I hadn't really thought much about it."

He closed his eyes for a moment, exposing the peculiar deep-violet coloration of his eyelids. "Badham and Son, Manufacturers," he said in a monotone, as if he were reading an advertisement. "Implements for Manicure and Pedicure, Number 17, Parsonage Lane"—and here he paused to flash open his eyes so that I felt them seize me like a pair of pincers—"Hertford."

Again I was thunderstruck. "But you don't mean to say that . . . that you suspect—?"

My conjecture was cut short by a sudden but deferential rap at the door. *"Entrez,"* Beersley called, the sneer he cultivated for conducting interrogations or dealing with natives and underlings scalloping his upper lip. The door swung to and a pair of shrunken little houseboys bowed into the room with our breakfast. Beersley, characteristically indifferent to the native distaste for preparing or consuming meat, had ordered kidneys, rashers, eggs, and toast with a pot of tea, jam, and catsup. He moved forward to the table, allowed himself to be seated, and then called rather sharply to the retreating form of the first servant. "You there," he said, pushing his plate away. The servant wheeled round as if he'd been shot, exchanged a stricken look with his compatriot stationed behind the table, and bowed low. "I want the nawab's food taster up here *tout de suite*—within the minute. Understand?"

"What is it, Beersley?" I said, inspecting the plate. "Looks all right to me." But he would say nothing until the food taster arrived.

From beyond the windows came the fiendish caterwauling and great terrible belly roars of the nawab's caged tigers as they impatiently awaited their breakfast. I stared down at the bloodied nail file a moment and then at the glistening china plate with its bulbous kidneys, lean red rashers, and golden eggs. When I looked up the food taster was standing in the doorway. He was a young man, worn about the eyes and thin as a beggar from the pressures and uncertainties of his job. He bowed his way nervously into the room and said in a tremulous voice, "You called for me, sahib?"

Beersley merely indicated the plate. "A bit of this kidney here," he said.

The man edged forward, clumsily hacked off a portion of the suspect kidney, and, closing his eyes, popped it into his mouth, chewed perfunctorily, and swallowed. As his Adam's apple bobbed on the recoil, he opened his eyes and smiled like a man who's passed a harrowing ordeal. But then, alarmingly, the corners of his mouth began to drop and his limbs to tremble. Within ten seconds he was clutching his stomach, and within the minute he was stretched out prone on the floor, dead as a pharaoh.

Things had taken a nasty turn. That evening, as Beersley interrogated the kitchen staff with a ferocity and doggedness unusual even for him, I found myself sniffing suspiciously at my bottle of porter, and though my stomach protested vigorously, I refused even to glance at the platter of *jalebis* the nawab's personal chef had set before me. Beersley was livid. He raged, threatened, cajoled. The two houseboys who had brought the fatal kidney were so shaken that they confessed to all manner of peccancies, including the furtive eating of meat on the part of the one, and an addiction to micturating in the nawab's soup on the part of the other—and yet clearly they were innocent of any complicity in the matter of the kidney. It was nearly midnight when Beersley dismissed the last of the kitchen servants—the third chutney spicer's assistant—and turned to me with a face drawn with fatigue. "Planty," he said, "I shall have your kidnapper for you by tea tomorrow."

He was at it all night. I woke twice—at half past three and close on to six—and saw the light burning in his window across the courtyard. He was indefatigable when he was on the scent, and as I plumped the pillows and drifted off, I knew he would prove true to his word. Unfortunately, in the interval the nawab lost two more children.

The whole house was in a state of agitation the following afternoon when Beersley summoned the nawab and his begum, Messrs. Patel and Bagwas, Hugh Tureen, Miss Compton-Divot, and several other members of the household staff to "an enlightenment session" in the nawab's library. Miss Compton-Divot, wearing a conventional English gown with bustle, sash, and uplifted bosom, stepped shyly into the room, like a fawn emerging from the bracken to cross the public highway. This was the first glimpse Beersley had allowed himself of her since the night of the entertainment and its chilling aftermath, and I saw him turn sharply away as she entered. Hugh Tureen, the game hunter, strode confidently across the room while Mr. Patel and Mr. Bagwas huddled together in a corner over delicate little demitasses of tea and chatted village gossip. In contrast, the nawab seemed upset, angry even. He marched into the room, a little brown butterball of a man, followed at a distance by his wife, and confronted Beersley before the latter could utter a word. "I am at the end of my stamina and patience," he sputtered. "It's been nearly a week since you've arrived and the criminals are still at it. Last night it was the twins, Indira and er"—here he conferred in a brief whisper with his wife—"Indira and Sushila. Who will it be tonight?"

Outside, the monsoon recommenced with a sudden crashing fall of rain that smeared the windows and darkened the room till it might have been dusk. I listened to it hiss in the gutters like a thousand coiled snakes.

Beersley gazed down on the nawab with a look of such contempt, I almost feared he would kick him aside as one might kick an importunate cur out of the roadway, but instead he merely folded his arms and said, "I can assure you, sir, that the kidnapper is in this very room and shall be brought to justice before the hour is out."

The ladies gasped, the gentlemen exclaimed: "What?" "Who?" "He can't be serious?" I found myself swelling with pride. Though the case was as foggy to me as it had been on the night of our arrival, I knew that Beersley, in his brilliant and inimitable way, had solved it. When the hubbub had died down, Beersley requested that the nawab take a seat so that he might begin. I leaned back comfortably in my armchair and awaited the denouement.

"First," Beersley said, clasping his hands behind his back and rocking to and fro on the balls of his feet, "the facts of the case. To begin with, we have a remote, half-beggared duchy under the hand of a despotic prince known for his self-indulgence and the opulence of his court—"

At once the nawab leaped angrily to his feet. "I beg your par-

don, sir, but I find this most offensive. If you cannot conduct your
investigation in a civil and properly respectful manner, I shall
have to ask you to . . . to—"

"Please, please, please," Beersley was saying as he motioned
the nawab back into his seat, "be patient and you'll soon see the
method in all this. Now, as I was saying: we have a little out-of-
the-way state despoiled by generations of self-serving rulers,
rulers whose very existence is sufficient to provoke widespread
animosity if not enmity among the populace. Next we have the
mysterious and unaccountable disappearance of the current
nawab's heirs and heiresses—that is, Gopal, Abha, Shanker,
Santha, Bhupinder, Bimal and Manu, Govind, Vallabhbhi Shiva,
and now Indira and Sushila—beginning on a moonless night two
weeks ago to this day, the initial discovery of such disappearance
made by the children's governess, one Miss Elspeth Compton-
Divot."

At the mention of the children, the begum, who was seated to
my left, began to whimper softly. Miss Compton-Divot boldly
held Beersley's gaze as he named her, the two entrepreneurs—
Bagwas and Patel—leaned forward attentively, and Hugh Tureen
yawned mightily. As for myself, I began to feel rather sleepy. The
room was terrifically hot despite the rain, and the glutinous
breeze that wafted up from the punkah bathed me in sweat.

"Thus far," Beersley continued, "we have a kidnapper whose
motives remained obscure—but then the kidnapper turned murderer, and as he felt me close on his trail he attempted murder
once again. And let me remind you of the method employed in
both cases—a foul and feminine method, I might add—that is,
the use of poison. I have here," he said, producing the nail file,
"the weapon used to kill the servant set to watch over the nawab's
flock. It is made of steel and was manufactured in England—in
Hertford, to be precise." At this point, Beersley turned to the
governess and addressed her directly. "Is it not true, Miss Compton-Divot, that you were born and raised in Hertfordshire and
that but six months ago you arrived in India seeking employment?"

The governess's face lost its color in that instant. "Yes," she stammered, "it is true, but—"

"And," Beersley continued, approaching to within a foot of her chair and holding the nail file out before him as if it were a hot poker, "do you deny that this is your nail file, brought with you from England for some malignant purpose?"

"I don't!" she shouted in obvious agitation. "Or rather, I do. I mean, yes, it is my nail file, but I lost it—or . . . or someone stole it—some weeks ago. Certainly you don't think that I—?"

"That you are the murderer, Miss Compton-Divot?"

Her face was parchment, her pretty neck and bosom as white as if they'd never seen the light of day.

"No, my dear, not the murderer," Beersley said, straightening himself and pacing back across the room like a great stalking cat, "but are murderer and kidnapper one and the same? But hold on a minute, let us consider the lines of the greatest poet of them all, one who knew as I do how artifice and deceit seethe through the apparent world and how tough-minded and true one must be to unconfound the illusion from the reality. 'There was an awful rainbow once in heaven: / We know her woof,'" he intoned, and I realized that something had gone wrong, that his voice had begun to drag and his lids to droop. He fumbled over the next line or two, then paused to collect himself and cast his unsteady gaze out over the room. "'Philosophy will clip an Angel's wings, / Conquer all mysteries by rule and line, / Empty the haunted air, and gnomed mine—'"

Here I cut him off. "Beersley," I demanded, "get on with it, old boy." It was the opium. I could see it now. Yes, he'd been up all night with the case and with his pellucid mind, but with his opium bowl too.

He staggered back at the sound of my voice and shook his head as if to clear it, and then, whirling round, he pointed a terrible riveting finger at the game hunter and shrieked: "Here, here is your murderer!"

Tureen, a big florid fellow in puttees and boots, sprang from his chair in a rage. "What? You dare to accuse me, you . . . you preposterous little worm?" He would have fallen on Beersley and, I believe, torn him apart, had not the nawab's Sikhs interceded.

"Yes, Hugh Tureen," Beersley shouted, a barely suppressed rage shaking his voice in emotional storm, "you who've so long fouled yourself with the blood of beasts, you killed for the love of her, for the love of this, this"—and here the word literally burst from his lips like the great Lord's malediction on Lucifer— "Lamia!"

A cry went round the room. "Oh yes, and she—black heart, foul seductress—led you into her web just as she led you," he shouted, whirling on the nawab, "Yadavindra Singh. Yes, meeting with you secretly in foul unlawful embrace, professing her love while working in complicity with this man"—indicating Bagwas— "and your damned ragged fakir, to undermine your corrupt dynasty, to deprive you of your heirs, poison your wife in her sleep, and succeed to the throne as the fourth begum of Sivani-Hoota!"

Everyone in the room was on his feet. There were twenty disputations, rain crashed at the windows, Tureen raged in the arms of the Sikhs, and the nawab looked as if he were in the throes of an apoplectic fit. Over it all came the voice of Beersley, gone shrill now with excitement. "Whore!" he screamed, descending on the governess. "Conspiring with Bagwas, tempting him with your putrid charms and the lucre the nawab gave out in exchange for your favors. Yes, drugging the children and night nurses with your, quote, hot chocolate!" Beersley swung round again, this time to face the begum, who looked as confused as if she'd awakened to find herself amid the Esquimaux in Alaska. "And you, dear sinned-against lady: your little ones are dead, smothered by Bagwas and his accomplice Patel, sealed in rubber at the plant, and shipped in bulk to Calcutta. Look for them there, so that at least they may have a decent burial."

I was at Beersley's side now, trying to fend off the furious rushes of his auditors, but he seemed to have lost control. "Tureen!" he shrieked, "you fool, you jackanapes! You believed in this harlot, this Compton-Divot, this feminine serpent! Believed her when she lay in your disgusting arms and promised you riches

when she found her way to the top! Good God!" he cried, breaking past me and rushing again at the governess, who stood shrink-
ing in the corner, "'Lamia! Begone, foul dream!'"

It was then that the nawab's Sikhs turned on my unfortunate
companion and pinioned his arms. The nawab, rage trembling
through his corpulent body, struck Beersley across the mouth
three times in quick succession, and as I threw myself forward to
protect him, a pair of six-foot Sikhs drew their daggers to warn me
off. The rest happened so quickly I can barely reconstruct it.
There was the nawab, foaming with anger, his speech about decency, citizens of the crown, and rural justice, the mention of tar
and feathers, the hasty packing of our bags, the unceremonious
bum's rush out the front gate, and then the long, wearying trek in
the merciless rain to the Sivani-Hoota station.

Some weeks later, an envelope with the monogram EC-D arrived in the evening mail at my bungalow in Calcutta. Inside I
found a rather wounding and triumphant letter from Miss Compton-Divot. Beersley, it seemed, had been wrong on all counts.
Even in identifying her with the woman he had once loved, which
I believe now lay at the root of his problem in this difficult case.
She was in fact the daughter of a governess herself, and had had
no connection whatever with Squire Trelawney—whom she knew
by reputation in Hertfordshire—or his daughter. As for the case
of the missing children, she had been able, with the aid of Mr.
Bagwas, to solve it herself. It seemed that practically the only
suspicion in which Beersley was confirmed was his mistrust of the
sadhu. Miss Compton-Divot had noticed the fellow prowling
about the upper rooms in the vicinity of the children's quarters
one night, and had determined to keep a close watch on him.
Along with Bagwas, she was able to tail the specious holy man to
his quarters in the meanest street of Sivani-Hoota's slums. There
they hid themselves and watched as he transformed himself into a
ragged beggar with a crabbed walk who hobbled through the dark
streets to his station, among a hundred other beggars, outside the
colonnades of the Colonial Office. To their astonishment, they saw
that the beggars huddled round him—all of whom had been de-

prived of the power of speech owing to an operation too gruesome to report here—were in fact the children of the nawab. The beggar master was promptly arrested and the children returned to their parents.

But that wasn't all: there remained the motive. When dragged before the nawab in chains and condemned to death by *peine fort et dure*, the beggar master spat forth his venom. "Don't you recognize me?" he taunted the nawab. "Look closer." Understanding animated the nawab's features and a low exclamation escaped his lips: "Rajendra!" he gasped. "Yes," sneered the beggar master, "the same. The man you wronged thirty-five years ago when you set your filthy minions on me, burned my house and barn to the ground, and took my wife for your own first begum. She turned her back on me for your promises, and you turned me out of the state to wander begging the rest of my life. I have had my revenge." The nawab had broken down in tears, the beggar master was hauled off to be tortured to death, and the nine tongueless children were brought home to be instructed in sign language by Miss Compton-Divot, who became engaged to marry Mr. Bagwas the following week.

And so ends the baffling and ever-surprising case of the Beggar Master of Sivani-Hoota. I did not show the governess's letter to Beersley, incidentally. I felt that he'd been under an unnatural strain over the course of the past several months, and determined instead to take him for a rest cure to a little hotel in the grassy hills of the Punjab, a place that, so they say, bears a striking resemblance to Hertfordshire.

On for the Long Haul

There was nothing wrong with his appendix—no stitch in the side, no inflammation, no pain—but Bayard was having it out. For safety's sake. He'd read an article once about an anthropologist who'd gone to Malaysia to study the social habits of the orangutan and died horribly when her appendix had burst three hundred miles from the nearest hospital; as she lay writhing in her death agony the distraught apes had hauled her halfway up a jack-fruit tree, where she was found several days later by a photographer from *Life* magazine. The picture—splayed limbs, gouty face, leaves like a mouthful of teeth—was indelible with him. She'd been unprepared, that anthropologist, inattentive to the little details that can make or break you. Bayard was taking no such chances.

At their first meeting, the surgeon had been skeptical. "You're going to Montana, Mr. Wemp, not Borneo. There are hospitals there, all the modern facilities."

"It's got to go, doctor," Bayard had quietly insisted, looking up with perfect composure from the knot of his folded hands.

"Listen, Mr. Wemp. I've got to tell you that every surgical procedure, however routine, involves risk"—the doctor paused to let this sink in—"and I really feel the risks outweigh the gains in this case. All the tests are negative—we have no indication of a potential problem here."

"But doctor—" Bayard felt himself at a loss for words. How explain to this earnest, assured man with the suntanned wife, the Mercedes, and the house in Malibu that all of Los Angeles, San Francisco, New York—civilization itself—was on the brink of a catastrophe that would make the Dark Ages look like a Sunday-afternoon softball game? How intimate the horrors that lay ahead, the privation, the suffering? He remembered Aesop's fable about the ant and the grasshopper. Some would be prepared, others would not. "You just don't understand how isolated I'm going to be," he said finally.

Isolated, yes. Thirty-five acres in Bounceback, Montana, population thirty-seven. The closest town with a hospital, bank, or restaurant was Missoula, a two-and-a-half-hour drive, an hour of it on washboard dirt. Bayard would have his own well, a cleared acre for vegetable farming, and a four-room cabin with wood stove, electrical generator, and a radiation-proof cellar stocked with a five-year supply of canned and freeze-dried foodstuffs. The whole thing was the brainchild of Sam Arkson, a real-estate developer who specialized in subsistence plots, bomb shelters, and survival homes. Bayard's firm had done some PR work for one of Arkson's companies—Thrive, Inc.—and as he looked into the literature of catastrophe, Bayard had found himself growing ever more uncertain about the direction of his own life. *Remember the gas crisis?* asked one of Arkson's pamphlets. *An inconvenience, right? The have-nots stepping on the haves. But what about the food crisis around the corner? Have you thought about what you'll do when they close up the supermarkets with a sign that says "Sorry, Temporarily Out of Food"?*

Bayard would never forget the day he'd come across that pamphlet. His palms had begun to sweat as he read on, gauging the effect of nuclear war on the food and water supply, thinking of life without toilet paper, toothpaste, or condiments, summoning images of the imminent economic depression, the starving masses, the dark-skinned marauding hordes pouring across our borders from the south to take, take, take with their greedy, desperate, clutching hands. That night he'd gone home in a cold sweat, visions of apocalypse dancing in his head. Fran made him a drink, but he couldn't taste it. The girls showed him their schoolwork—the sweet, ingenuous loops of their penmanship, the pale watercolors and gold stars—and he felt the tears start up in his eyes. They were doomed, he was doomed, the world sinking like a stone. After they'd gone to bed he slipped out to the kitchen and silently pulled back the refrigerator door. Inside he found a head of deliquescing lettuce, half a gallon of milk, mayonnaise, mustard, chutney, a jar of capers so ancient it might have been unearthed in a tomb, a pint of butter-brickle ice cream, and a single Mexicali Belle TV dinner. The larder yielded two cans of pickled Chinese mushrooms, half a dozen packages of artificial rice pudding, and a lone box of Yodo Crunch cereal, three-quarters empty. He felt sick. Talk about a prolonged siege—they didn't even have breakfast.

That night his dreams had tentacles. He woke feeling strangled. The coffee was poisonous, the newspaper rife with innuendo, each story, each detail cutting into him with the sharp edge of doom. A major quake was on the way, the hills were on fire, there was murder and mayhem in Hollywood, AIDS was spreading to the heterosexual population, Kaddafi had the bomb. Outside sat the traffic. Three million cars, creeping, spitting, killing the atmosphere, inching toward gridlock. The faces of the drivers were impassive. Shift, lurch, advance, stop, shift, lurch. Didn't they know the whole world had gone hollow, rotten like a tooth? Didn't they know they were dead? He looked into their eyes and saw empty sockets, looked into their faces and saw the death's head. At work it was no better. The secretaries greeted him as if money mattered, as if there were time to breathe, go out to Chan Dara for lunch, and get felt up in the Xerox room; his colleagues were as bland as cue balls, nattering on about baseball, stocks, VCRs, and food processors. He staggered down the hallway as if he'd been hit in the vitals, slamming into the sanctuary of his office like a hunted beast. And there, on his desk, as if it were the bony pointed finger of the Grim Reaper himself, was Arkson's pamphlet.

By two-thirty that afternoon he was perched on a chair in Sam Arkson's San Diego office, talking hard-core survival with the impresario himself. Arkson sat behind a desk the size of a trampoline, looking alternately youthful and fissured with age—he could have been anywhere from thirty-five to sixty. Aggressively tanned and conscientiously muscled, his hair cut so close to the scalp it might have been painted on, he resembled nothing so much as a professional sweat meister, Vic Tanny fighting the waistline bulge, Jack La Lanne with a Mohawk. He was dressed in fatigues and wore a khaki tie. "So," he said, leaning back in his chair and sizing up Bayard with a shrewd, unforgiving gaze, "are you on for the long haul or do you just need a security blanket?"

Bayard was acutely conscious of his paunch, the whiteness of his skin, the hair that trailed down his neck in soft, frivolous coils. He felt like a green recruit under the burning gaze of the drill instructor, like an awkward dancer trying out for the wrong role. He coughed into his fist. "The long haul."

Arkson seemed pleased. "Good," he said, a faint smile playing across his lips. "I thought at first you might be one of these halfway types that wants a bomb shelter under the patio or something." He gave Bayard a knowing glace. "They might last a month or two after the blast," he said, "but what then? And what if it's not war we're facing but worldwide economic collapse? Are they going to eat their radiation detectors?"

This was a joke. Bayard laughed nervously. Arkson cut him off with a contemptuous snort and a wave of his hand that consigned all the timid, slipshod, halfway Harrys of the world to an early grave. "No," he said, "I can see you're the real thing, a one-hundred-percenter, no finger in the dike for you." He paused. "You're a serious person, Bayard, am I right?"

Bayard nodded.

"And you've got a family you want to protect?"

Bayard nodded again.

"Okay"—Arkson was on his feet, a packet of brochures in his hand—"we're going to want to talk hidden location, with the space, seeds, fertilizer, and tools to grow food and the means to hunt it, and we're going to talk a five-year renewable stockpile of survival rations, medical supplies, and specie—and of course weaponry."

"Weaponry?"

Arkson had looked at him as if he'd just put a bag over his head. "Tell me," he said, folding his arms so that the biceps swelled beneath his balled fists, "when the bust comes and you're sitting on the only food supply in the county, you don't really think your neighbors are going to breeze over for tea and polite chitchat, do you?"

Though Bayard had never handled a gun in his life, he knew the answer: there was a sickness on the earth and he'd have to harden himself to deal with it.

Suddenly Arkson was pointing at the ceiling, as if appealing to a higher authority to back him up. "You know what I've got up there on the roof?" he said, looming over Bayard like an inquisitor. Bayard hadn't the faintest idea.

"A Brantly B2B."

Bayard gave him a blank look.

"A chopper. Whirlybird. You know: upski-downski. And guess who flies it?" Arkson spread the brochures out on the desk in front of him, tapping a forefinger against the glossy photograph of a helicopter floating in a clear blue sky beneath the rubric ESCAPE CRAFT. "That's right, friend: me. I fly it. Leave nothing to chance, that's my motto." Bayard thumbed through the brochure, saw minijets, hovercraft, Cessnas, seaplanes, and ultralights.

"I can be out of town in ten minutes. Half an hour later I'm in my compound—two hundred fenced acres, three security men, goats, cows, chickens, pigs, corn as high as your chin, wheat, barley, rye, artesian wells, underground gas and water tanks—and an arsenal that could blow away the PLO. Listen," he said, and his eyes were like a stalking cat's, "when the shit hits the fan they'll be eating each other out there."

Bayard had been impressed. He was also terrified, sick with the knowledge of his own impotence and vulnerability. The blade was poised. It could fall today, tonight, tomorrow. They had to get out. "Fran," he called as he hurried through the front door, arms laden with glossy brochures, dire broadsides, and assorted survival tomes from Arkson Publications, Ltd. "Fran!"

Fran had always been highstrung—neurotic, actually—and the sort of pure, unrefined paranoia that had suddenly infested Bayard was second nature to her. Still, she would take some persuading—he was talking about uprooting their entire life, after all—and it was up to Bayard to focus that paranoia and bring it to bear on the issue at hand. She came out of the sunroom in a tentlike swimsuit, a large, solid, plain-faced woman in her late thirties, trailing children. She gave him a questioning look while the girls, chanting "Daddy, Daddy," foamed round his legs. "We've got to talk," was all he could say.

Later, after the children had been put to bed, he began his campaign. "We're sitting on a powder keg," he said as she bent over the dishwasher, stacking plates. She looked up, blinking behind the big rectangular frames of her glasses like a frogman coming up for air. "Pardon?"

"L.A., the whole West Coast. It's the first place the Russians'll hit—if the quake doesn't drop us into the ocean first. Or the banks go under. You've read about the S&Ls, right?"

She looked alarmed. But, then, she alarmed easily. Chronically overprotected as a child, cloistered in a parochial school run along the lines of a medieval nunnery, and then consigned to a Catholic girls' college that made it look liberal, she believed with all her heart in the venality of man and the perfidy and rottenness of the world. On the rare occasions when she left the house she clutched her purse like a fullback going through a gap in the line, saw all pedestrians—even white-haired grandmothers—as potential muggers, and dodged Asians, Latinos, Pakistanis, and Iranians as if they were the hordes of Genghis Khan. "What in God's name are you talking about?" she said.

"I'm talking about Montana."

"Montana?"

At this point Bayard had simply fetched his trove of doom literature and spread it across the kitchen table. "Read," he said, knowing full well the books and pamphlets could speak far more eloquently than he. In the morning he'd found her hunched over the table still, the ashtray full beside her, a copy of *Doom Newsletter* in her hand, *Panic in the Streets* and *How to Kill*, volumes I–IV, face down beside a steaming coffee mug. "But what about the girls?" she said. "What about school, ballet lessons, tennis, swimming?"

Melissa was nine, Marcia seven. The move to the hinterlands would be disruptive for them, maybe traumatic—Bayard didn't deny it—but then, so would nuclear holocaust. "Ballet lessons?" he echoed. "What good do you think ballet lessons are going to be when maniacs are breaking down the door?" And then, more gently: "Look, Fran, it's going to be hard for all of us, but I just don't see how we can stay here now that our eyes have been opened— it's like sitting on the edge of a volcano or something."

She was weakening, he could feel it. When he got home from the office she was sunk into the sofa, her eyes darting across the page before her like frightened animals. Arkson had called. Four times. "Mrs. Wemp, Fran," he'd shouted over the wire as if the barbarians were at the gate, "you've got to listen to me. I have a place for you. Nobody'll find you. You'll live forever. Sell that deathtrap and get out now before it's too late!" Toward the end of the week she went through an entire day without changing out of her nightgown. Bayard pressed his advantage. He sent the girls to the babysitter and took the day off from work to ply her with pamphlets, rhetoric and incontrovertible truths, and statistics on everything from the rising crime rate to nuclear kill ratios. As dusk fell that evening, the last choked rays of sunlight irradiating the smog till it looked like mustard gas coming in over the trenches, she capitulated. In a voice weak with terror and exhaustion, she called him into the bedroom, where she lay still as a corpse. "All right," she croaked. "Let's get out."

After Fran, the surgeon was easy. For fifteen minutes Bayard had quietly persisted while the doctor demurred. Finally, throwing his trump card, the surgeon leaned forward and said: "You're aware your insurance won't cover this, Mr. Wemp?"

Bayard had smiled. "No problem," he said. "I'll pay cash."

Two months later he and Fran sported matching abdominal scars, wore new flannel shirts and down vests, talked knowledgeably of seed sets, fertilizer, and weed killer, and resided in the distant rugged reaches of the glorious Treasure State, some four hundred miles from ground zero of the nearest likely site of atomic devastation. The cabin was a good deal smaller than what they were used to, but then, they were used to luxury condominiums, and the cabin sacrificed luxury—comfort, even—for utility. Its exterior was simulated log, designed to make the place look like a trapper's cabin to the average marauder, but the walls were reinforced with steel plates to a thickness that would withstand bazooka or antitank gun. In the basement, which featured four-foot-thick concrete walls and lead shielding, was the larder. Ranks of hermetically sealed canisters mounted the right-hand wall, each with a reassuring shelf life of ten years or more: bulk grains, wild rice, textured vegetable protein, yogurt powder, matzo meal, hardtack, lentils, bran, Metamucil. Lining the opposite wall, precisely stacked, labeled and alphabetized, were the freeze-dried entrées, from *abbacchio alla cacciatora* and *boeuf bourguignonne* to shrimp Creole, turkey Tetrazzini, and *ziti alla romana*. Bayard took comfort in their very names, as a novice might take comfort in the names of the saints: Just In Case freeze-dried linguine with white clam sauce, tomato crystals from Lazarus Foods, canned truffles from Gourmets for Tomorrow, and Arkson's own Stash Brand generic foodstuffs, big plain-labeled cans that read CATSUP, SAUERKRAUT, DETERGENT, LARD. In the evenings, when the house was as quiet as the far side of the moon, Bayard would slip down into the shelter, pull the airtight door closed behind him, and spend hours contemplating the breadth, variety, and nutritional range of his cache. Sinking back in a padded armchair, his heartbeat decelerating, breathing slowed to a whisper, he would feel the calm of the womb descend on him. Then he knew the pleasures of the miser, the hoarder, the burrowing squirrel, and he felt as free from care as if he were wafting to and fro in the dark amniotic sea whence he sprang.

Of course, such contentment doesn't come cheap. The whole package—land, cabin, four-wheel-drive vehicle, arms and munitions, foodstuffs, and silver bars, De Beers diamonds, and cowrie shells for barter—had cost nearly half a million. Arkson, whose corporate diversity put him in a league with Gulf & Western, had been able to provide everything, lock, stock, and barrel, right down to the church-key opener in the kitchen drawer and the reusable toilet paper in the bathroom. There were radiation suits, flannels, and thermal underwear from Arkson Outfitters, and weapons—including a pair of Russian-made AK 47s smuggled out of Afghanistan and an Israeli grenade launcher—from Arkson Munitions. In the driveway, from Arkson Motors, Domestic and Import, was the four-wheel-drive Norwegian-made Olfputt TC 17, which would run on anything handy, from paint thinner to rubbing alcohol, climb the north face of the Eiger in an ice storm, and pull a plow through frame-deep mud. The cabin's bookshelves were mostly given over to the how-to, survival, and self-help tomes in which Arkson Publications specialized, but there were reprints of selected classics—*Journal of the Plague Year, Hiroshima,* and *Down and Out in London and Paris*—as well. Arkson made an itemized list, tallied the whole thing up, and presented the bill to Bayard and Fran in the San Diego office.

Fran was so wrought up at this point she barely gave it a glance. She kept looking over her shoulder at the door as if in expectation of the first frenzied pillagers, and then she would glance down at the open neck of her purse and the .22-caliber Beretta Arkson had just handed her ("My gift to you, Fran," he'd said; "learn to use it"). Bayard himself was distracted. He tried to look judicious, tried to focus on the sheet of paper before him with the knowing look one puts on for garage mechanics presenting the bill for arcane mechanical procedures and labor at the rate of a hundred and twenty dollars an hour, but he couldn't. What did it matter? Until he was ensconced in his cabin he was like a crab without its shell. "Seems fair," he murmured.

Arkson had come round the desk to perch on the near edge and take his hand. "No bargain rate for survival, Bayard," he said, "no fire sales. If the price seems steep, just think of it this way: Would you put a price on your life? Or the lives of your wife and children?" He'd paused to give Bayard a saintly look, the look of the young Redeemer stepping through the doors of the temple. "Just be thankful that you two had the financial resources—and the foresight—to protect yourself."

Bayard had looked down at the big veiny tanned hand clutching his own and shaken it mechanically. He felt numb. The past few weeks had been hellish, what with packing up, supervising the movers, and making last-minute trips to the mall for things like thread, Band-Aids, and dental floss—not to mention agonizing over the sale of the house, anticipating Fran's starts and rushes of panic, and turning in his resignation at the Hooper-Munson Co., where he'd put in fourteen years and worked himself up to Senior Vice President in Charge of Reversing Negative Corporate Image. Without Arkson it would have been impossible. He'd soothed Fran, driven the children to school, called the movers, cleaners, and painters, and then gone to work on Bayard's assets with the single-mindedness of a general marshaling troops. Arkson Realty had put the condo on the market and found a buyer for the summer place in Big Bear, and Arkson, Arkson, and Arkson, Brokers, had unloaded Bayard's holdings on the stock exchange with a barely significant loss. When combined with Fran's inheritance and the money Bayard had put away for the girls' education, the amount realized would meet Thrive, Inc.'s price and then some. It was all for the best, Arkson kept telling him, all for the best. If Bayard had second thoughts about leaving his job and dropping out of society, he could put them out of his mind: society, as he'd known it, wouldn't last out the year. And as far as money was concerned, well, they'd be living cheaply from here on out.

"Fran," Arkson was saying, taking her hand now too and linking the three of them as if he were a revivalist leading them forward to the purifying waters, "Bayard . . ." He paused again, overcome with emotion. "Feel lucky."

Now, two months later, Bayard could stand on the front porch

of his cabin, survey the solitary expanse of his property with its
budding aspen and cottonwood and glossy conifers, and take
Arkson's parting benediction to heart. He did feel lucky. Oh, perhaps on reflection he could see that Arkson had shaved him on one
item or another, and that the doom merchant had kindled a blaze
under him and Fran that put them right in the palm of his hand,
but Bayard had no regrets. He felt secure, truly secure, for the
first time in his adult life, and he bent contentedly to ax or hoe,
glad to have escaped the Gomorrah of the city. For her part, Fran
seemed to have adjusted well too. The physical environment beyond the walls of her domain had never much interested her, and
so it was principally a matter of adjusting to one set of rooms as
opposed to another. Most important, though, she seemed more
relaxed. In the morning, she would lead the girls through their
geography or arithmetic, then read, sew, or nap in the early afternoon. Later she would walk round the yard—something she
rarely did in Los Angeles—or work in the flower garden she'd
planted outside the front door. At night, there was television, the
signals called down to earth from the heavens by means of the
satellite dish Arkson had providently included in the package.

The one problem was the girls. At first they'd been excited, the
whole thing a lark, a vacation in the woods, but as the weeks wore
on they became increasingly withdrawn, secretive, and, as Bayard
suspected, depressed. Marcia missed Mrs. Sturdivant, her second-grade teacher; Melissa missed her best friend Nicole, Disneyland, Baskin and Robbins, and the beach, in that order. Bayard
saw the pale, sad ovals of their faces framed in the gloom of the
back bedroom as they hovered over twice-used coloring books,
and he felt as if a stake had been driven through his heart. "Don't
worry," Fran said, "give them time. They'll make the adjust-
ment." Bayard hoped so. Because there was no way they were
going back to the city.

One afternoon—it was mid-June, already hot, a light breeze
discovering dust and tossing it on the hoods and windshields of
the cars parked along the street—Bayard was in the lot outside
Chuck's Wagon in downtown Bounceback, loading groceries into

the back of the Olfputt, when he glanced up to see two men stepping out of a white Mercedes with California plates. One of them
was Arkson, in his business khakis and tie. The other—tall and
red-faced, skinny as a refugee in faded green jumpsuit and work
boots—Bayard had never seen before. Both men stretched themselves, and then the stranger put his hands on his hips and slowly
revolved a full three hundred and sixty degrees, his steady, expressionless gaze taking in the gas station, saloon, feed store, and
half-deserted streets as if he'd come to seize them for nonpayment
of taxes. Bayard could barely contain himself. "Sam!" he called.
"Sam Arkson!" And then he was in motion, taking the lot in six
animated strides, his hand outstretched in greeting.

At first Arkson didn't seem to recognize him. He'd taken the
stranger's arm and was pointing toward the mountains like a tour
guide when Bayard called out his name. Half turning, as if at some
minor disturbance, Arkson gave him a preoccupied look, then
swung back to say something under his breath to his companion.
By then Bayard was on him, pumping his hand. "Good to see you,
Sam."

Arkson shook numbly. "You too," he murmured, avoiding Bayard's eyes.

There was an awkward silence. Arkson looked constipated. The
stranger—his face was so red he could have been apoplectic, ter-
minally sunburned, drunk—glared at Bayard as if they'd just exchanged insults. Bayard's gaze shifted uneasily from the stranger's
eyes to the soiled yellow beret that lay across his head like a
cheese omelet and then back again to Arkson. "I just wanted
to tell you how well we're doing, Sam," he stammered, "and . . .
and to thank you—I mean it, really—for everything you've
done for us."

Arkson brightened immediately. If a moment earlier he'd
looked like a prisoner in the dock, hangdog and tentative, now he
seemed his old self. He smiled, ducked his head, and held up his
palm in humble acknowledgment. Then, running his fingers over
the stubble of his crown, he stepped back a pace and introduced
the ectomorphic stranger. "Rayfield Cullum," he said, "Bayard
Wemp."

"Glad to meet you," Bayard said, extending his hand.

The stranger's hands never left his pockets. He stared at Bayard a moment out of his deepset yellow eyes, then turned his head to spit in the dirt. Bayard's hand dropped like a stone.

"I'd say you two have something in common," Arkson said mysteriously. And then, leaning forward and dropping his voice: "Rayfield and I are just ironing out the details on the plot next to yours. He wants in this week—tomorrow, if not sooner." Arkson laughed. The stranger's eyes lifted to engage Bayard's; his face remained expressionless.

Bayard was taken by surprise. "Plot?" he repeated.

"East and south," Arkson said, nodding. "You'll be neighbors. I've got a retired couple coming in the end of the month from Saratoga Springs—they'll be purchasing the same package as yours directly to the north of you, by that little lake."

"Package?" Bayard was incredulous. "What is this, Levittown, Montana, or something?"

"Heh-heh, very funny, Bayard." Arkson had put on his serious look, life and death, the world's a jungle, La Lanne admonishing his audience over the perils of flab. "The crunch comes, Bayard," he said, "you could support fifty people on those thirty-five acres, what with the game in those woods and the fertility of that soil. You know it as well as I do."

Now Cullum spoke for the first time, his voice a high, nagging rasp, like static. "Arkson," he said, driving nails into the first syllable, "I ain't got all day."

It was then that Melissa, giggling like a machine and with a pair of ice-cream cones thrust up like torches over her head, came tearing around the side of the building, her sister in pursuit. Marcia was not giggling. She was crying in frustration, wailing as if her heart had been torn out, and cutting the air with a stick. "Melissa!" Bayard shouted, but it was too late. Her skinny brown legs got tangled and she pitched forward into Cullum, who was just then swiveling his head round at the commotion. There was the scrape of sneakers on gravel, the glare of the sun poised motionless overhead, and then the wet, rich, fecal smear of chocolate-fudge ice cream—four scoops—on the seat of Cullum's jumpsuit. Cullum's knee buckled under the impact, and he jumped back as if he'd been struck by a snake. "Godamnit!" he roared, and Bayard could see that his hands were shaking. "Goddamnit to hell!"

Melissa lay sprawled in the dirt. Stricken face, a thin wash of red on her scraped knee. Bayard was already bending roughly for her, angry, an apology on his lips, when Cullum took a step forward and kicked her twice in the ribs. "Little shit," he hissed, his face twisted with lunatic fury, and then Arkson had his broad arms around him, pulling him back like a handler with an attack dog.

Melissa's mouth was working in shock, the first hurt breathless shriek caught in her throat; Marcia stood white-faced behind them; Cullum was spitting out curses and dancing in Arkson's arms. Bayard might have lifted his daughter from the dirt and pressed her to him, he might have protested, threatened, waved his fist at this rabid dog with the red face, but he didn't. No. Before he could think he was on Cullum, catching him in the center of that flaming face with a fist like a knob of bone. Once, twice, zeroing in on the wicked little dog eyes and the fleshy dollop of the nose, butter, margarine, wet clay, something giving with a crack, and then a glancing blow off the side of the head. He felt Cullum's workboots flailing for his groin as he stumbled forward under his own momentum, and then Arkson was driving him up against the Mercedes and shouting something in his face. Suddenly freed, Cullum came at him, beret askew, blood bright in his nostrils, but Arkson was there, pinning Bayard to the car and shooting out an arm to catch hold of the skinny man's shirt. "Daddy!" Melissa shrieked, the syllables broken with shock and hurt.

"You son of a bitch!" Bayard shouted.

"All right now, knock it off, will you?" Arkson held them at arm's length like a pair of fighting cocks. "It's just a misunderstanding, that's all."

Bleeding, shrunk into his jumpsuit like a withered tortoise, Cullum held Bayard's gaze and dropped his voice to a hiss. "I'll kill you," he said.

Fran was aghast. "Is he dangerous?" she said, turning to peer
over her spectacles at Bayard and the girls as they sat at the
kitchen table. She was pouring wine vinegar from a three-gallon
jug into a bowl of cucumber spears. Awkwardly. "I mean, he
sounds like he escaped from a mental ward or something."

Bayard shrugged. He could still taste the tinny aftershock the
incident had left in the back of his throat. A fight. He'd been
involved in a fight. Though he hadn't struck anyone in anger since
elementary school, hadn't even come close, he'd reacted instinctively in defense of his children. He sipped his gimlet and felt a
glow of satisfaction.

"This is the man we're going to have next door to us?" Fran set
the bowl on the table beside a platter of reconstituted stir-fried
vegetables and defrosted tofu. The girls were subdued, staring
down their straws into glasses of chocolate milk. "Well?" Fran's
eyes searched him as she sat down across the table. "Do you think
I can have any peace of mind with this sort of . . . of violence and
lawlessness on my doorstep? Is this what we left the city for?"

Bayard speared a square of tofu and fed it into his mouth. "It's
hardly on our doorstep, Fran," he said, gesturing with his fork.
"Besides, I can handle him, no problem."

A week passed. Then two. Bayard saw no more of Arkson, or of
Cullum, and the incident began to fade from his mind. Perhaps
Cullum had soured on the deal and gone off somewhere else—or
back to the hole he'd crawled out of. And what if he did move in?
Arkson was right: there was so much land between them they
might never lay eyes on one another, let alone compete for resources. At any rate, Bayard was too busy to worry about it. Mornings, it was second-grade geography and fourth-grade history,
which meant relearning his state capitals and trying to keep his de
Sotos, Coronados, and Cabeza de Vacas straight. Afternoons, he
kept busy with various home-improvement projects—constructing a lopsided playhouse for the girls, fencing his vegetable garden against the mysterious agent that masticated everything he
planted right down to the root, splitting and stacking wood, fumbling over the instructions for the prefab aluminum toolshed he'd
mail-ordered from the Arkson Outfitters catalogue. Every third

day he drove into Bounceback for groceries (he and Fran had decided to go easy on the self-subsistence business until such time as
society collapsed and made it imperative) and on weekends the
family would make the long trek down to Missoula for a restaurant
meal and a movie. It was on one of these occasions that they
bought the rabbits.

Bayard was coming out of the hardware store with a box of two-
penny nails, a set of socket wrenches, and a hacksaw when he
spotted Fran and the girls across the street, huddled over a man
who seemed to be part of the sidewalk. The man, Bayard saw as
he crossed the street to join them, was long-haired, bearded, and
dirty. He had a burlap sack beside him, and the sack was moving.
"Here, here," said the man, grinning up at them, and then he
plunged his hand into the bag and drew out a rabbit by the ears.
The animal's paws were bound with rubber bands, its fur was rat-
colored. "This one here's named Duke," the man said, grinning.
"He's trained."

Long-whiskered, long-eared, and long-legged, it looked more
like a newborn mule than a rabbit. As the man dangled it before
the girls, its paws futilely kicking and eyes big with terror, Bayard
almost expected it to bray. "Good eatin', friend," the man said,
giving Bayard a shrewd look.

"Daddy," Melissa gasped, "can we buy him? Can we?"

The man was down on his knees, fumbling in the sack. A moment later he extracted a second rabbit, as lanky, brown, and
sickly-looking as the first. "This one's Lennie. He's trained too."

"Can we, Daddy?" Marcia chimed in, tugging at his pant leg.

Bayard looked at Fran. The girls held their breath. "Five
bucks," the man said.

Down the street sat the Olfputt, gleaming like a gigantic toaster
oven. Two women, a man in a cowboy hat, and a boy Melissa's age
stood staring at it in awe and bewilderment. Bayard jingled the
change in his pocket, hesitating. "For both," the man said.

Initially, the rabbits had seemed a good idea. Bayard was no
psychologist, but he could see that these gangling flat-footed ro-
dents, with their multiplicity of needs, with their twitching noses
and grateful mouths, might help draw the girls out of themselves.

He was right. From the moment they'd hustled the rabbits into the car, cut their bonds, and pressed them to their scrawny chests while Fran fretted over ticks, tularemia, and relapsing fever, the girls were absorbed with them. They fed them grass, lettuce, and the neat little pellets of rabbit food that so much resembled the neat little pellets the animals excreted. They cuddled, dressed, and brushed them. They helped Bayard construct a pair of interlocking chicken-wire cages and selected the tree from which they would hang, their thin serious faces compressed with concern over weasels, foxes, coons, coyotes. Melissa devoted less time to tormenting her sister and bemoaning the absence of her school friends; Marcia seemed less withdrawn.

For his part, Bayard too found the new pets compelling. They thumped their feet joyously when he approached their cages with lettuce or parsley, and as they nuzzled his fingers he gazed out over his cleared acre to the trees beyond and thought how this was only the beginning. He would have goats, chickens, pigs, maybe even a cow or a horse. The way he saw it, a pet today was meat on the hoof tomorrow. Hadn't they eaten horses during the First World War? Mules, oxen, dogs? Not to mention rabbits. Of course, these particular rabbits were an exception. Though in theory they were to be skinned, stewed, and eaten in time of distress, though they represented a hedge against hard times and a life-sustaining stock of protein, Bayard looked into their quiet, moist eyes and knew he would eat lentils first.

The following week Bayard took the family into Missoula for a double sci-fi/horror feature (which only helped confirm him in his conviction that the world was disintegrating) and dinner at the local Chinese restaurant. It was after dark when they got home and the Olfputt's headlights swung into the yard to illuminate two tiny figures hanging like wash from the simulated beam that ran the length of the front porch. Melissa spotted them first. "What's that?" she said.

"Where?"

"There, up on the porch."

By the time Bayard saw them it was too late. Fran had seen them too—disheveled ears and limp paws, the puny little car-

casses twisting slowly round their monofilament nooses—and
worse, the seven-year-old, rousing herself from sleep, had caught
a nightmarish glimpse of them before he could flick off the lights.
"My God," Fran whispered. They sat there a moment, the dark
suffocating, no gleam of light for miles. Then Marcia began to
whimper and Melissa called out his name sharply, as if in accusation, as if he alone were responsible for all the hurts and perver-
sions of the world.

Bayard felt he was sinking. Pork fried rice and duck sauce tore
at the pit of his stomach with a hellish insistence, Fran was hyperventilating, and the girls' lamentations rose in intensity from
piteous bewildered bleats to the caterwauling of demons. Frightened, angry, uncomprehending, he sat there in utter blackness,
his hands trembling on the wheel. When finally he turned on the
parking lights and pushed open the door, Fran clutched his arm
with the grip of a madwoman. "Don't go out there," she hissed.

"Don't be silly," Bayard said.

"No," she sobbed, clawing at him as if she were drowning. Her
eyes raged at him in the dim light, the girls were weeping and
moaning, and then she was pressing something into his hand,
heavy, cold, instrument of death. "Take this."

Six or seven pickups were parked outside the T&T Cocktail Bar
when Bayard rolled into downtown Bounceback. It was half past
eleven, still hot, the town's solitary street light glowing like a
myopic eye. As he crossed the street to the telephone outside
Chuck's Wagon, Bayard could make out a number of shadowy
figures in broad-brimmed hats milling around in front of the bar.
There was a murmur of disembodied voices, the nagging whine of
a country fiddle, stars overhead, the glow of cigarettes below.
Drunks, he thought, hurrying past them. Their lives wouldn't be
worth a carton of crushed eggs when the ax fell.

Bayard stalked up to the phone, tore the receiver from its cradle, and savagely dialed the number he'd scribbled across a paper
napkin. He was angry, keyed up, hot with outrage. He listened to
the phone ring once, twice, three times, as he cursed under his
breath. This was too much. His wife was sick with fear, his chil-

dren were traumatized, and all he'd worked for—security, self-sufficiency, peace of mind—was threatened. He'd had to prowl round his own home like a criminal, clutching a gun he didn't know how to use, jumping at his own shadow. Each bush was an assassin, each pocket of shadow a crouching adversary, the very trees turned against him. Finally, while Fran and the girls huddled in the locked car, he'd cut down Lennie and Duke, bundled the lifeless bodies in a towel, and hid them out back. Then Fran, her face like a sack of flour, had made him turn on all the lights till the house blazed like a stage set, insisting that he search the closets, poke the muzzle of the gun under the beds, and throw back the doors of the kitchen cabinets like an undercover cop busting drug peddlers. When he'd balked at this last precaution—the cabinets couldn't have concealed anything bigger than a basset hound —she'd reminded him of how they'd found Charlie Manson under the kitchen sink. "All right," he'd said after searching the basement, "there's nobody here. It's okay."

"It was that maniac, wasn't it?" Fran whispered, as if afraid she'd be overheard.

"Daddy," Melissa cried, "where's Lennie, and . . . and Duke?" The last word trailed off in a broken lamentation for the dead, and Bayard felt the anger like a hot nugget inside him.

"I don't know," he said, pressing Melissa to him and massaging her thin, quaking little shoulders. "I don't know." Through the doorway he could see Marcia sitting in the big armchair, sucking her thumb. Suddenly he became aware of the gun in his hand. He stared down at it for a long moment, and then, almost unconsciously, as if it were a cigarette lighter or a nail clipper, he slipped it into his pocket.

Now he stood outside Chuck's Wagon, the night breathing down his neck, the telephone receiver pressed to his ear. Four rings, five, six. Suddenly the line engaged and Arkson, his voice shrunk round a kernel of suspicion, answered with a quick tentative "Yeah?"

"Sam? It's me, Bayard."

"Who?"

"Bayard Wemp."

There was a pause. "Oh yeah," Arkson said finally, "Bayard. What can I do for you? You need anything?"

"No, I just wanted to ask you—"

"Because I know you're going to be short on hardware for harvesting, canning, and all that, and I've got a new line of meat smokers you might want to take a look at—"

"Sam!" Bayard's voice had gone shrill, and he fought to control it. "I just wanted to ask you about that guy in the beret, you know, the one you had with you up here last month—Cullum?"

There was another pause. Bayard could picture his mentor in a flame-retardant bathrobe, getting ready to turn in on a bed that converted to a life raft in the event that a second flood came over the earth while he lay sleeping. "Uh-huh. Yeah. What about him?"

"Well, did he ever buy the place? I mean, is he up here now?"

"Listen, Bayard, why not let bygones be bygones, huh? Rayfield is no different than you are—except maybe he doesn't like children, is all. He's a one-hundred-percenter, Bayard, on for the long haul like you. I'm sure he's forgot all about that little incident—and so should you."

Bayard drew a long breath. "I've got to know, Sam."

"It takes all kinds, Bayard."

"I don't need advice, Sam. Just information. Look, I can go down to the county assessor's office in the morning and get what I want."

Arkson sighed. "All right," he said finally. "Yes. He moved in yesterday."

When he turned away from the phone, Bayard felt his face go hot. Survival. It was a joke. He owned thirty-five acres of untrammeled Wild West backwoods wilderness land and his only neighbor was a psychopath who kicked children in the stomach and mutilated helpless animals. Well, he wasn't going to allow it. Society might be heading for collapse, but there were still laws on the books. He'd call the sheriff, take him to court, have him locked up.

He was halfway to his car, just drawing even with the open door of the T&T, when he became aware of a familiar sound off to his

left—he turned, recognizing the distinctive high whine of an
Olfputt engine. There, sitting at the curb, was an Olfputt pickup,
looking like half an MX missile with a raised bed grafted to the
rear end. He stopped, puzzled. This was no Ford, no Chevy, no
Dodge. The Olfputt was as rare in these parts as a palanquin—
he'd never seen one himself till Arkson . . . Suddenly he began to
understand.

The door swung open. Cullum's face was dark—purple as a
birthstain in the faint light. The engine ticked, raced, and then fell
back as the car idled. The headlights seemed to clutch at the
street. "Hey, hey," Cullum said. "Mr. Rocky Marciano. Mr.
Streetfight."

Bayard became aware of movement in the shadows around him.
The barflies, the cowboys, had gathered silently, watching him.
Cullum stood twenty feet away, a rifle dangling at his side. Bayard
knew that rifle, just as he'd known the Olfputt. Russian-made, he
thought. AK 47. Smuggled out of Afghanistan. He felt Fran's little
pistol against his thigh, weighing him down like a pocketful of
change. His teeth were good, his heartbeat strong. He had a five-
year supply of food in his basement and a gun in his pocket.
Cullum was waiting.

Bayard took a step forward. Cullum spat in the dirt and raised
the rifle. Bayard could have gone for his gun, but he didn't even
know how to release the safety catch, let alone aim and fire the
thing, and it came to him that even if he did know how to handle
it, even if he'd fired it a thousand times at cans, bottles, rocks, and
junkyard rats, he would never use it, not if all the hungry hordes
of the earth were at his door.

But Cullum would. Oh yes, Cullum would. Cullum was on for
the long haul.

The Hector Quesadilla Story

He was no Joltin' Joe, no Sultan of Swat, no Iron Man. For one thing, his feet hurt. And God knows no legendary immortal ever suffered so prosaic a complaint. He had shin splints too, and corns and ingrown toenails and hemorrhoids. Demons drove burning spikes into his tailbone each time he bent to loosen his shoelaces, his limbs were skewed so awkwardly that his elbows and knees might have been transposed and the once-proud knot of his *frijole*-fed belly had fallen like an avalanche. Worse: he was old. Old, old, old, the graybeard hobbling down the rough-hewn steps of the senate building, the ancient mariner chewing on his whiskers and stumbling in his socks. Though they listed his birthdate as 1942 in the program, there were those who knew better: it was way back in '54, during his rookie year for San Buitre, that he had taken Asunción to the altar, and even in those distant days, even in Mexico, twelve-year-olds didn't marry.

When he was younger—really young, nineteen, twenty, tearing up the Mexican League like a saint of the stick—his ears were so sensitive he could hear the soft rasping friction of the pitcher's fingers as he massaged the ball and dug in for a slider, fastball, or change-up. Now he could barely hear the umpire bawling the count in his ear. And his legs. How they ached, how they groaned and creaked and chattered, how they'd gone to fat! He ate too much, that was the problem. Ate prodigiously, ate mightily, ate as if there were a hidden thing inside him, a creature all of jaws with an infinite trailing ribbon of gut. *Huevos con chorizo* with beans, *tortillas, camarones* in red sauce, and a twelve-ounce steak for breakfast, the chicken in *mole* to steady him before afternoon games, a sea of beer to wash away the tension of the game and prepare his digestive machinery for the flaming *machaca*-and-pepper salad Asunción prepared for him in the blessed evenings of the home stand.

Five foot seven, one hundred eighty-nine and three-quarters pounds. Hector Hernán Jesús y María Quesadilla. Little Cheese, they called him. Cheese, Cheese, Cheesus, went up the cry as he stepped in to pinch-hit in some late-inning crisis, Cheese, Cheese, Cheesus, building to a roar until Chavez Ravine resounded as if with the holy name of the Saviour Himself when he stroked one of the clean line-drive singles that were his signature or laid down a bunt that stuck like a finger in jelly. When he fanned, when the bat went loose in the fat brown hands and he went down on one knee for support, they hissed and called him *Viejo*.

One more season, he tells himself, though he hasn't played regularly for nearly ten years and can barely trot to first after drawing a walk. One more. He tells Asunción too—One more, one more —as they sit in the gleaming kitchen of their house in Boyle Heights, he with his Carta Blanca, she with her mortar and pestle for grinding the golden, petrified kernels of maize into flour for the tortillas he eats like peanuts. *Una más*, she mocks. What do you want, the Hall of Fame? Hang up your spikes, Hector.

He stares off into space, his mother's Indian features flattening his own as if the legend were true, as if she really had taken a spatula to him in the cradle, and then, dropping his thick lids as he takes a long slow swallow from the neck of the bottle, he says: Just the other day, driving home from the park, I saw a car on the freeway, a Mercedes with only two seats, a girl in it, her hair out back like a cloud, and you know what the license plate said? His eyes are open now, black as pitted olives. Do you? She doesn't. Cheese, he says. It said Cheese.

Then she reminds him that Hector Jr. will be twenty-nine next month and that Reina has four children of her own and another on the way. You're a grandfather, Hector—almost a great-grand-father, if your son ever settled down. A moment slides by, filled with the light of the sad, waning sun and the harsh Yucatano dialect of the radio announcer. *Hombres* on first and third, one down. *Abuelo*, she hisses, grinding stone against stone until it makes his teeth ache. Hang up your spikes, *abuelo*.

But he doesn't. He can't. He won't. He's no grandpa with hair the color of cigarette stains and a blanket over his knees, he's no toothless old gasser sunning himself in the park—he's a big-leaguer, proud wearer of the Dodger blue, wielder of stick and glove. How can he get old? The grass is always green, the lights always shining, no clocks or periods or halves or quarters, no punch-in and punch-out: this is the game that never ends. When the heavy hitters have fanned and the pitchers' arms gone sore, when there's no joy in Mudville, taxes are killing everybody, and the Russians are raising hell in Guatemala, when the manager paces the dugout like an attack dog, mind racing, searching high and low for the canny veteran to go in and do single combat, there he'll be—always, always, eternal as a monument—Hector Quesadilla, utility infielder, with the .296 lifetime batting average and service with the Reds, Phils, Cubs, Royals, and L.A. Dodgers.

So he waits. Hangs on. Trots his aching legs round the outfield grass before the game, touches his toes ten agonizing times each morning, takes extra batting practice with the rookies and slump-

ing millionaires. Sits. Watches. Massages his feet. Waits through
the scourging road trips in the Midwest and along the East Coast,
down to muggy Atlanta, across to stormy Wrigley, and up to frigid
Candlestick, his gut clenched round an indigestible cud of meat-
loaf and instant potatoes and wax beans, through the terrible night
games with the alien lights in his eyes, waits at the end of the
bench for a word from the manager, for a pat on the ass, a roar, a
hiss, a chorus of cheers and catcalls, the marimba pulse of bat
striking ball, and the sweet looping arc of the clean base hit.

And then comes a day, late in the season, the homeboys battling for the pennant with the big-stick Braves and the sneaking
Jints, when he wakes from honeyed dreams in his own bed that's
like an old friend with the sheets that smell of starch and soap and
flowers, and feels the pain stripped from his body as if at the touch
of a healer's fingertips. Usually he dreams nothing, the night a
blank, an erasure, and opens his eyes on the agonies of the martyr
strapped to a bed of nails. Then he limps to the toilet, makes a
poor discolored water, rinses the dead taste from his mouth, and
staggers to the kitchen table, where food, only food, can revive in
him the interest in drawing another breath. He butters tortillas
and folds them into his mouth, spoons up egg and melted jack
cheese and *frijoles refritos* with the green *salsa*, lashes into his
steak as if it were cut from the thigh of Kerensky, the Atlanta relief
ace who'd twice that season caught him looking at a full-count
fastball with men in scoring position. But not today. Today is different, a sainted day, a day on which sunshine sits in the windows
like a gift of the Magi and the chatter of the starlings in the
crapped-over palms across the street is a thing that approaches the
divine music of the spheres. What can it be?

In the kitchen it hits him: *pozole* in a pot on the stove, *carnitas*
in the saucepan, the table spread with sweetcakes, *buñuelos*, and
the little marzipan *dulces* he could kill for. *Feliz cumpleaños*,
Asunción pipes as he steps through the doorway. Her face is lit
with the smile of her mother, her mother's mother, the line of gift
givers descendant to the happy conquistadors and joyous Aztecs.
A kiss, a *dulce*, and then a knock at the door and Reina, fat with
life, throwing her arms around him while her children gobble up

the table, the room, their grandfather, with eyes that swallow their faces. Happy birthday, Daddy, Reina says, and Franklin, her youngest, is handing him the gift.

And Hector Jr.?

But he doesn't have to fret about Hector Jr., his firstborn, the boy with these same great sad eyes who'd sat in the dugout in his Reds uniform when they lived in Cincy and worshiped the pudgy icon of his father until the parish priest had to straighten him out on his hagiography; Hector Jr., who studies English at USC and day and night writes his thesis on a poet his father has never heard of, because here he is, walking in the front door with his mother's smile and a store-wrapped gift—a book, of course. Then Reina's children line up to kiss the *abuelo*—they'll be sitting in the box seats this afternoon—and suddenly he knows so much: he will play today, he will hit, oh yes, can there be a doubt? He sees it already. Kerensky, the son of a whore. Extra innings. Koerner or Manfredonia or Brooksie on third. The ball like an orange, a mango, a muskmelon, the clean swipe of the bat, the delirium of the crowd, and the gimpy *abuelo*, a big-leaguer still, doffing his cap and taking a tour of the bases in a stately trot, Sultan for a day.

Could things ever be so simple?

In the bottom of the ninth, with the score tied at 5 and Reina's kids full of Coke, hotdogs, peanuts, and ice cream and getting restless, with Asunción clutching her rosary as if she were drowning and Hector Jr.'s nose stuck in some book, Dupuy taps him to hit for the pitcher with two down and Fast Freddie Phelan on second. The eighth man in the lineup, Spider Martinez from Muchas Vacas, D.R., has just whiffed on three straight pitches, and Corcoran, the Braves' left-handed relief man, is all of a sudden pouring it on. Throughout the stadium a hush has fallen over the crowd, the torpor of suppertime, the game poised at apogee. Shadows are lengthening in the outfield, swallows flitting across the face of the scoreboard, here a fan drops into his beer, there a big mama gathers up her purse, her knitting, her shopping bags and parasol, and thinks of dinner. Hector sees it all. This is the moment of catharsis, the moment to take it out.

As Martinez slumps toward the dugout, Dupuy, a laconic, em-
bittered man who keeps his suffering inside and drinks Gelusil
like water, takes hold of Hector's arm. His eyes are red-rimmed
and paunchy, doleful as a basset hound's. Bring the runner in,
champ, he rasps. First pitch fake a bunt, then hit away. Watch
Booger at third. Uh-huh, Hector mumbles, snapping his gum.
Then he slides his bat from the rack—white ash, tape-wrapped
grip, personally blessed by the archbishop of Guadalajara and his
twenty-seven acolytes—and starts for the dugout steps, knowing
the course of the next three minutes as surely as his blood knows
the course of his veins. The familiar cry will go up—Cheese,
Cheese, Cheesus—and he'll amble up to the batter's box, knocking imaginary dirt from his spikes, adjusting the straps of his golf
gloves, tugging at his underwear, and fiddling with his batting
helmet. His face will be impenetrable. Corcoran will work the ball
in his glove, maybe tip back his cap for a little hair grease, and
then give him a look of psychopathic hatred. Hector has seen it
before. Me against you. My record, my career, my house, my
family, my life, my mutual funds and beer distributorship against
yours. He's been hit in the elbow, the knee, the groin, the head.
Nothing fazes him. Nothing. Murmuring a prayer to Santa Griselda, patroness of the sun-blasted Sonoran village where he was
born like a heat blister on his mother's womb, Hector Hernán
Jesús y María Quesadilla will step into the batter's box, ready for
anything.

But it's a game of infinite surprises.

Before Hector can set foot on the playing field, Corcoran suddenly doubles up in pain, Phelan goes slack at second, and the
catcher and shortstop are hustling out to the mound, tailed an
instant later by trainer and pitching coach. First thing Hector
thinks is groin pull, then appendicitis, and finally, as Corcoran
goes down on one knee, poison. He'd once seen a man shot in the
gut at Obregón City, but the report had been loud as a thun-
derclap, and he hears nothing now but the enveloping hum of the
crowd. Corcoran is rising shakily, the trainer and pitching coach
supporting him while the catcher kicks meditatively in the dirt,
and now Mueller, the Atlanta *cabeza*, is striding big-bellied out of

the dugout, head down as if to be sure his feet are following orders. Halfway to the mound, Mueller flicks his right hand across his ear quick as a horse flicking its tail, and it's all she wrote for Corcoran.

Poised on the dugout steps like a bird dog, Hector waits, his eyes riveted on the bullpen. Please, he whispers, praying for the intercession of the Niño and pledging a hundred votary candles—at least, at least. Can it be?—yes, milk of my mother, yes—Kerensky himself strutting out onto the field like a fighting cock. Kerensky!

Come to the birthday boy, Kerensky, he murmurs, so certain he's going to put it in the stands he could point like the immeasurable Bambino. His tired old legs shuffle with impatience as Kerensky stalks across the field, and then he's turning to pick Asunción out of the crowd. She's on her feet now, Reina too, the kids come alive beside her. And Hector Jr., the book forgotten, his face transfigured with the look of rapture he used to get when he was a boy sitting on the steps of the dugout. Hector can't help himself: he grins and gives them the thumbs-up sign.

Then, as Kerensky fires his warm-up smoke, the loudspeaker crackles and Hector emerges from the shadow of the dugout into the tapering golden shafts of the late-afternoon sun. That pitch, I want that one, he mutters, carrying his bat like a javelin and shooting a glare at Kerensky, but something's wrong here, the announcer's got it screwed up: BATTING FOR RARITAN, NUMBER 39, DAVE TOOL. What the—? And now somebody's tugging at his sleeve and he's turning to gape with incomprehension at the freckle-faced batboy, Dave Tool striding out of the dugout with his big forty-two-ounce stick, Dupuy's face locked up like a vault, and the crowd, on its feet, chanting Tool, Tool, Tool! For a moment he just stands there, frozen with disbelief. Then Tool is brushing by him and the idiot of a batboy is leading him toward the dugout as if he were an old blind fisherman poised on the edge of the dock.

He feels as if his legs have been cut out from under him. Tool! Dupuy is yanking him for Tool? For what? So he can play the lefty-righty percentages like some chess head or something? Tool, of all people. Tool, with his thirty-five home runs a season and lifetime BA of .234; Tool, who's worn so many uniforms they had to expand the league to make room for him—what's he going to do? Raging, Hector flings down his bat and comes at Dupuy like a cat tossed in a bag. You crazy, you jerk, he sputters. I woulda hit him, I woulda won the game. I dreamed it. And then, his voice breaking: It's my brithday, for Christ's sake!

But Dupuy can't answer him, because on the first pitch Tool slams a real worm burner to short and the game is going into extra innings.

By seven o'clock, half the fans have given up and gone home. In the top of the fourteenth, when the visitors came up with a pair of runs on a two-out pinch-hit home run, there was a real exodus, but then the Dodgers struck back for two to knot it up again. Then it was three up and three down, regular as clockwork. Now, at the end of the nineteenth, with the score deadlocked at 7 all and the players dragging themselves around the field like gut-shot horses, Hector is beginning to think he may get a second chance after all. Especially the way Dupuy's been using up players like some crazy general on the Western Front, yanking pitchers, juggling his defense, throwing in pinch runners and pinch hitters until he's just about gone through the entire roster. Asunción is still there among the faithful, the foolish, and the self-deluded, fumbling with her rosary and mouthing prayers for Jesus Christ Our Lord, the Madonna, Hector, the home team, and her departed mother, in that order. Reina too, looking like the survivor of some disaster, Franklin and Alfredo asleep in their seats, the *niñitas* gone off somewhere—for Coke and dogs, maybe. And Hector Jr. looks like he's going to stick it out too, though he should be back in his closet writing about the mystical so-and-so and the way he illustrates his poems with gods and men and serpents. Watching him, Hector can feel his heart turn over.

In the bottom of the twentieth, with one down and Gilley on first—he's a starting pitcher but Dupuy sent him in to run for Manfredonia after Manfredonia jammed his ankle like a turkey and had to be helped off the field—Hector pushes himself up

from the bench and ambles down to where Dupuy sits in the corner, contemplatively spitting a gout of tobacco juice and saliva
into the drain at his feet. Let me hit, Bernard, come on, Hector
says, easing down beside him.

Can't, comes the reply, and Dupuy never even raises his head.
Can't risk it, champ. Look around you—and here the manager's
voice quavers with uncertainty, with fear and despair and the dull
edge of hopelessness—I got nobody left. I hit you, I got to play
you.

No, no, you don't understand—I'm going to win it, I swear.

And then the two of them, like old bankrupts on a bench in
Miami Beach, look up to watch Phelan hit into a double play.

A buzz runs through the crowd when the Dodgers take the field
for the top of the twenty-second. Though Phelan is limping, Thorkelsson's asleep on his feet, and Dorfman, fresh on the mound, is
the only pitcher left on the roster, the moment is electric. One
more inning and they tie the record set by the Mets and Giants
back in '64, and then they're making history. Drunk, sober, and
then drunk again, saturated with fats and nitrates and sugar, the
crowd begins to come to life. Go, Dodgers! Eat shit! Yo Mama!
Phelan's a bum!

Hector can feel it too. The rage and frustration that had con-
sumed him back in the ninth are gone, replaced by a dawning
sense of wonder—he could have won it then, yes, and against his
nemesis Kerensky too—but the Niño and Santa Griselda have
been saving him for something greater. He sees it now, knows it
in his bones: he's going to be the hero of the longest game in
history.

As if to bear him out, Dorfman, the kid from Albuquerque, puts
in a good inning, cutting the bushed Braves down in order. In the
dugout, Doc Pusser, the team physician, is handing out the little
green pills that keep your eyes open and Dupuy is blowing into a
cup of coffee and staring morosely out at the playing field. Hector
watches as Tool, who'd stayed in the game at first base, fans on
three straight pitches, then he shoves in beside Dorfman and tells
the kid he's looking good out there. With his big cornhusker's ears

and nose like a tweezer, Dorfman could be a caricature of the green rookie. He says nothing. Hey, don't let it get to you, kid—I'm going to win this one for you. Next inning or maybe the inning after. Then he tells him how he saw it in a vision and how it's his birthday and the kid's going to get the victory, one of the biggest of all time. Twenty-four, twenty-five innings maybe.

Hector had heard of a game once in the Mexican League that took three days to play and went seventy-three innings, did Dorfman know that? It was down in Culiacán. Chito Marití, the converted bullfighter, had finally ended it by dropping down dead of exhaustion in center field, allowing Sexto Silvestro, who'd broken his leg rounding third, to crawl home with the winning run. But Hector doesn't think this game will go that long. Dorfman sighs and extracts a bit of wax from his ear as Pantaleo, the third-string catcher, hits back to the pitcher to end the inning. I hope not, he says, uncoiling himself from the bench; my arm'd fall off.

Ten o'clock comes and goes. Dorfman's still in there, throwing breaking stuff and a little smoke at the Braves, who look as if they just stepped out of *The Night of the Living Dead*. The home team isn't doing much better. Dupuy's run through the whole team but for Hector, and three or four of the guys have been in there since two in the afternoon; the rest are a bunch of ginks and gimps who can barely stand up. Out in the stands, the fans look grim. The vendors ran out of beer an hour back, and they haven't had dogs or kraut or Coke or anything since eight-thirty.

In the bottom of the twenty-seventh Phelan goes berserk in the dugout and Dupuy has to pin him to the floor while Doc Pusser shoves something up his nose to calm him. Next inning the balls-and-strikes ump passes out cold, and Dorfman, who's beginning to look a little fagged, walks the first two batters but manages to weasel his way out of the inning without giving up the go-ahead run. Meanwhile, Thorkelsson has been dropping ice cubes down his trousers to keep awake, Martinez is smoking something suspicious in the can, and Ferenc Fortnoi, the third baseman, has begun talking to himself in a tortured Slovene dialect. For his part, Hector feels stronger and more alert as the game goes on. Though he hasn't had a bite since breakfast he feels impervious to the pangs of hunger, as if he were preparing himself, mortifying his flesh like a saint in the desert.

And then, in the top of the thirty-first, with half the fans asleep and the other half staring into nothingness like the inmates of the asylum of Our Lady of Guadalupe, where Hector had once visited his halfwit uncle when he was a boy, Pluto Morales cracks one down the first-base line and Tool flubs it. Right away it looks like trouble, because Chester Bubo is running around right field looking up at the sky like a birdwatcher while the ball snakes through the grass, caroms off his left foot, and coasts like silk to the edge of the warning track. Morales meanwhile is rounding second and coming on for third, running in slow motion, flat-footed and hump-backed, his face drained of color, arms flapping like the undersized wings of some big flightless bird. It's not even close. By the time Bubo can locate the ball, Morales is ten feet from the plate, pitching into a face-first slide that's at least three parts collapse, and that's it, the Braves are up by one. It looks black for the hometeam. But Dorfman, though his arm has begun to swell like a sausage, shows some grit, bears down, and retires the side to end the historic top of the unprecedented thirty-first inning.

Now, at long last, the hour has come. It'll be Bubo, Dorfman, and Tool for the Dodgers in their half of the inning, which means that Hector will hit for Dorfman. I been saving you, champ, Dupuy rasps, the empty Gelusil bottle clenched in his fist like a hand grenade. Go on in there, he murmurs, and his voice fades away to nothing as Bubo pops the first pitch up in back of the plate. Go on in there and do your stuff.

Sucking in his gut, Hector strides out onto the brightly lit field like a nineteen-year-old, the familiar cry in his ears, the haggard fans on their feet, a sickle moon sketched in overhead as if in some cartoon strip featuring drunken husbands and the milkman. Asunción looks as if she's been nailed to the cross, Reina wakes with a start and shakes the little ones into consciousness, and Hector Jr. staggers to his feet like a battered middleweight coming out for the fifteenth round. They're all watching him. The fans whose lives are like empty sacks, the wife who wants him home in front of the TV, his divorced daughter with the four kids and another on the way, his son, pride of his life, who reads for the doctor of philosophy while his crazy *padrecito* puts on a pair of long stockings and chases around after a little white ball like a case of arrested development. He'll show them. He'll show them some *cojones*, some true grit and desire: the game's not over yet.

On the mound for the Braves is Bo Brannerman, a big mustachioed machine of a man, normally a starter but pressed into desperate relief service tonight. A fine pitcher—Hector would be the first to admit it—but he just pitched two nights ago and he's worn thin as wire. Hector steps up to the plate, feeling legendary. He glances over at Tool in the on-deck circle, and then down at Booger, the third-base coach. All systems go. He cuts at the air twice and then watches Brannerman rear back and release the ball: strike one. Hector smiles. Why rush things? Give them a thrill. He watches a low outside slider that just about bounces to even the count, and then stands like a statue as Brannerman slices the corner of the plate for strike two. From the stands, a chant of *Viejo, Viejo*, and Asunción's piercing soprano, Hit him, Hector!

Hector has no worries, the moment eternal, replayed through games uncountable, with pitchers who were over the hill when he was a rookie with San Buitre, with pups like Brannerman, with big-leaguers and Hall of Famers. Here it comes, Hector, 92 MPH, the big *gringo* trying to throw it by you, the matchless wrists, the flawless swing, one terrific moment of suspended animation—and all of a sudden you're starring in your own movie.

How does it go? The ball cutting through the night sky like a comet, arching high over the center fielder's hapless scrambling form to slam off the wall while your legs churn up the base paths, you round first in a gallop, taking second, and heading for third . . . but wait, you spill hot coffee on your hand and you can't feel it, the demons apply the live wire to your tailbone, the legs give out and they cut you down at third while the stadium erupts in howls of execration and abuse and the *niñitos* break down, faces flooded with tears of humiliation, Hector Jr. turning his back in disgust and Asunción raging like a harpie, *Abuelo! Abuelo! Abuelo!*

Stunned, shrunken, humiliated, you stagger back to the dugout in a maelstrom of abuse, paper cups, flying spittle, your life a waste, the game a cheat, and then, crowning irony, that bum Tool, worthless all the way back to his washerwoman grandmother and the drunken muttering whey-faced tribe that gave him suck, stands tall like a giant and sends the first pitch out of the park to tie it. Oh, the pain. Flat feet, fire in your legs, your poor tired old heart skipping a beat in mortification. And now Dupuy, red in the face, shouting: The game could be over but for you, you crazy gimpy old beaner washout! You want to hide in your locker, bury yourself under the shower-room floor, but you have to watch as the next two men reach base and you pray with fervor that they'll score and put an end to your debasement. But no, Thorkelsson whiffs and the new inning dawns as inevitably as the new minute, the new hour, the new day, endless, implacable, world without end.

But wait, wait: who's going to pitch? Dorfman's out, there's nobody left, the astonishing thirty-second inning is marching across the scoreboard like an invading army, and suddenly Dupuy is standing over you—no, no, he's down on one knee, begging. Hector, he's saying, didn't you use to pitch down in Mexico when you were a kid, didn't I hear that someplace? Yes, you're saying, yes, but that was—

And then you're out on the mound, in command once again, elevated like some half-mad old king in a play, and throwing smoke. The first two batters go down on strikes and the fans are rabid with excitement, Asunción will raise a shrine, Hector Jr. worships you more than all the poets that ever lived, but can it be? You walk the next three and then give up the grand slam to little Tommy Oshimisi! Mother of God, will it never cease? But wait, wait, wait: here comes the bottom of the thirty-second and Brannerman's wild. He walks a couple, gets a couple out, somebody reaches on an infield single and the bases are loaded for you, Hector Quesadilla, stepping up to the plate now like the Iron Man himself. The wind-up, the delivery, the ball hanging there like a *piñata*, like a birthday gift, and then the stick flashes in your hands like an archangel's sword, and the game goes on forever.

Whales Weep

They say the sea is cold, but the sea contains
the hottest blood of all. . . .
—D. H. LAWRENCE, "Whales Weep Not"

I don't know what it was exactly—the impulse toward preservation in the face of flux, some natal fascination with girth—who can say? But suddenly, in the winter of my thirty-first year, I was seized with an overmastering desire to seek out the company of whales. That's right: whales. Flukes and blowholes. Leviathan. Moby Dick.

People talked about the Japanese, the Russians. Factory ships, they said. Dwindling numbers and a depleted breeding stock, whales on the wane. I wanted desperately to see them before they sang their swan song, before they became a mere matter of record, cards in an index, skeletal remains strung out on coat hangers and suspended from the high concave ceilings of the Smithsonian like blueprints of the past. More: I wanted to know them, smell them, touch them. I wanted to mount their slippery backs in the

high seas, swim amongst them, come to understand their expan-
sive gestures, sweeping rituals, their great whalish ecstasies and
stupendous sorrows.

This cetaceamania was not something that came on gradually, a
predilection that developed over a period of months into interest,
awareness, and finally absorption—not at all. No: it took me by
storm. Of course I'd been at least marginally aware of the plight of
whales and dolphins for years, blitzed as I was by pleas from the
Sierra Club, the National Wildlife Federation, and the Save the
Whales people. I gave up tuna fish. Wrote a letter to my con-
gressman. Still, I'd never actually seen a whale and can't say that I
was any more concerned about cetaceans than I was about the
mountain gorilla, inflation, or the chemicals in processed foods.
Then I met Harry Macey.

It was at a party, somewhere in the East Fifties. One of those
seasonal affairs: Dom Pérignon, cut crystal, three black girls whining over a prerecorded disco track. Furs were in. Jog togs. The
hustle. Health. I was with Stephanie King, a fashion model. She
was six feet tall, irises like well water, the *de rigueur* mole at the
corner of her mouth. Like most of the haute couture models
around town, she'd developed a persona midway between Girl
Scout and vampire. I did not find it at all unpalatable.

Stephanie introduced me to a man in beard, blazer, and bi-
focals. He was rebuking an elderly woman for the silver-fox boa
dangling from her neck. "Disgusting," he snarled, working himself into a froth. "Savage and vestigial. What do you think we've
developed synthetics for?" His hair was like the hair of Kennedys,
boyish, massed over his brow, every strand shouting for attention;
his eyes were cold and messianic. He rattled off a list of endan-
gered species, from snail darter to three-toed sloth, his voice
sucking mournfully at each syllable as if he were a rabbi uttering
the secret names of God. Then he started on whales.

I cleared my throat and held out my hand. "Call me Roger," I
said.

He didn't even crack a smile. Just widened his sphere of influence to include Stephanie and me. "The blue whale," he was saying, flicking the ash from his cigarette into the ashtray he held

supine in his palm, "is a prime example. One hundred feet long, better than a quarter of a million pounds. By far and away the largest creature ever to inhabit the earth. His tongue alone weighs three tons, and his penis, nine and a half feet long, would dwarf a Kodiak bear. And how do we reward this exemplar of evolutionary impetus?" He paused and looked at me like a quiz-show host. Stephanie, who had handed her lynx maxicoat to the hostess when we arrived, bowed twice, muttered something unintelligible, and wandered off with a man in dreadlocks. The old woman was asleep. I shrugged my shoulders.

"We hunt him to the brink of extinction, that's how. We boil him down and convert him into margarine, pet food, shoe polish, lipstick."

This was Harry Macey. He was a marine biologist connected with NYU and, as I thought at the time, something of an ass. But he did have a point. Never mind his bad breath and egomania; his message struck a chord. As he talked on, lecturing now, his voice modulating between anger, conviction, and a sort of evangelical fervor, I began to develop a powerful, visceral sympathy with him. Whales, I thought, sipping at my champagne. Magnificent, irreplaceable creatures, symbols of the wild and all that, brains the size of ottomans, courting, making love, chirping to one another in the fathomless dark—just as they'd been doing for sixty million years. And all this was threatened by the greed of the Japanese and the cynicism of the Russians. Here was something you could throw yourself into, an issue that required no soul-searching, good guys and bad as clearly delineated as rabbits and hyenas.

Macey's voice lit the deeps, illuminated the ages, fired my enthusiasm. He talked of the subtle intelligence of these peaceful, lumbering mammals, of their courage and loyalty to one another in the face of adversity, of their courtship and foreplay and the monumental suboceanic sex act itself. I drained my glass, shut my eyes, and watched an underwater *pas de deux:* great shifting bulks pressed to one another like trains in collision, awesome, staggering, drums and bass pounding through the speakers until all I could feel through every cell of my body was that fearful, seismic humping in the depths.

———

Two weeks later I found myself bobbing about in a rubber raft somewhere off the coast of British Columbia. It was raining. The water temperature was thirty-four degrees. A man unlucky enough to find himself immersed in such water would be dead of exposure inside of five minutes. Or so I was told.

I was given this morsel of information by either Nick, Gary, or Ernie, my companions in the raft. All three were in their mid-twenties, wild-eyed and bearded, dressed in Norwegian sweaters, rain slickers, and knit skullcaps. They were aficionados of rock and roll, drugs, airplanes, and speedboats. They were also dangerous lunatics dedicated to thrusting themselves between the warheads of six-foot, quadri-barbed, explosive harpoons and the colossal rushing backs of panic-stricken whales.

At the moment, however, there were no whales to be seen. Living whales, at any rate. The carcasses of three sei whales trailed behind the rictus of a Russian factory ship, awaiting processing. A low cloud cover, purple-gray, raveled out from horizon to horizon like entrails on a butcher's block, while the Russian ship loomed above us, its endless rust-streaked bows high as the Jersey palisades, the stony Slavic faces of the Russian seamen ranged along the rail like a string of peas. There were swells eight feet high. All around us the sea was pink with the blood of whales and sliced by the great black dorsal fins of what I at first took to be sharks. A moment later I watched a big grinning killer whale rush up out of the depths and tear a chunk of meat the size of a Holstein from one of the carcasses.

Nick was lighting his pipe. "Uh," I said, "shouldn't we be getting back to the ship?"

If he heard me, he gave no sign of it. He was muttering under his breath and jerking angrily at his knuckles. He took a long, slow hit from a tarnished flask, then glared up at the stoic Russian faces and collectively gave them the finger. "Murderers!" he shouted. "Cossack faggots!"

I was on assignment for one of the news magazines, and I'd managed to come up with some expense money from *Audubon* as well. The news magazine wanted action shots of the confrontation between the whalers and Nick, Gary, and Ernie; *Audubon* wanted some wide-angles of spouting whales for an article by some cetologist studying the lung capacity of the minke. I'd talked them into the assignment. Like a fool. For the past few years I'd been doing pretty well on the fashion circuit (I'd done some Junior Miss things for J. C. Penney and Bloomingdale's and freelanced for some of the women's magazines), but had begun to feel that I was missing something. Call it malaise, call it boredom. I was making a living, but what was I doing for the generations of mankind? Saving the whales—or at least doing my part in it—seemed a notch or two higher on the ethical scale than inflaming the lust of pubescent girls for snakeskin boots and fur collars. And what's more, I was well equipped to do it, having begun my career as a naturalist.

That's right: I too had my youthful illusions. I was just six months out of college when I did my study of the bearded tit for the *National Geographic*, and I was flushed with success and enthusiasm. The following year *Wildlife* sent me up the Xingu to record the intimate life of the capybara. I waded through swamps, wet to my waist, crouched behind blinds for days on end, my skin black with mosquitoes though I didn't dare slap them for fear of spooking my quarry. I was bitten by three different species of arachnids. I contracted bilharziasis. It was then that I decided to trade in my telephoto lens and devote myself to photographing beautiful women with haunted eyes in clean, airy studios.

Nick was on his feet now, fighting for balance as the waves tossed our raft. "Up Brezhnev!" he shrieked, the cords in his neck tight as hawsers.

Suddenly one of the Russians reared back and threw something at us, something round and small. I watched its trajectory as it shot out over the high bow of the ship and arced gracefully for us. It landed with a rush of air and a violent elastic hiss like a dozen rubber bands snapping simultaneously. The missile turned out to be a grapefruit, frozen hard as a brick. It tore a hole through the floor of the raft.

———

After the rescue, I spent a few days in a hospital in Vancouver, then flew back to New York. Gary—or was it Ernie?—lost two toes. I took a nasty crack over the eyebrow that required nineteen stitches and made me look either rakish or depraved, depending on your point of view. The photos, for which I'd been given an advance, were still in the camera—about thirty fathoms down. Still, things wouldn't have been so bad if it weren't for the headaches. Headaches that began with a quick stab at something beneath the surface of the eye and then built with a steadily mounting pressure until the entire left side of my head felt like a helium balloon and I began to understand that I was no longer passionate on the subject of whales. After all, the only whales I'd managed to catch sight of were either dead, dying, or sprinting for their lives in a rush of foam. Where was the worth and beauty in that? And where, I wondered, was the affirmation these diluvian and mystical beasts were supposed to inject into my own depleted life?

The night I got in, Stephanie showed up at my apartment with a bottle of Appleton's rum. We made piña coladas and love. There was affirmation in that. In the morning, 7:00 A.M., Harry Macey was at the door in a warm-up suit. He whistled at the stitching over my eye, compared me unfavorably wth Frankenstein's monster, offered me a dried lemon peel, and sat down at the kitchen table. "All right," he barked, "let's have it—all the details. Currents, sightings, the Russian take—everything." I reconstructed the trip for him over Red Zinger and granola, while he nodded and spooned, spooned and nodded, filing mental notes. But before I'd even got halfway he cut me off, jumped up from the table, and told me there was someone I just had to meet, right away, no arguments, a person I could really relate to.

I looked up from my granola, head throbbing. He was standing over me, shot through with energy, tugging at his ear, blowing the steam from his teacup, all but dancing. "I know you're going to love him," he said. "The man knows whales inside and out."

Eyolf Holluson lived in a two-room apartment on East Twenty-sixth Street. He was eighty-six years old. We mounted the steps two at a time—all five flights—and stood outside the door while Harry counted his heartbeats. "Forty-four a minute," he said, matter-of-factly. "Nothing when you consider the lungfish, but not bad for a man of thirty-nine." In the process, my own heart seemed to have migrated to my head, where it was pounding like a letterpress over my left eye.

A voice, high and nasal, shaken with vibrato, echoed from behind the door. "Harry?"

Harry answered in the affirmative, the voice indicated that the door was open, and we stepped into a darkened room lit only by flashing Christmas bulbs and smelling of corned beef and peppermint. On the far side of the room, lost in the folds of a massive, dun-colored armchair draped with layers of doily and antimacassar, sat Eyolf. Before him was a TV tray, and beyond that a color TV, pictures flashing, sound turned off.

"Eyolf," Harry said, "I'd like you to meet a friend of mine—he's come to talk about whales."

The old man turned and squinted up at me over the top of his steel-rimmed spectacles, then turned back to the tray. "Oh yah," he said. "Yust finishing up my breakfast." He was eating corned beef, plum tomatoes from the can, dinner mints.

Harry prompted him. "Eyolf fished whales for fifty-seven years —first with the Norwegian fleet, and then, when they packed it in, with the Portuguese off the Canary Islands."

"The old way," Eyolf said, his mouth a stew of mint and tomato. "Oars and harpoons."

We crossed the room and settled into a spongy loveseat that smelled of cat urine. Harry produced a pocket-sized tape recorder, flicked it on, and placed it on the TV tray beside the old man's plate. Then he sank back into the loveseat, crossed his legs at the knee, and said, "Tell us about it, Eyolf."

The old man was wearing a plaid bathrobe and slippers. His frame was big, flesh wasted, his skin the color and texture of beef jerky. He talked for two hours, the strange nasal voice creaking like oars in their locks, rising and falling like the tide. He told us of a sperm whale that had overturned a chase boat in the Sea of Japan, of shipmates towed out of sight and lost in the Antarctic, of a big Swede who lost his leg in a fight with flensing knives. With a crack of his knees he rose up out of the chair and took a harpoon down from the wall, cocked his arm, and told us how he'd stuck a thousand whales, hot blood spurting in his face over the icy spume, how it tasted and how his heart rushed with the chase. "You stick him," he said, "and it's like sticking a woman. Better."

There was a copy of the *Norsk Hvalfangst-Tildende* on the table. Behind me, mounted on hooks, was a scrimshaw pipe, and beside it a huge blackened sheet of leather, stiff with age. I ran my finger along its abrasive edge, wondering what it was—a bit of fluke, tongue?—and yet somehow, in a dim grope of intuition, knowing.

Eyolf was spinning a yarn about a sperm whale that had surfaced beneath him with an eighteen-foot squid clenched in its jaws when he turned to me. "I think maybe you are wondering what is this thing like a bullfighter's cape hanging from Eyolf's wall?" I nodded. "A present from the captain of the *Freya*, nearly forty years back, it was. In token of my take of finback and bowhead over a period of two, three hectic weeks. Hectic, oh yah. Blood up to my knees—hot first, then cold. There was blood in my shoes at night."

"The leather, Eyolf," Harry said. "Tell Roger about it."

"Oh yah," he said, looking at me now as if I were made of plastic. "This here is off of the biggest creater on God's earth. The sulphur-bottom, what you call the blue. I keep it here for vigor and long life."

The old man gingerly lifted it from the wall and handed it to me. It was the size of a shower curtain, rigid as tree bark. Eyolf was smiling and nodding. "Solid, no?" He stood there, looking down at me, trembling a bit with one of his multiple infirmities.

"So what is it?" I said, beginning to lose patience.

"You don't know?" He was picking his ear. "This here is his foreskin."

Out on the street Harry said he had a proposition for me. A colleague of his was manning a whale watch off the Península Valdés on the Patagonian coast. He was studying the right whale on its breeding grounds and needed some high-quality photographs to accompany the text of a book he was planning. Would I take the assignment for a flat fee?

My head throbbed at the thought of it. "Will you come along with me?"

Harry looked surprised. "Me?" Then he laughed. "Hell no, are you kidding? I've got classes to teach, I'm sitting on a committee to fund estuarine research, I'm committed for six lectures on the West Coast."

"I just thought—"

"Look, Roger—whales are fascinating and they're in a lot of trouble. I'm hoping to do a monograph on the reproductive system of the rorquals, in fact, but I'm no field man. Actually, pelagic mammals are almost as foreign to my specialty area as elephants."

I was puzzled. "Your specialty area?"

"I study holothurians. My dissertation was on the sea cucumber." He looked a little abashed. "But I think big."

———

The Patagonian coast of Argentina is a desolate, godforsaken place, swept by perpetual winds, parched for want of rain, home to such strange and hardy creatures as the rhea, crested tinamou, and Patagonian fox. Darwin anchored the *Beagle* here in 1832, rowed ashore and described a dozen new species. Wildlife abounded. The rocks were crowded with birds—kelp and dolphin gulls, cormorants in the thousands, the southern lapwing, redbacked hawk, tawny-throated dotterel. Penguins and sea lions lolled among the massed black boulders and bobbed in the green swells, fish swarmed offshore, and copepods—ten billion for each star in the sky—thickened the Falkland current until it took on the consistency of porridge. Whales gathered for the feast. Rights, finbacks, minkes—Darwin watched them spouting and lobtailing, sounding and surfacing, courting, mating, calving.

Nothing has changed here—but for the fact that there are fewer whales now. The cormorants and penguins and seals are still there, numbers uncountable, still battening on the rich *potage* that washes the littoral. And still undisturbed by man—with one small exception. The Tsunamis. Shuhei, Grace, and their three daughters. For five months out of the year the Tsunamis occupy the Península Valdés, living in a concrete bunker, eating pots of rice, beans, and fish, battling the wind and the loneliness, watching whales.

Stephanie and I landed with the supply plane, not two hundred feet from the Tsunami bunker. It was August, and the right whales were mating. During the intervening months I'd nursed my split head, drained pitchers of piña coladas, and gone back to the Junior Miss circuit. But I kept in touch with Harry Macey, read ravenously on the subject of whales, joined Greenpeace, and flew to Tokyo for the trial of six members of a cetacean terrorist group accused of harpooning a Japanese industrialist at the Narita airport. I attended lectures, looked at slides, visited Nantucket. At night, after a long day in the studio, I closed my eyes and whales slipped through the Stygian sea of my dreams. There was no denying them.

Grace was waiting for us as the Cessna touched down: hooded sweatshirt, blue jeans, eyes like polished walnut. The girls were there too—Gail, Amy, and Melia—bouncing, craning their necks, rabid with excitement at the prospect of seeing two new faces in the trackless waste. Shuhei was off in the dunes somewhere, in a welter of sonar dishes, listening for whales.

I shook hands with Grace; Stephanie, in a blast of perfume and windswept hair, pecked her cheek. Stephanie was wearing seal-skin boots, her lynx coat, and a "Let Them Live" T-shirt featuring the flukes of a sounding whale. She had called me two days before

I was scheduled to leave and said that she needed a vacation. Okay, I told her, glad to have you. She found a battery-operated hair dryer and a pith helmet at the Abercrombie & Fitch closeout sale, a wolf-lined parka at Max Bogen, tents, alcohol stoves, and freeze-dried Stroganoff at Paragon; she mail-ordered a pair of khaki puttees and sheepskin mukluks from L. L. Bean, packed up her spare underwear, eyeshadow, three gothic romances, and six pounds of dried apricots, and here she was, in breezy Patagonia, ready for anything.

"Christ!" I shouted, over the roar of the wind. "Does it always blow like this?" It was howling in off the sea, a steady fifty knots.

Grace was grinning, hood up, hair in her face. With her oblate eyes and round face and the suggestion of the hood, she looked like an Eskimo. "I was just going to say," she shouted, "this is calm for the Península Valdés."

That night we sat around the Franklin stove, eating game pie and talking whale. Grace was brisk and efficient, cooking, serving, clearing up, joking, padding round the little room in shorts and white sweat socks. Articulated calves, a gap between the thighs: earth mother, I thought. Shuhei was brooding and hesitant, born in Osaka (Grace was from L.A.). He talked at length about his project, of chance and probability, of graphs, permutations, and species-replacement theory. He was dull. When he attempted a witticism—a play on "flukes," I think it was—it caught us unaware and he turned red.

Outside the wind shrieked and gibbered. The girls giggled in their bunks. We burned our throats on Shuhei's sake and watched the flames play over the logs. Stephanie was six feet long, braless and luxuriant. She yawned and stretched. Shuhei was looking at her the way an indigent looks at a veal cutlet.

"Well," I said, yawning myself. "Guess we better turn in."

We'd pitched our tent just before dark, and it had blown down three times since. Now, as we made for the door, Shuhei became insistent. "No, no," he said, all but blocking our way. "Stay in here tonight—with us."

Grace looked up from her sake. "Yes," she said. "We insist."

———

I woke to the sound of whales. A deep, resonant huffing and groaning I could feel in my bones, a sound like trombones and English horns. It was light. I glanced round and saw that the Tsunamis were gone, hurriedly pulled on my clothes, grabbed my camera, and slipped out the door. There was no need to wake Stephanie.

The sky was overcast and the wind was still blowing a steady gale—it threw sand in my face as I made my way down to the cove where the Tsunamis kept their inflatable raft. There were birds everywhere—gulls whitening the sky, cormorants diving for fish, penguins loitering among the rocks as if they'd been carved of wood. Elephant seals and their pups sprawled on the beach; right whales spouted in the bay. It was like a *National Geographic Special.* I took a few shots of the seals, then worked my way down the shoreline until I found Grace and Melia perched atop a sand dune with a pair of binoculars and a notepad. Grace was wearing a windbreaker, white shorts, and a scarf; Melia was six years old.

Grace waved. "Want to go out in the boat?" she called.

I stood in water up to my knees, bracing the raft, while Grace pulled the starter cord and Melia held my Bronica. As we lurched off into the persistent swells I found myself thinking of Nick, Gary, and Ernie, but my initial fears proved unfounded: Grace was a faultless and assured pilot. We cut diagonally across the bay toward a distant sand spit. Gulls keened overhead, seals barked, spray flew, and then, before I could even get my camera focused, a big right pounded the water with his massive flukes, not thirty feet from us. "That was Bob Tail," Grace said, laughing.

I was wiping the spray from my lens. "How could you tell?"

"Easy. There's a piece missing from his left fluke."

We cruised the bay, and I was introduced to thirty whales or so, some recognized by name, others anonymous. I saw Gray Spot, Cyclops, Farrah Fawcett, and Domino, and actually got close enough to touch one of them. He was skimming the surface, black as a barge and crusted over with barnacles and lice, the huge yellowed mesh of his baleen exposed like the insides of a piano. Grace wheeled the raft round on him, throttle cranked down to idle, and as we came up alongside him I reached out and patted his cool, smooth hide. It was like patting a very wet horse the size of a house. I laid my open palm against the immensity of the whale's flank and for one mad moment thought I could feel the blood coursing through him, the colossal heart beating time with the roll of the tides and the crash of distant oceans; I felt I was reaching out and touching the great steaming heart of the planet itself. And then, in a rush of foam, he was gone.

For the next two weeks I spent mornings, afternoons—and when the light was good—evenings out on the bay. Stephanie came out with us once or twice, but preferred beachcombing with the girls; Shuhei was busy with the other boat, running up to Punta Tombo and back—something to do with his sonar dishes. He was gathering data on the above-water sounds of the right whale, while Grace was busy surveying the local population for size, color, distinguishing characteristics. She was also intent on observing their breeding behavior.

One afternoon we came upon a female floating belly up. Two males—one an adolescent no more than two-thirds her size—were nudging her, shoving at her great inert form with their callused snouts like a pair of beavers trying to maneuver a log. Grace cut the engine and pulled out her notepad. "Is she dead?" I asked.

Grace laughed. The sun was climbing, and she held up a hand to shade her eyes as she looked at me. "They're mating," she said. "Or about to."

"A *ménage à trois?*"

She explained it, patiently. The female was rejecting her suitors, heaving her working parts from the water to avoid being taken forcibly. The reason for the cold flipper was anybody's guess. Perhaps she was tired, or suffering from a cold, or simply discriminating. She did have a problem, though. Since she couldn't breathe while inverted, she'd have to right herself every fifteen minutes or so to take a quick breath. And then they'd be on her.

The first time she rolled over we recognized her as Domino, so named for the symmetrical arrangement of callosities on her forehead. She was an adept coquette: rolling, spouting, filling her lungs, and turning belly up again before her suitors had a chance. I made some sort of joke about the prom and the back seat of a Studebaker. Grace giggled, the raft bobbed, we had peanut-butter sandwiches—and waited.

Grace told me about growing up over her father's sushi bar in Little Tokyo, about dropping out of veterinary school to study oceanography at Miami, about Osaka and Shuhei. I told her about the crested tit and the capybara, and was in the middle of a devastatingly witty aperçu of the Junior Miss world when suddenly the raft was rammed from behind and tossed into the air like a bit of driftwood. A third male, big as an express train, had come charging past us in the heat of his passion, intent on Domino. We were shaken, but unhurt. The raft was right side up, the camera round my neck, the notepad in Grace's lap.

Meanwhile, it became clear that the interloper was not about to stand on ceremony. He chased off his rivals, pounded the water to a froth with his tail, forced Domino over, and ravished her. It was frightening, appalling, fascinating—like nothing I'd ever imagined. They re-enacted the birth of Surtsey, the consolidation of the moon, the eruption of Vesuvius. He slid beneath her, belly to belly, locked his flippers in hers and pitched into her. Leviathan indeed.

I was swollen with emotion, transported, ticking with excitement. So awestruck I hadn't taken a single photograph. Grace's hand was on my knee. The raft rose and settled, rose and settled, as if keeping time with each monumental thrust and heave. Some-how—I have no clear recollection of how it happened—we were naked. And then we were on the floor of the raft, gently undulating rubber, the cries of gulls, salt sea spray, locked in a mystery and a rhythm that defied the drift of continents and the receding of the waters.

———

A month later, in New York, I ran into Harry Macey at a bar. "So what gives with Grace and Shuhei?" he said.

"What do you mean?"

I hadn't heard? There'd been some sort of blowup between them. A vicious temper. Stormy. Hadn't I noticed? Well, he'd really taken it to her: black eye, scratched cornea, right arm in a sling. She was in San Francisco with the children. He was in Miami, brooding. The project was dead.

Harry ground out his cigarette in the ashtray he held in his palm. "Did you notice any strain between them when you were down there?"

"None."

He grinned. "Cabin fever, I guess, huh? I mean, I take it it's pretty bleak down there." He ordered me another drink. "So listen," he said. "You interested in flying out to the Azores? There's a big broil going on over that little local whaling operation—the Portuguese thing."

I downed my drink in a gulp. I felt like a saboteur, a killer, the harpoonist crouched in the bow of the rushing boat. "If you want to know the truth," I said, holding his eyes, "I'm just a little bit tired of whales right now."

The New Moon Party

There was a blizzard in the Dakotas, an earthquake in Chile, and a solar eclipse over most of the Northern Hemisphere the day I stepped up to the governor's podium in Des Moines and announced my candidacy for the highest post in the land. As the lunar shadow crept over the Midwest like a stain in water, as noon became night and the creatures of the earth fell into an unnatural frenzy and the birds of the air fled to premature roosts, I stood in a puddle of TV lights, Lorna at my side, and calmly raked the incumbent over the coals. It was a nice campaign ploy—I think I used the term "penumbra" half a dozen times in my speech—but beyond that I really didn't attach too much significance to the whole thing. I wasn't superstitious. I wore no chains or amulets, I'd never had a rabbit's foot, I attended church only because my constituents expected me to. Of portents, I knew nothing.

My awakening—I've always liked to refer to it as my "lunar epiphany"—came at the dog end of a disappointing campaign in the coach section of a DC 10 somewhere between Battle Creek and Montpelier. It was two months before the convention, and we were on our way to Vermont to spill some rhetoric. I was picking at something the airline optimistically called *salade Madrid*, my feet hurt, my digestion was shot, and the latest poll had me running dead last in a field of eight. My aides—a bunch of young Turks and electoral strong-arm men who wielded briefcases like swords and had political ambitions akin to Genghis Khan's—were daintily masticating their rubbery *coq au vin* and trying to use terms like "vector," "interface," and "demographic volatility" in a single sentence. They were dull as doorknobs, dry as the dust on the textbooks that had given them life. Inspiration? They couldn't have inspired a frog to croak. No, it was Lorna, former Rose Queen and USC song girl and the sweetest, lovingest wife a man could want, who was to lift me that night to the brink of inspiration even as I saw myself swallowed up in defeat.

The plane dipped, the lights flickered, and Lorna laid one of her pretty white hands on my arm. "Honey," she whispered, with that soft throbbing City-of-Industry inflection that always made me think of surf caressing the pylons of the Santa Monica pier, "will you look at that moon?"

I stabbed at my salad in irritation, a speech about Yankee gumption, coydog control, and support prices for maple-sugar pinwheels tenting my lap, and took a hasty glance at the darkened porthole. "Yeah?" I said, and I'm sure there was more than a little edge to my voice: Couldn't she see that I was busy, worn out, heartbroken, and defeated? Couldn't she see I was like the old lion with a thorn in his paw, surrounded by wolves and jackals and facing his snaggle-toothed death in the political jungle? "What of it?" I snarled.

"Oh, I don't know," she murmured, her voice dreamy, seductive almost (had she been reading those women's magazines again?). "It just looks so old and shabby."

I squinted through that dark little porthole at the great black fathomless universe and saw the moon, palely glowing, looked at the moon probably for the first time in twenty years. Lorna was right. It did look pretty cheesy.

She hummed a few bars of "Shine On, Harvest Moon," and then turned to me with those big pale eyes—still beautiful, still enough to move me after all these years—and said, "You know, if that moon was a loveseat I'd take it out to the garage and send to Bloomingdale's for a new one."

One of my aides—Colin or Carter or Rutherford, I couldn't keep their names straight—was telling a joke in dialect about three Mexican gardeners and an outhouse, another was spouting demographic theory, and the stewardess swished by with a smell of perfume that hit me like a twenty-one-gun salute. It was then—out of a whirl of thoughts and impressions like cream whipped in a blender—that I had my moment of grace, of inspiration, the moment that moves mountains, solves for x, and makes a musical monument of the "Hymn to Joy," the moment the mass of humankind lives an entire lifetime for and never experiences. "Of course," I blurted, upending the salad in my excitement, "yes," and I saw all the campaign trails of all the dreary, pavement-pounding, glad-handing years fall away beneath me like streamers from heaven, like tickertape, as I turned to kiss Lorna as if I were standing before the cheering hordes on Inauguration Day.

Colin or Carter or Rutherford turned to me and said, "What is it, George—are you all right?"

"The New Moon," I said.

Lorna was regarding me quizzically. A few of the other aides turned their heads.

I was holding my plastic cup of 7-Up aloft as if it were crystal, as if it were filled with Taittinger or Dom Pérignon. "To the New Moon!" I said with a fire and enthusiasm I hadn't felt in years. "To the New Moon Party!"

———

The American people were asleep. They were dead. The great, the giving, the earnest, energetic, and righteous American people had thrown in the towel. Rape, murder, cannibalism, political up-

heaval in the Third World, rock and roll, unemployment, pup-
pies, mothers, Jackie, Michael, Liza: nothing moved them. Their
worst fears, most implausible dreams, and foulest conceptions
were all right there in the metro section, splashed across the ever-
swelling megalopic eye of the TV screen in living color and
clucked over by commentators who looked as alike as bowling
pins. Scandal and horror were as mundane as a yawn before bed;
honor, decency, heroism, and enterprise were looked on as
quaint, largely inapplicable notions that expressed an inexcusable
naïveté about the way of the world. In short, no one gave a good
goddamn about anything. Myself included. So how blame them
when they couldn't tell the candidates apart, didn't bother to turn
out at the polls, neither knew nor cared whether the honorable
Mr. P. stood for Nazi rebirth or federally funded electronic walk-
ers for the aged and infirm?

I'd seen it all, and nothing stirred me, either. Ultraism, conser-
vatism, progressivism, communism, liberalism, neofascism, parties of the right, left, center, left of center, and oblate poles: who
cared? I didn't even know why I was running. I'd served my two
terms as a fresh-faced, ambitious young representative during the
Eisenhower years, fought through three consecutive terms in the
senatorial wars, wielded the sword of power and influence in
the most armor-plated committees on the Hill, and been twice
elected governor of Iowa on a platform that promised industrial
growth, environmental protection, and the eradication of corn
blight through laser technology. And yet, for all that, I wasn't
satisfied. I guess, even at sixty-one, I was still afflicted with those
hungry pangs of ambition that every boy who can't play center
field for the Yankees will never wholly shake: I wanted to be top
dog, kick off my shoes in the Oval Office, and stir up a fuss wher-
ever I went; I wanted to climb high atop the mountain and look
down on the creeping minuscule figures of queens, rock stars,
matinee idols, and popes. It was a cold life in a comfortless universe; I didn't believe in God, afterlife, or leprechauns. I wanted
to make my mark on history—what else was there?

And so I—we—came up with the issue that would take the
country—no, the world itself—by storm. From the moment of

my epiphany on that rattling howling DC 10 I never said another
word about taxes, inflation, Social Security, price supports, or the
incumbent's lamentable record on every key issue from the de-
centralization of the Boy Scouts to relations with the Soviet
Union. No, I talked only of the New Moon. The moon *we* were
going to build, to create, to hurl into the sky to take its place
among the twinkling orbs of the night and recover the dignity and
economic stability of America in the process. Jupiter had twelve
moons, Saturn ten, Uranus five. What were we? Where was our
global pride when we could boast but one craggy, acne-ridden
bulb blighting the nighttime sky? *A New Moon. A New Moon
Soon:* it was on my lips like a battle cry.

In Montpelier they thought I'd gone mad. An audience of
thirty-seven had turned out at the local ag school to hear me talk
about coydogs and maple-sugar pinwheels, but I gave them a dose
of the New Moon instead. I strode out onto the stage like a man
reborn (which I was), shredded my prepared speech, and flung it
like confetti over their astonished heads, my arms spread wide,
the spontaneous, thrilling message of the lunar gospel pouring
from me in evangelical fervor. LUNACY, mocked the morning
headlines. THORKELSSON MOONSTRUCK. But the people listened. They murmured in Montpelier, applauded lightly—hands
chapped and dry as cornhusks—in Rutland. In Pittsburgh, where
I really began to hit my stride (I talked of nothing but the steel it
would take to piece together the superstructure of the new satellite), they got up on tables and cheered. The American people
were tired of party bickering, vague accusations, and even vaguer
solutions; they were sick to death of whiz-kid economists, do-
nothing legislatures, and the nightmare specter of nuclear war.
They wanted joy, simplicity, a goal as grand as Manifest Destiny
and yet as straightforward and unequivocal as a bank statement.
The New Moon gave it to them.

By the time the convention rolled around, the New Moon was
waxing full. I remember the way the phones rang off the hook:
would we take a back seat to Fritz, throw our support to John,
accept the VP nomination on a split-issue platform? Seven weeks
earlier no one had even deigned to notice us—half the time we

didn't even get press coverage. But New Moon fever was sweeping the country—we'd picked up a bundle of delegates, won in Texas, Ohio, and California, and suddenly we were a force to reckon with.

"George," Colin was saying (I'm sure it was Colin, because I'd canned Carter and Rutherford to avoid the confusion), "I still say we've got to broaden our base. The one issue has taken us leagues, I admit it, but—"

I cut him off. I was George L. Thorkelsson, former representative, former senator, and current governor of the Mesopotamia of the Midwest, the glorious, farinaceous, black-loamed hogbutt of the nation, and I wasn't about to listen to any defeatist twaddle from some Ivy League pup. "Hey diddle, diddle," I said, "the cat and the fiddle." I was feeling pretty good.

It was then that Gina—Madame Scutari, that is—spoke up. Lorna and I had discovered her in the kitchen of Mama Gina's, a Nashville pasta house, during the Tennessee primary. She'd made an *abbacchio alla cacciatora* that knocked my socks off, and when we'd gone back to congratulate her she'd given me a look of such starstruck devotion I felt like the new Messiah. It seemed that the Madame (who wasn't Italian at all, but Hungarian) was a part-time astrologist and clairvoyant, and had had a minor seizure at the very moment of my epiphany in the DC 10—her left arm had gone numb and she'd pitched forward into a platter of antipasto with the word "lunar" on her lips. She told us all this in a rush of malapropisms and tortured syntax, while cauldrons of marinara sauce bubbled around her and her faintly mustachioed upper lip rose and fell like a shuttlecock. Then she'd leaned forward to whisper in my ear like a priestess of the oracle. *Leo,* she'd said, hitting my sign on the nose, *Scorpio in the ascendant.* Then she drew up her rouged face and gave me a broad Magyar wink and I could feel her lips moving against my ear: *A New Moon Soon,* she rasped. From that moment on she'd become one of my closest advisers.

Now she cleared her throat with a massive dignity, her heavy arms folded over her bust, and said, in that delicate halting accent that made you feel she could read the future like a Neapolitan

menu, "Not to worry, Georgie: I see you rising like the lion coming into the tenth house."

"But George"—Colin was nearly whining—"gimmicks are
okay, but they can only take you so far. Think of the political
realities."

Lorna and the Madame exchanged a look. I watched as a smile
animated my wife's features. It was a serene smile, visionary, the
smile of a woman who already saw herself decked out in a gown
like a shower of gold and presiding over tea in the Blue Room.

I turned to Colin and tersely reminded him of the political realities his late colleagues were currently facing. "We need no naysayers here," I added. "You're either on the bus or you're off it."
He looked at me as if he were about to say something he would
regret, but the Madame cut him off, her voice elevated yet soft,
the syllables falling together with a kiss that cut through the confusion and the jangling of telephones like a benediction: "Promise
them the moon," she said.

The convention itself was child's play. We'd captured the imag-
ination of the country, restored the average working man's faith in
progress, given America a cause to stand up and shout about. We
split the thing down the middle and I took my delegates outside
the party to form the first significant rump party since the days of
Henry Wallace. We were the New Moon Party and they came to
us in droves. Had anyone ever stopped to consider how many
amateur astrologers there were out there? How many millions
who guided their every move—from love affairs to travel plans to
stock purchases and the most auspicious time for doing their
nails—according to the conjunction of the planets and the phases
of the moon? Or how many religious fanatics and sci-fi freaks there
were, Trekkies, lunatics, werewolves, extraterrestrialists, saucer
nuts, and the like? Not to mention women, who've had to carry
that white-goddess baggage around with them since the dawn of
time. Well, here was an issue that could unite them all. Nixon had
put men on the moon; I was going to bring the moon to men. And
women.

Oh, there were the usual cries of outrage and anathema, the

usual blockheads, whiners, and pleaders, but we paid them no heed. NASA was behind us, one hundred percent. So were U.S. Steel, the AFL-CIO, the Teamsters, Silicon Valley, Wall Street and Big Oil, and just about anyone else in the country who worked for a living. A New Moon. Just think of the jobs it would create!

The incumbent—a man twelve years my senior who looked as if he'd been stuffed with sand—didn't stand a chance. Oh, they painted him up and pointed him toward the TV monitors and told him when to laugh or cry or make his voice tremble with righteousness, and they had him recite the usual litany about the rights of the rich and the crying need for new condos on Maui, and they prodded him to call the New Moon a hoax, a technological impossibility, a white elephant, and a liberal-humanist threat to the integrity of the interplanetary heavens, but all to no avail. It almost hurt me to see his bowed head, smeared blusher, and plasticized hair as he conceded defeat to a national TV audience after I'd swept every precinct in the country with the exception of a handful in Santa Barbara, where he'd beaten me by seventeen votes, but what the hell. This was no garden party, this was politics.

———

Sadly, however, unity and harmony are not the way of the world, and no leader, no matter how visionary—not Napoleon, not Caesar, not Mohammed, Louis XVI, Jim Jones, or Jesus of Nazareth—can hope to stave off the tide of discord, malcontent, envy, hatred, and sheer seething anarchy that inevitably rises up to crush him with the force of a tidal wave. And so it was, seven years later, my second term drawing to a close and with neither hope nor precedent for a third, that I found the waves crashing at very doorstep. I, who had been the most heralded chief executive in the country's history, I, who had cut across social strata, party differences, ethnic divisions, and international mistrust with my vision of a better world and a better future, was well on my way to becoming the most vilified world leader since Attila the Hun.

Looking back on it, I can see that perhaps my biggest mistake was in appointing Madame Scutari to my Cabinet. The problem wasn't so much her lack of experience—I understand that now—but her lack of taste. She took something truly grand—a human monument before which all the pyramids, Taj Mahals, and World Trade Centers paled by comparison—and made it tacky. For that I will never forgive her.

At any rate, when I took office back in January of '85, I created a new Cabinet post that would reflect the chief priority of my administration—I refer to the now infamous post of secretary for Lunar Affairs—and named Gina to occupy it. Though she'd had little formal training, she knew her stars and planets cold, and she was a woman of keen insight and studied judgment. I trusted her implicitly. Besides which, I was beleaguered by renegade scientists, gypsies, sci-fi hacks (one of whom was later to write most of my full-moon addresses to the nation), amateur inventors, and corporation execs, all clamoring for a piece of the action—and I desperately needed someone to sort them out. Gina handled them like diners without reservations.

The gypsies, Trekkies, diviners, haruspexes, and the like were apparently pursuing a collective cosmic experience, something that would ignite the heavens; the execs—from U.S. Steel to IBM to Boeing to American Can—wanted contracts. After all, the old moon was some 2,160 miles in diameter and eighty-one quintillion tons of dead weight, and they figured whatever we were going to do would take one hell of a lot of construction. Kaiser proposed an aluminum-alloy shell filled with Styrofoam, to be shuttled piecemeal into space and constructed by robots on location. The Japanese wanted to mold it out of plastic, while Firestone saw a big synthetic golf-ball sort of thing and Con Ed pushed for a hollow cement globe that could be used as a repository for nuclear waste. And it wasn't just the big corporations, either—it seemed every crank in the country was suddenly a technological wizard. A retired gym teacher from Sacramento suggested an inflatable ball made of simulated pigskin, and a pizza magnate from Brooklyn actually proposed a chicken-wire sphere coated with raw dough. *Bake it with lasers or something*, he wrote, *it'll harden like rock.*

Believe me. During those first few heady months in office the proposals must have come in at the rate of ten thousand a day.

If I wasn't equipped to deal with them (I've always been an idea man myself), Gina was. She conferred before breakfast, lunched three or four times a day, dined and brunched, and kept a telephone glued to her head as if it were a natural excrescence. "No problem," she told me. "I'll have a proposal for you by June."

She was true to her word.

I remember the meeting at which she presented her findings as keenly as I remember my mother's funeral or the day I had my gall bladder removed. We were sitting around the big mahogany table in the conference room, sipping coffee. Gina flowed through the door in a white caftan, her arms laden with clipboards and blueprints, looking pleased with herself. She took a seat beside Lorna, exchanged a bit of gossip with her in a husky whisper, then leaned across the table and cleared her throat. "Glitter," she said, "that's what we want, Georgie. Something bright, something to fill up the sky and screw over the astrological charts forever." Lorna, who'd spent the afternoon redesigning the uniforms of the Scouts of America (they were known as Space Cadets now, and the new unisex uniforms were to feature the spherical New Moon patch over the heart), sat nodding at her side. They were grinning conspiratorially, like a pair of matrons outfitting a parlor.

"Glitter?" I echoed, smiling into the face of their enthusiasm. "What did you have in mind?"

The Madame closed her heavy-lidded gypsy eyes for a moment, then flashed them at me like a pair of blazing guns. "The Bonaventure Hotel, Georgie—in L.A.? You know it?"

I shook my head slowly, wondering what she was getting at.

"Mirrors," she said.

I just looked at her.

"Fields of them, Georgie, acres upon acres. Just think of the reflective power! Our moon, *your* moon—it'll outshine that old heap of rock and dust ten times over."

Mirrors. The simplicity of it, the beauty. I felt the thrill of her inspiration, pictured the glittering triumphant moon hanging there like a jewel in the sky, bright as a supernova, bright as the star of Bethlehem. No, brighter, brighter by far. The flash of it would illuminate the darkest corners, the foulest alleys, drive back the creatures of darkness and cut the crime rate exponentially. George L. Thorkelsson, I thought, light giver. "Yes," I said, my voice husky with emotion, "yes."

But Filencio Salmón, author of *The Ravishers of Pentagord* and my chief speech writer, rose to object. "Wees all due respet, Meeser Presiden, these glass globe goin' to chatter like a gumball machine the firs' time a meteor or anytin' like that run into it. What you wan eeze sometin' strong, Teflon maybe."

"Not shiny enough," Gina countered, exchanging a hurt look with Lorna. Obviously she hadn't thought very deeply about the thing if she hadn't even taken meteors into account. Christ, she was secretary for Lunar Affairs, with two hundred JPL eggheads, selenologists, and former astronauts on her staff, and that was the best she could come up with?

I leaned back in my chair and looked over the crestfallen faces gathered round the table—Gina, Lorna, Salmón, my national security adviser, the old boy in the Philip Morris outfit we sent out for sandwiches. "Listen," I said, feeling wise as Solomon, "the concept is there—we'll work out a compromise solution."

No one said a word.

"We've got to. The world's depending on us."

We settled finally on stainless steel. Well buffed, and with nothing out there to corrode it, it would have nearly the same reflective coefficient as glass, and it was one hell of a lot more resistant. More expensive too, but when you've got a project like this, what's a hundred billion more or less? Anyway, we farmed out the contracts and went into production almost immediately. We had decided, after the usual breast-beating, shouting matches, resignations, and reinstatements, on a shell of jet-age plastic strengthened by steel girders, and a façade—one side only—of stainless-steel plates the size of Biloxi, Mississippi. Since we were only going up about eighty thousand miles, we figured we could get away with a sphere about one-third the size of the old moon: its proximity to earth would make it appear so much larger.

I don't mean to minimize the difficulty of all this. There were obstacles both surmountable and insurmountable, technologies to be invented, resources to be tapped, a great wealthy nation to be galvanized into action. My critics—and they were no small minority, even in those first few euphoric years—insisted that the whole thing was impossible, a pipe dream at best. They were defeatists, of course, like Colin (for whom, by the way, I found a nice little niche in El Salvador as assistant to the ambassador's body-count man), and they didn't faze me in the least. No, I figured that if in the space of the six years of World War II man could go from biplanes and TNT to jets and nuclear bombs, anything was possible if the will was there. And I was right. By the time my first term wound down we were three-quarters of the way home, the economy was booming, the unemployment rate approaching zero for the first time since the forties, and the Cold War defrosted. (The Russians had given over stockpiling missiles to work on their own satellite project. They were rumored to be constructing a new planet in Siberia, and our reconnaissance photos showed that they were indeed up to something big—something, in fact, that looked like a three-hundred-mile-long eggplant inscribed at intervals with the legend NOVAYA SMOLENSK.) Anyway, as most of the world knows, the Republicans didn't even bother to field a candidate in '88, and New Moon fever had the national temperature hovering up around the point of delirium.

Then, as they say, the shit hit the fan.

———

To have been torn to pieces like Orpheus or Mussolini, to have been stretched and broken on the rack or made to sing "Hello, Dolly" at the top of my lungs while strapped naked to a carny horse driven through the House of Representatives would have been pleasure compared to what I went through the night we unveiled the New Moon. What was to have been my crowning triumph—my moment of glory transcendent—became instead my most ignominious defeat. In an hour's time I went from savior to fiend.

For seven years, along with the rest of the world, I'd held my breath. Through all that time, through all the blitz of TV and newspaper reports, the incessant interviews with project scientists and engineers, the straw polls, moon crazes, and marketing ploys, the New Moon had remained a mystery. People knew how big it was, they could plot its orbit and talk of its ascending and descending nodes and how many million tons of materials had gone into its construction—but they'd yet to see it. Oh, if you looked hard enough you could see that something was going on up there, but it was as shadowy and opaque as the blueprint of a dream. Even with a telescope—and believe me, many's the night I spent at Palomar with a bunch of professional stargazers, or out on the White House lawn with the Questar QM 1 Lorna gave me for Christmas—you couldn't make out much more than a dark circle punched out of the great starry firmament as if with a cookie cutter.

Of course, we'd planned it that way. Right from the start we'd agreed that the best policy was to keep the world guessing—who wanted to see a piecemeal moon, after all, a moon that grew square by square in the night sky like some crazy checkerboard or something? This was no department store going up on West Twenty-third Street—this was something extraordinary, unique, this was the quintessence of man's achievement on the planet, and it should be served up whole or not at all. It was Salmón, in a moment of inspiration, who came up with the idea of putting the reflecting plates on the far side, facing out on the deeps of the universe, and then swinging the whole business around by means of initial-thrust and retro-rockets for a triumphant—and politically opportune—unveiling. I applauded him. Why not? I thought. Why not milk this thing for everything it was worth?

The night of the unveiling was clear and moonless. Lorna sat beside me on the dais, regal and resplendent in a Halston moonglow gown that cost more than the combined gross product of any six towns along the Iowa-Minnesota border. Gina was there too, of course, looking as if she'd just won a fettuccine cook-off in Naples, and the audience of celebrities, foreign ambassadors, and politicos gathered on the south lawn numbered in the thousands. Outside

the gates, in darkness, three-quarters of a million citizens milled
about with spherical white-moon candles, which were to be lit at
the moment the command was given to swing the New Orb into
view. Up and down the Eastern Seaboard, in Quebec and Ontario, along the ridge of the Smokies, and out to the verge of the
Mississippi, a hush fell over the land as municipalities big and
small cut their lights.

Ferenc Syzgies, the project's chief engineer, delivered an interminable speech peppered with terms like "photometric function"
and "fractional pore space," Anita Bryant sang a couple of spir-
ituals, and finally Luciano Pavarotti rose to do a medley of "Moon
River," "Blue Moon," and "That's Amore." Lorna leaned over and
took my hand as the horns stepped in on the last number. "Nervous?" she whispered.

"No," I murmured, but my throat had thickened till I felt I was
going to choke. They'd assured me there would be no foul-ups—
but nothing like this had ever been attempted before, and who
could say for sure?

"When-a the moon-a hits your eye like a big pizza pie," sang
Pavarotti, "that's *amore*." The dignitaries shifted in their seats,
Lorna was whispering something I couldn't hear, and then Co-
burn, the VP, was introducing me.

I stood and stepped to the podium to spontaneous, thrilling and
sustained applause, Salmón's speech clutched in my hand, the
shirt collar chafing at my neck like a garrote. Flashbulbs popped,
the TV cameras seized on me like the hungry eyes of great mechanical insects, faces leaped out of the crowd: here a senator I
loathed sitting cheek by jowl with a lobbyist from the Sierra Club,
there a sour-faced clergyman I'd prayed beside during a dreary
rally seven years earlier. The glowing, corn-fed visage of Miss
Iowa materialized just beneath the podium, and behind her sat
Coretta King, Tip O'Neill, Barbra Streisand, Carl Sagan, and
Mickey Mantle, all in a row. The applause went on for a full five
minutes. And then suddenly the audience were on their feet and
singing "God Bless America" as if their lives depended on it.
When they were finished, I held up my hands for silence and
began to read.

Salmón had outdone himself. The speech was measured, hysterical, opaque, and lucid. My voice rang triumphantly through the PA system, rising in eulogy, trembling with visionary fervor, dropping to an emotion-choked whisper as I found myself taking on everything from the birth of the universe to Conestoga wagons and pioneer initiative. I spoke of interstellar exploration, of the movie industry and Dixieland jazz, of the great selfless, uncontainable spirit of the American people, who, like latter-day Prometheuses, were giving over the sacred flame to the happy, happy generations to come. Or something like that. I was about halfway through when the New Orb began to appear in the sky over my shoulder.

The first thing I remember was the brightness of it. Initially there was just a sliver of light, but the sliver quickly grew to a crescent that lit the south lawn as if on a July morning. I kept reading. "The gift of light," I intoned, but no one was listening. As the thing began to swing round to full, the glare of it became insupportable. I paused to gaze down at the faces before me: they were awestruck, panicky, disgusted, violent, enraptured. People had begun to shield their eyes now; some of the celebrities and musicians slipped on sunglasses. It was then that the dogs began to howl. Faintly at first, a primal yelp here or there, but within thirty seconds every damn hound, mongrel, and cur in the city of Washington was baying at the moon as if they hadn't eaten in a week. It was unnerving, terrifying. People began to shout, and then to shove one another.

I didn't know what to do. "Well, er," I said, staring into the cameras and waving my arm with a theatrical flourish, "ladies and gentlemen, the New Moon!"

Something crazy was going on. The shoving had stopped as abruptly as it had begun, but now, suddenly and inexplicably, the audience started to undress. Right before me, on the platform, in the seats reserved for foreign diplomats, out over the seething lawn, they were kicking off shoes, hoisting shirt fronts and brassieres, dropping cummerbunds and Jockey shorts. And then, incredibly, horribly, they began to clutch at one another in passion, began to stroke, fondle, and lick, humping in the grass, plunging

into the bushes, running around like nymphs and satyrs at some
mad bacchanal. A senator I'd known for forty years went by me in
a dead run, pursuing the naked wife of the Bolivian ambassador;
Miss Iowa disappeared beneath the rhythmically heaving buttocks
of the sour-faced clergyman; Lorna was down to a pair of six-
hundred-dollar bikini briefs and I suddenly found to my horror
that I'd begun to loosen my tie.

Madness, lunacy, mass hypnosis, call it what you will: it was a
mess. Flocks of birds came shrieking out of the trees, cats appeared from nowhere to caterwaul along with the dogs, congress-
men rolled about on the ground, grabbing for flesh and yipping
like animals—and all this on national television! I felt lightheaded,
as if I were about to pass out, but then I found I had an erection
and there before me was this cream-colored thing in a pair of high-
heeled boots and nothing else, Lorna had disappeared, it was
bright as noon in Miami, dogs, cats, rats, and squirrels were howling like werewolves, and I found that somehow I'd stripped down
to my boxer shorts. It was then that I lost consciousness. Merci-
fully.

———

These days, I am not quite so much in the public eye. In fact, I
live in seclusion. On a lake somewhere in the Northwest, the
Northeast, or the Deep South, my only company a small cadre of
Secret Service men. They are laconic sorts, these Secret Service
men, heavy of shoulder and head, and they live in trailers set up
on a ridge behind the house. To a man, they are named Greg or
Craig.

As those who read this will know, all our efforts to modify the
New Moon (Coburn's efforts, that is: I was in hiding) were
doomed to failure. Syzgies's replacement, Klaus Erkhardt the
rocket expert, had proposed tarnishing the stainless-steel plates
with payloads of acid, but the plan had proved unworkable, for
obvious reasons. Meanwhile, a coalition of unlikely bedfellows—
Syria, Israel, Iran, Iraq, Libya, Great Britain, Argentina, the
Soviet Union, and China among them—had demanded the "im-

mediate removal of this plague upon our heavens," and in this country we came as close to revolution as we had since the 1770s.

Coburn did the best he could, but the following November, Colin, Carter, and Rutherford jumped parties and began a push to re-elect the man I'd defeated in '84 on the New Moon ticket. He was old—antediluvian, in fact—but not appreciably changed in either appearance or outlook, and he was swept into office in a landslide. The New Moon, which had been blamed for everything from causing rain in the Atacama to fomenting a new baby boom, corrupting morals, bestializing mankind, and making the crops grow upside down in the Far East, was obliterated by a nuclear thunderbolt a month after he took office.

On reflection, I can see that I was wrong—I admit it. I was an optimist, I was aggressive, I believed in man and in science, I challenged the heavens and dared to tamper with the face of the universe and its inscrutable design—and I paid for it as swiftly and surely as anybody in all the tragedies of Shakespeare, Sophocles, and Dashiell Hammett. Gina dropped me like a plate of hot lasagna and went back to her restaurant, Colin stabbed me in the back, and Coburn, once he'd taken over, refused to refer to me by name—I was known only as his "predecessor." I even lost Lorna. She left me after the debacle of the unveiling and the impeachment that followed precipitately on its heels, left me to "explore new feelings," as she put it. "I've got to get it out of my system," she told me, a strange glow in her eyes. "I'm sorry, George."

Hell yes, I was wrong. But just the other night I was out on the lake with one of the Secret Service men—Greg, I think it was—fishing for yellow perch, when the moon—the age-old, scar-faced, native moon—rose up out of the trees like an apparition. It was yellow as the underbelly of the fish on the stringer, huge with atmospheric distortion. I whistled. "Will you look at that moon," I said.

Greg just stared at me, noncommittal.

"That's really something, huh?" I said.

No response.

He was smart, this character—he wouldn't touch it with a tenfoot pole. I was just talking to hear myself anyway. Actually, I was thinking the damn thing did look pretty cheesy, thinking maybe where I'd gone wrong was in coming up with a new moon instead of just maybe bulldozing the old one or something. I began to picture it: lie low for a couple years, then come back with a new ticket—*Clean Up the Albedo, A New Face for an Old Friend, Save the Moon!*

But then there was a tug on the line, and I forgot all about it.

Not a Leg to Stand On

Calvin Tompkins is just lifting the soda bottle to his lips when the German-made car brakes in front of the house and the woman with the mean little eyes and the big backside climbs out in a huff. "Where'd you get that?" she demands, shoving through the hinge-sprung gate on feet so small it's astonishing they can support her. The old man doesn't know what to say. He can tell you the dimensions of the biggest hotdog ever made or Herbert Hoover's hat size, but sometimes, with the rush of things, it's all he can do to hold up his end of a conversation. Now he finds himself entirely at a loss as the big woman sways up the rotted steps to the rot-gutted porch and snatches the bottle out of his hand.

"Patio soda!" The way she says it is an indictment, her voice pinched almost to a squeal and the tiny feet stamping in outrage. "I am the only one that sells it for ten miles around here, and I want to know where you got it. Well?"

Frail as an old rooster, Calvin just gapes up at her.

She stands there a moment, her lips working in rage, the big shoulders, bosom, and belly poised over the old man in the wheelchair like an avalanche waiting to happen, then flings the bottle down in disgust. "*Mein Gott*, you people!" she says, and suddenly her eyes are wet.

It is then that Ormand, shadowed by Lee Junior, throws back the screen door with a crash and lurches out onto the porch. He's got a black bottle of German beer in his hand and he's unsteady on his feet. "What the hell's goin' on here?" he bellows, momentarily losing his footing in the heap of rags, cans, and bottles drifted up against the doorframe like detritus. Never graceful, he catches himself against the near post and sets the whole porch trembling, then takes a savage swipe at a yellow K-Mart oilcan and sends it rocketing out over the railing and up against the fender of the rusted, bumper-blasted Mustang that's been sitting alongside the house as long as the old man can remember.

"You know what is going on," the woman says, holding her ground. "You know," she repeats, her accent thickening with her anger, "because you are a thief!"

Ormand is big, unshaven, dirty. At twenty-two, he already has a beer gut. "Hell I am," he says, slurring his words, and the old man realizes he's been helping himself to the pain pills again. Behind Ormand, Lee Junior bristles. He too, Calvin now sees, is clutching a black bottle.

"Thief!" the woman shouts, and then she begins to cry, her face splotched with red, the big bosom heaving. Watching her, the old man feels a spasm of alarm: why, she's nothing but a young girl. Thirty years old, if that. For a keen, sharp instant her grief cuts at him like a saw, but then he finds himself wondering how she got so fat. Was it all that blood sausage and beer she sells? All that potato salad?

Now Lee Junior steps forward. "You got no right to come

around here and call us names, lady—this is private property."
He is standing two feet from her and he is shouting. "Why don't
you get your fat ass out of here before you get hurt, huh?"

"Yeah," Ormand spits, backing him up. "You can't come around
here harassing this old man—he's a veteran, for Christ's sake. You
keep it up and I'm going to have to call the police on you."

In that instant, the woman comes back to life. The lines of her
face bunch in hatred, the lips draw back from her teeth, and suddenly she's screaming. "*You* call the police on *me!?* Don't make
me laugh." Across the street a door slams. People are beginning to
gather in their yards and driveways, straining to see what the
commotion is about. "Pigs! Filth!" the woman shrieks, her little
feet dancing in anger, and then she jerks back her head and spits
down the front of Lee Junior's shirt.

The rest is confusion. There's a struggle, a stew of bodies, the
sound of a blow. Lee Junior gives the woman a shove, somebody
slams into Calvin's wheelchair, Ormand's voice cracks an octave,
and the woman cries out in German; the next minute Calvin finds
himself sprawled on the rough planks, gasping like a carp out of
water, and the woman is sitting on her backside in the dirt at the
foot of the stairs.

No one helps Calvin up. His arm hurts where he threw it out to
break his fall, and his hip feels twisted or something. He lies very
still. Below him, in the dirt, the woman just sits there mewling
like a baby, her big lumpy yellow thighs exposed, her socks gray
with dust, the little doll's shoes worn through the soles and
scuffed like the seats on the Number 56 bus.

"Get the hell out of here!" Lee Junior roars, shaking his fist.
"You . . . you fat-assed"—here he pauses for the hatred to rise up
in him, his face coiled round the words—"Nazi bitch!" And then,
addressing himself to Mrs. Tuxton's astonished face across the
street, and to Norm Cramer, the gink in the Dodgers cap, and all
the rest of them, he shouts: "And what are you lookin' at, all of
you? Huh?"

Nobody says a word.

———

Two days later Calvin is sitting out on the porch with a brand-new white plaster cast on his right forearm, watching the sparrows in the big bearded palm across the way and rehearsing numbers by way of mental exercise—5,280 feet in a mile, eight dry quarts in a peck—when Ormand comes up round the side of the house with a satchel of tools in his hand. "Hey, Calvin, what's doin'?" he says, clapping a big moist hand on the old man's shoulder. "Feel like takin' a ride?"

Calvin glances down at his cast with its scrawl of good wishes—"Boogie Out!" Lee Junior had written—and then back at Ormand. He is thinking, suddenly and unaccountably, of the first time he laid eyes on the Orem place. Was it two years ago already? Yes, two years, come fall. He'd been living with that Mexicano family out in the Valley—rice and beans, rice and beans, till he thought he'd turn into a human burrito or blow out his insides or something—and then his daughter had found Jewel's ad in the paper and gone out and made the arrangements.

"What do you say?" Ormand is leaning over him now. "Calvin?"

"A ride?" Calvin says finally. "Where to?"

Ormand shrugs. "Oh, you know: around."

Don't expect anything fancy, she'd told him, as if he had anything to say about it. But when they got there and were actually sitting in the car out front where they had a good view of the blistered paint, dead oleanders, trash-strewn yard, and reeling porch, she was the one who got cold feet. She started in on how maybe he wouldn't like these people and how maybe she ought to look a little further before they decided, but then *Bang!* went the screen door and Big Lee and Ormand ambled down the steps in T-shirts and engineer boots. Big Lee folded a stick of Red Man and tucked it up alongside his teeth, Ormand was clutching a can of Safeway beer like it was grafted onto him, and both of them were grinning as if they'd just shared a dirty joke in the back of the church. And then Big Lee was reaching his callused hand in through the window to shake with Calvin. Glad to meet you, neighbor, he murmured, turning his head to spit.

Shit, Calvin had said, swiveling round to look his daughter in the eye, I like these people.

Two minutes later they're out in the street, Ormand swinging back the door of his primer-splotched pickup, the pale bulb of Mrs. Tuxton's face just visible beyond the curtains over her kitchen sink. Even with Ormand's help, the old man has trouble negotiating the eight-inch traverse from the wheelchair to the car seat, what with his bum leg and fractured forearm and the general debility that comes of living so long, but once they're under way he leans back, half closes his eyes, and gives himself up to the soothing wash of motion. Trees flit overhead, streaks of light and moving shadow, and then an open stretch and the sun, warm as a hand, on the side of his face.

Yes, he likes these people. They might have their faults—Ormand and Lee Junior are drunk three-quarters of the time (that is, whenever they're not sleeping) and they gobble up his pain pills like M&Ms—but down deep he feels more kinship with them than he does with his own daughter. At least they'll talk to him and treat him like a human being instead of something that's been dead and dug up. Hell, they even seem to like him. When they go out visiting or whatever it is they do—house to house, dusty roads, day and night—they always want to take him along. So what if he has to sit there in the car sometimes for an hour or more? At least he's out of the house.

When he looks up, they're in a strange neighborhood. Stucco houses in shades of mustard and aquamarine, shabby palms, campers and trailers and pickups parked out front. Ormand has got a fresh beer and his eyes are shrunk back in his head. He stabs at the radio buttons and a creaky fiddle comes whining through the dashboard speaker. "You been noddin' out there a bit, huh, Calvin?" he says.

The old man's teeth hurt him all of a sudden, hurt him something fierce, so that the water comes to his eyes—he wants to cry out with the pain of it, but his arm begins to throb in counterpoint and pretty soon his hip starts kicking up where he twisted it and all he can do is just clamp his jaws shut in frustration. But when the car rolls to a stop beneath a dusty old oak and Ormand slips out the door with his satchel and says, "Just hang out here for a bit, okay, Calvin? I'll be right back," the old man finds the image

of the German woman rising up in his mind like a river-run log
that just won't stay down, and his voice comes back to him.
"Where *did* you get that soda, anyways?" he says.

"I tell you, Dad, I just don't trust these people. Now, you look
what's happened to your arm, and then there's this whole business of Lee going to jail—"
Calvin is sitting glumly over a bowl of tepid corn chowder in the
Country Griddle, toying with his spoon and sucking his teeth like
a two-year-old. Across the bright Formica table, his daughter
breaks off her monologue just long enough to take a sip of coffee
and a quick ladylike nip at her tuna on rye. She's wearing an off-
white dress, stockings, false eyelashes, and an expression about
midway between harried and exasperated.
"He was innocent," Calvin says.
His daughter gives him an impatient look. "Innocent or not,
Dad, the man is in jail—in prison—for armed robbery. And I
want to know who's paying the bills and taking car of the place—I
want to know who's looking after you."
"Armed robbery? The man had a screwdriver in his hand, for
Christ's sake—"
"Sharpened."
"What?"
"I said it was a sharpened screwdriver."
For a moment, Calvin says nothing. He fiddles with the salt
shaker and watches his daughter get the Dad-you-know-you're-
not-supposed-to look on her face, and then, when he's got her off
guard, he says, "Jewel."
"Jewel? Jewel what?"
"Takes care of the place. Pays the bills. Feeds me." And she
does a hell of a job of it too, he's about to add, when a vast and
crushing weariness suddenly descends on him. Why bother? His
daughter's up here on her day off to see about his arm and snoop
around till she finds something rotten. And she'll find it, all right,
because she's nothing but a sack of complaints and suspicions. Her
ex-husband is second only to Adolf Hitler for pure maliciousness,
her youngest is going to a psychiatrist three times a week, and her

oldest is flunking out of college, she's holding down two jobs to pay for the station wagon, figure-skating coaches, and orthopedic shoes, and her feet hurt. How could she even begin to understand what he feels for these people?

"Yes, and she drinks too. And that yard—it looks like something out of 'Li'l Abner.'" She's waving her sandwich now, gesturing in a way that reminds him of her mother, and it makes him angry, it makes him want to throw her across his knee and paddle her. "Dad," she's saying, "listen. I've heard of this place up near me—a woman I know whose mother is bedridden recommended it and she—"

"A nursing home."

"It's called a 'gerontological care facility' and it'll cost us seventy-five dollars more a month, but for my peace of mind—I mean, I just don't feel right about you being with these people any more."

He bends low over his chowder, making a racket with the spoon. So what if Jewel drinks? (And she does, he won't deny it—red wine mainly, out of the gallon jug—and she's not afraid to share it, either.) Calvin drinks too. So does the president. And so does the bossy, tired-looking woman sitting across the table from him. It doesn't mean a damn thing. Even with Lee in jail, even with her two big out-of-work nephews sitting down at the table and eating like loggers or linebackers or something, Jewel manages. And with no scrimping, either. Eggs for breakfast, bologna and American cheese on white for lunch with sweet butter pickles, and meat—real meat—for supper. Damn Mexicans never gave him meat, that's for shit sure.

"Dad? Did you hear what I said? I think it's time we made a change."

"I'm going nowhere," he says, and he means it, but already the subject has lost interest for him. Thinking of Jewel has got him thinking of her ham hocks and beans, and thinking of ham hocks and beans has got him thinking of Charlottesville, Virginia, and a time before he lost his leg when he and Bobbie Bartro were drunk on a bottle of stolen bourbon and racing up the street to his mother's Sunday-afternoon sit-down dinner, where they slid into their seats and passed the mashed potatoes as if there were noth-

ing more natural in the world. Off on the periphery of his consciousness he can hear his daughter trumpeting away, stringing
together arguments, threatening and cajoling, but it makes no difference. His mind is made up.

"Dad? Are you listening?"

Suddenly the lights are blinding him, the jukebox is scalding his
ears, and the weariness pressing down on him like a truckload of
cement. "Take me home, Berta," he says.

He wakes to darkness, momentarily disoriented. The dreams
have come at him like dark swooping birds, lifting him, taking him
back, dropping him in scene after scene of disorder, threat, and
sorrow. All of a sudden he's sunk into the narrow hospital bed in
San Bernardino, fifty years back, his head pounding with the ache
of concussion, his left leg gone at the knee. *What kind of motorcycle was it?* the doctor asks. And then he's in Bud's Grocery and
General Store in Charlottesville, thirteen years old, and he's got a
salami in one hand and a sixty-pound-pull hunting bow in the
other and no money, and he's out the door and running before
Bud can even get out from behind the counter. And then finally,
in the moment of waking, there's Ruth, his wife, down on the
kitchen floor in a spasm, hurt bad somewhere down in the deep of
her. But wait: somehow all of a sudden she's grown fat, rearranged
her features and the color of her hair—somehow she's transformed herself into the Patio-soda woman. Big, big, big. Thighs
like buttermilk. *You people,* she says.

There's a persistent thumping in the floorboards, like the beat
of a colossal heart, and the occasional snatch of laughter. He hears
Ormand's voice, Jewel's. Then another he doesn't recognize.
Ormand. Lee Junior. Laughter. Pushing himself up to a sitting
position, he swings his legs around and drops heavily into the
wheelchair. Then he fumbles for his glasses—1:30, reads the
dimly glowing face of the clock—and knocks over the cup with his
partial plate in it. He's wearing his striped pajamas. No need to
bother about a bathrobe.

"Hey, Calvin—what's happening!" Ormand shouts as the old
man wheels himself into the living room. Lee Junior and Jewel are

sitting side by side on the couch; the Mexican kid—Calvin can never remember his name—is sprawled on the floor smoking a big yellow cigarette, and Ormand is hunched over a bottle of tequila in the easy chair. All three color TVs are on and the hi-fi is scaring up some hellacious caterwauling nonsense that sets his teeth on edge. "Come on in and join the party," Jewel says, holding up a bottle of Spañada.

For a moment he just sits there blinking at them, his eyes adjusting to the light. The numbers are in his head again—batting averages, disaster tolls, the dimensions of the Grand Coulee Dam—and he doesn't know what to say. "C'mon, Calvin," Ormand says, "loosen up."

He feels ridiculous, humbled by age. Bony as a corpse in the striped pajamas, hair fluffed out like cotton balls pasted to his head, glasses glinting in the lamplight. "Okay," he murmurs, and Jewel is up off the couch and handing him a paper cup of the sweetened red wine.

"You hear about Rod Chefalo?" the Mexican says.

"No," says Lee Junior.

"Ormand, you want to put on a movie or something I can watch?" Jewel says. One TV set, the biggest one, shows an auto race, little cars plastered with motor-oil stickers whizzing round a track as if in a children's game; the other two feature brilliantined young men with guitars.

"Drove that beat Camaro of his up a tree out in the wash."

"No shit? He wind up in the hospital or what?"

"What do you want to watch, Aunt Jewel? You just name it. I don't give a shit about any of this."

After a while, Calvin finds himself drifting. The wine smells like honeydew melons and oranges and tastes like Kool-Aid, but it gives him a nice little burn in the stomach. His daughter's crazy, he's thinking as the wine settles into him. These are good people. Nice to sit here with them in the middle of the night instead of being afraid to leave his room, like when he was with those Mexicans, or having some starched-up bitch in the nursing home dousing the lights at eight.

"You know she went to the cops?" Lee Junior's face is like something you'd catch a glimpse of behind a fence.

"The cops?" The Mexican kid darts his black eyes round the room, as if he expects the sheriff to pop up from behind the couch. "What do you mean, she went to the cops?"

"They can't do a thing," Ormand cuts in. "Not without a search warrant."

"That's right." Lee Junior reaches for his can of no-name beer, belching softly and thumping a fist against his sternum. "And to get one they need witnesses. And I tell you, any of these shitheels on this block come up against me, they're going to regret it. Don't think they don't know it either."

"That fat-assed Kraut," Ormand says, but he breaks into a grin, and then he's laughing. Lee Junior joins him and the Mexican kid makes some sort of wisecrack, but Calvin misses it. Jewel, her face noncommittal, gets up to change the channel.

"You know what I'm thinkin'?" Ormand says, grinning still. Jewel's back is turned, and Calvin can see the flicker of green and pink under her right arm as she flips through the channels on the big TV. Lee Junior leans forward and the Mexican kid waves the smoke out of his eyes and props himself up on one elbow, a cautious little smile creeping into the lower part of his face. "What?" the Mexican kid says.

Calvin isn't there, he doesn't exist, the cardboard cup is as insubstantial as an eggshell in his splotched and veiny hand as he lifts it, trembling, to his lips.

"I'm thinking maybe she could use another lesson."

In the morning, early, Calvin is awakened by the crackle and stutter of a shortwave radio. His throat is dry and his head aches, three cups of wine gone sour in his mouth and leaden on his belly. With an effort, he pushes himself up and slips on his glasses. The noise seems to be coming from outside the house—static like a storm in the desert, tinny voices all chopped and diced. He parts the curtains.

A police cruiser sits at the curb, engine running, driver's door swung open wide. Craning his neck, Calvin can get a fix on the porch and the figures of Ormand—bare chest and bare feet—and a patrolman in the uniform of the LAPD. "So what's this all about?" Ormand is saying.

The officer glances down at the toes of his boots, then looks up and holds Ormand's gaze. "A break-in last night at the European Deli around the corner, 2751 Commerce Avenue. The proprietor"—and here he pauses to consult the metal-bound notepad in his hand—"a Mrs. Eva Henckle, thinks that you may have some information for us. . . ."

Ormand's hair is in disarray; his cheeks are dark with stubble. "No, Officer," he says, rubbing a hand over his stomach. "I'm sorry, but we didn't hear a thing. What time was that, did you say?"

The patrolman is young, no more than two or three years older than Ormand. In fact, he looks a bit like Ormand—if Ormand were to lose thirty pounds, stand up straight, get himself a shave, and cut the dark scraggly hair that trails down his back like something stripped from an animal. Ignoring the question, the patrolman produces a stub of pencil and asks one of his own. "You live here with your aunt, is that right?"

"Uh-huh."

"And a brother, Leland Orem, Junior—is that right?"

"That's right," Ormand says. "And like I said, we were all in last night and didn't hear a thing."

"Mother deceased?"

"Yeah."

"And your father?"

"What's that got to do with the price of beans?" Ormand's expression has gone nasty suddenly, as if he's bitten into something rotten.

For a moment, the patrolman is silent, and Calvin becomes aware of the radio again: the hiss of static, and a bored, disembodied voice responding to a second voice, equally bored and disembodied. "Do you know a Jaime Luis Torres?" the patrolman asks.

Ormand hesitates, shuffling his feet on the weathered boards a minute before answering. His voice is small. "Yes," he says.

"Have you seen him recently?"

"No," Ormand lies. His voice is a whisper.

"What was that?"

"I said no."

There is another pause, the patrolman looking into Ormand's eyes, Ormand looking back. "Mrs. Henckle's place has been burglarized four times in the last three months. She thinks you and your brother might be responsible. What do you say?"

"I say she's crazy." Ormand's face is big with indignation. The officer says nothing. "She's had it in for us ever since we were in junior high and she says Lee took a bottle of beer out of the cooler—which he never did. She's just a crazy bitch and we never had anythin' to do with her."

The patrolman seems to mull over this information a moment, thoughtfully stroking the neat clipped crescent of his mustache. Then he says, "She claims she's seen you and your brother out here on the porch drinking types of German beer and soda you can't get anywhere else around here—except at her place."

"Yeah?" Ormand snarls. "And what does that prove? You want to know, I bought that stuff in downtown L.A."

"Where?"

"This place I know, I'm not sure of the street, but I could drive you right to it, no sweat. She's just crazy, is all. She don't have a leg to stand on."

"Okay, Ormand," the officer says, snapping shut his notepad, "I've got it all down here. Mind if I step inside a minute and look around?"

"You got a search warrant?"

It's a long morning. Calvin sits up in bed, trying to read an article in *The Senior Citizen* about looking and feeling younger— "Get Out and Dance!" the headline admonishes—but he has trouble concentrating. The house is preternaturally quiet. Ormand and Lee Junior, who rarely rise before noon, slammed out the door half an hour after the patrolman left, and they haven't been back since. Jewel is asleep. Calvin can hear the harsh ratcheting snores from her room up the hall.

The thing that motivates him to pull on a flannel shirt and a pair of threadbare khaki pants and lower himself into the wheelchair is hunger—or at least that's what he tells himself. Most times when Jewel overindulges her taste for red wine and sleeps through the morning, Calvin stays put until he hears her moving about in the kitchen, but today is different. It's not just that he's feeling out of sorts physically, the cheap wine having scoured his digestive tract as relentlessly as a dose of the cathartic his mother used to give him when he had worms as a boy, but he's disturbed by the events of the preceding night and early morning as well. "She could use another lesson," Ormand had said, and then, first thing in the morning, the patrolman had shown up. Down deep, deeper even than the lowest stratum of excuses and denials he can dredge up, Calvin knows it's no coincidence.

The wheels rotate under his hands as he moves out into the hallway and eases past Jewel's room. He can see her through the half-open door, still in her dress and sneakers, her head buried in a litter of bedclothes. Next door is the bathroom—he's been in there three times already—and then, on the left, the kitchen. He rolls off the carpet and onto the smooth, spattered linoleum, gliding now, pulling right to skirt an overturned bag of garbage, and wheeling up to the sink for a sip of water.

The place is a mess. Unwashed cups, glasses, plates, and silverware litter the counter, and beer bottles too—the black ones. A jar of peanut butter stands open on the kitchen table, attracting flies. There's a smear of something on the wall, the wastebasket hasn't been emptied in a week, and the room reeks of sick-sweet decay. Calvin gulps a swallow or two of water from a cup scored with black rings. Eleven A.M. and hot already. He can feel the sweat where the glasses lie flat against his temples as he glides over to the refrigerator and swings back the door.

He'd been hoping for a leftover hamburger or a hard-boiled egg, but he isn't ready for this: the thing is packed, top to bottom, with cold cuts, big blocks of cheese, bratwurst and Tiroler. *Käse*, reads the label on a wedge of white cheese, *Product of Germany*. *Tilsiter*, reads another. *Schmelzkäse, Mainauer, Westfälischer Schinken*. For a long moment Calvin merely sits there, the cold

air in his face, the meats and blocks of cheese wrapped in white
butcher's paper stacked up taller than his head. Somehow, he
doesn't feel hungry any more. And then it hits him: something
like anger, something like fear.

The refrigerator door closes behind him with an airtight hiss,
flies scatter, an overturned cup on the floor spins wildly away from
his right wheel, and he's back in the hallway again, but this time
he's turning left, into the living room. Bottles, ashtrays, crumpled
newspapers, he ignores them all. On the far side of the room
stands a cheap plywood door, a door he's never been through: the
door to Ormand and Lee Junior's room. Sitting there evenings,
watching TV, he's caught a glimpse of the cluttered gloom beyond
the doorway as one or the other of the boys slams in or out, but
that's about it. They've never invited him in, and he's never much
cared. But now, without hesitation, he wheels himself across the
room, shoves down on the door latch with the heel of his hand,
and pushes his way in.

He's no fool. He knew what he would find. But still, the magni-
tude of it chokes up his throat and makes the blood beat in his
head like a big bass drum. From one end of the room to the other,
stacked up to the ceiling as if the place were a warehouse or something, are stereo sets, radios, TVs, power tools, toaster ovens, and
half a dozen things Calvin doesn't even recognize except to know
that they cost an arm and a leg. In one corner are cases of beer—
and, yes, Patio soda—and in the other, beneath a pair of huge PA
speakers, guns. Shotguns, rifles, semiautomatics, a sack full of
handguns with pearly and nickel-plated grips spilled on the floor
like treasure. He can't believe it. Or no, worse, he can. Shaken,
he backs out of the room and pulls the door shut.

The house is silent as a tomb. But wait: is that Jewel? Calvin's
underarms are soaked through, a bead of sweat drops from his
nose. The house stirs itself, floorboards creak of their own accord,
the refrigerator starts up with a sigh. Is that Ormand? No, there:
he can hear Jewel's snores again, stutter and wheeze, faint as the
hum of the flies. This is his chance: he knows what he must do.

Outside, the sun hits him like a slap in the face. Already his
shoulder sockets are on fire and the cast feels like an anchor

twisted round his arm. For an instant he sits there beside the door
as if debating with himself, the watery old eyes scanning the street
for Ormand's pickup. Then all at once he's in motion, rocking
across the loose floorboards, past the mounds of debris and down
the ramp Ormand fixed up for him at the back end of the porch.
Below, the ground is littered with tires and machine parts, with
rags and branches and refuse, and almost immediately he finds
himself hung up on something—part of an auto transmission, it
looks like—but he leans over to wrestle with it, heart in his
throat, fingers clawing at grease and metal, until he frees himself.
Then he's out the ramshackle gate and into the street.

It's not much of a hill—a five-degree grade maybe, and fifty or
sixty yards up—but to the old man it seems like Everest. So hot,
his seat stuck to the chair with his own wetness, salt sweat stinging
his eyes, arms pumping and elbows stabbing, on he goes. A station wagon full of kids thunders by him, and then one of those
little beetle cars; up ahead, at the intersection of Tully and Commerce, he can see a man on a bicycle waiting for the light to
change. Up, up, up, he chants to himself, everything clear, not a
number in his head, the good and bad of his life laid out before
him like an EKG chart. The next thing he knows, the hill begins
to even off and he's negotiating the sidewalk and turning the corner into the merciful shade of the store fronts. It's almost a shock
when he looks up and finds himself staring numbly at his gaunt,
wild-haired image in the dark window of Eva's European Deli.

The door stands open. For a long moment he hesitates, watching himself in the window. His face is crazy, the glint of his glasses
masking his eyes, a black spot of grease on his forehead. What am
I doing? he thinks. Then he wipes his hands on his pants and
swings his legs through the doorway.

At first he can see nothing: the lights are out, the interior dim.
There are sounds from the rear of the shop, the scrape of objects
being dragged across the floor, a thump, voices. "I got no insurance, I tell you." Plaintive, halting, the voice of the German
woman. "No money. And now I owe nearly two thousand dollars
for all this stock"—more heavy, percussive sounds—"all gone to
waste."

Now he begins to locate himself, objects emerging from the
gloom, shades drawn, a door open to the sun all the way down the
corridor in back. Christ, he thinks, looking round him. The display racks are on the floor, toppled like trees, cans and boxes and
plastic packages torn open and strewn from one end of the place to
the other. He can make out the beer cooler against the back wall,
its glass doors shattered and wrenched from the hinges. And here,
directly in front of him, like something out of a newsreel about
flooding along the Mississippi, a clutter of overturned tables,
smashed chairs, tangled rolls of butcher's paper, the battered cash
register and belly-up meat locker. But all this is nothing when
compared with the swastikas. Black, bold, stark, they blot everything like some killing fungus. The ruined equipment, the walls,
ceiling, floors, even the bleary reproductions of the Rhine and the
big hand-lettered menu in the window: nothing has escaped the
spray can.

"I am gone," the German woman says. "Finished. Four times is
enough."

"Eva, Eva, Eva." The second voice is thick and doleful, a
woman's voice, sympathy like going to the bathroom. "What can
you do? You know how Mike and I would like to see those people
in jail where they belong—"

"Animals," the German woman says.

"We know it's them—everybody on the block knows it—but
we don't have the proof and the police won't do a thing. Honestly,
I must watch that house ten hours a day but I've never seen a
thing proof positive." At that moment, Mrs. Tuxton's head comes
into view over the gutted meat locker. The hair lies flat against her
temples, beauty-parlor silver. Her lips are pursed. "What we
need is an eyewitness."

Now the German woman swings into view, a carton in her
arms. "Yah," she says, the flesh trembling at her throat, "and you
find me one in this . . . this stinking community. You're a bunch of
cowards—and you'll forgive me for this, Laura—but to let criminals run scot-free on your own block, I just don't understand it.
Do you know when I was a girl in Karlsruhe after the war and we

found out who was the man breaking into houses on my street, what we did? Huh?"

Calvin wants to cry out for absolution: I know, I know who did it! But he doesn't. All of a sudden he's afraid. The vehemence of this woman, the utter shambles of her shop, Ormand, Lee Junior, the squawk of the police radio: his head is filling up. It is then that Mrs. Tuxton swivels round and lets out a theatrical little gasp. "My God, there's someone here!"

In the next moment they're advancing on him, the German woman in a tentlike dress, the mean little eyes sunk into her face until he can't see them, Mrs. Tuxton wringing her hands and jabbing her pointy nose at him as if it were a knife. "You!" The German woman exclaims, her fists working, the little feet in their worn shoes kneading the floor in agitation. "What are you doing here?"

Calvin doesn't know what to say, his head crowded with numbers all of a sudden. Twenty thousand leagues under the sea, a hundred and twenty pesos in a dollar, sixteen men on a dead man's chest, yo-ho-ho and one-point-oh-five quarts to a liter. "I . . . I—" he stammers.

"The nerve," Mrs. Tuxton says.

"Well?" The German woman is poised over him now, just as she was on the day she slapped the soda from his hand—he can smell her, a smell like liverwurst, and it turns his stomach. "Do you know anything about this, eh? Do you?"

He does. He knows all about it. Jewel knows, Lee Junior knows, Ormand knows. They'll go to jail, all of them. And Calvin? He's just an old man, tired, worn out, an old man in a wheelchair. He looks into the German woman's face and tries to feel pity, tries to feel brave, righteous, good. But instead he has a vision of himself farmed out to some nursing home, the women in the white caps prodding him and humiliating him, the stink of fatality on the air, the hacking and moaning in the night—

"I'm . . . I'm sorry," he says.

Her face goes numb, flesh the color of raw dough. "Sorry?" she echoes. "Sorry?"

But he's already backing out the door.

Stones in My Passway, Hellhound on My Trail

I got stones in my passway
and my road seems black as night.
I have pains in my heart,
they have taken my appetite.
—ROBERT JOHNSON (1914?–1938)

Saturday night. He's playing the House Party Club in Dallas, singing his blues, picking notes with a penknife. His voice rides up to a reedy falsetto that gets the men hooting and then down to the cavernous growl that chills the women, the hard chords driving behind it, his left foot beating like a hammer. The club's patrons—field hands and laborers—pound over the floorboards like the start of the derby, stamping along with him. Skirts fly, straw hats slump over eyebrows, drinks spill, ironed hair goes wiry. Overhead two dim yellow bulbs sway on their cords; the light is suffused with cigarette smoke, dingy and brown. The floor is wet with spittle and tobacco juice. From the back room, a smell of eggs frying. And beans.

Huddie Doss, the proprietor, has set up a bar in the corner: two barrels of roofing nails and a pine plank. The plank supports a cluster of gallon jugs, a bottle of Mexican rum, a pewter jigger, and three lemons. Robert sits on a stool at the far end of the room, boxed in by men in kerchiefs, women in calico. The men watch his fingers, the women look into his eyes.

It is 1938, dust bowl, New Deal. FDR is on the radio, and somebody in Robinsonville is naming a baby after Jesse Owens. Once, on the road to Natchez, Robert saw a Pierce Arrow and talked about it for a week. Another time he spent six weeks in Chicago and didn't know the World's Fair was going on. Now he plays his guitar up and down the Mississippi, and in Louisiana, Texas, and Arkansas. He's never heard of Hitler and he hasn't eaten in two days.

When he was fifteen he watched a poisoned dog tear out its entrails. It was like this:

They were out in the fields when a voice shouted, "Loup's gone mad!," and then he was running with the rest of them, down the slope and across the red dust road, past the shanties and into the gully where they dumped their trash, the dog crying high over the sun and then baying deep as craters in the moon. It was a coonhound, tawny, big-boned, the color of a lion. Robert pushed through the gathering crowd and stood watching as the animal dragged its hindquarters along the ground like a birthing bitch, the ropy testicles strung out behind. It was mewling now, the high-pitched cries sawing away at each breath, and then it was baying again, howling death until the day was filled with it, their ears and the pits of their stomachs soured with it. One of the men said in a terse, angry voice, "Go get Turkey Nason to come on down here with his gun," and a boy detached himself from the crowd and darted up the rise.

It was then that the dog fell heavily to its side, ribs heaving, and began to dig at its stomach with long racing thrusts of the rear legs. There was yellow foam on the black muzzle, blood bright in the nostrils. The dog screamed and dug, dug until the flesh was raw and its teeth could puncture the cavity to get at the gray intestine, tugging first at a bulb of it and then fastening on a lank strand like dirty wash. There was no sign of the gun. The woman beside Robert began to cry, a sound like crumpling paper. Then one of the men stepped in with a shovel in his hand. He hit the dog once across the eyes and the animal lunged for him. The shovel fell twice more and the dog stiffened, its yellow eyes gazing round the circle of men, the litter of bottles and cans and rusted machinery, its head lolling on the lean, muscular neck, poised for one terrible moment, and then it was over. Afterward Robert came close: to look at the frozen teeth, the thin, rigid limbs, the green flies on the pink organs.

Between sets Robert has been out back with a girl named Beatrice, and Ida Mae Doss, Huddie's daughter, is not happy about it. As he settles back down on the stool and reaches for his guitar, he looks up at the pine plank, the barrels, Ida Mae stationed behind the bar. She is staring at him—cold, hard, her eyes like razors. What can he do? He grins, sheepish. But then Beatrice steams in, perfumed in sweat, the blue print shift clinging like a wet sheet. She sashays through the knot of men milling around Robert and says, "Why don't you play something sweet?" Robert pumps the neck of the guitar, strikes the strings twice, and then breaks into "Phonograph Blues":

> And we played it on the sofa and we played it 'side the wall,
> But, boys, my needle point got rusty and it will not play at all.

The men nudge one another. Ida Mae looks daggers. Beatrice flounces to the center of the floor, raises her arms above her head, and begins a slow grinding shuffle to the pulse of the guitar.

No one knows how Robert got his guitar. He left Letterman's farm when he was sixteen, showed up a year and a half later with a new Harmony Sovereign. He walked into the Rooster Club in Robinsonville, Mississippi, and leaned against the wall while Walter Satter finished out his set. When Satter stepped up to the bar, Robert was at his elbow. "I heard your record," Robert said. He was short, skinny, looked closer to twelve than eighteen.

"You like it?"

"Taught me a lot."

Satter grinned.

"Mind if I sit in on the next set?"

"Sure—if you think you can go on that thing."

Robert sat in. His voice was a shower, his guitar a storm. The sweet slide leads cut the atmosphere like lightning at dusk. Satter played rhythm behind him for a while, then stepped down.

The lemons are pulp, the rum decimated, jugs lighter. Voices drift through the open door, fireflies perforate the dark rafters. It is hot as a jungle, dark as a cave. The club's patrons are quieter now—some slouched against the walls, others leaning on the bar, their fingers tapping like batons. Beatrice is an exception. She's still out in the center of the floor, head swaying to the music, heels kicking, face bright with perspiration—dancing. A glass in her hand. But suddenly she lurches to the left, her leg buckles, and she goes down. There is the shrill of breaking glass, and then silence. Robert has stopped playing. The final chord rings in the air, decapitated; a sudden unnatural silence filters through the smoke haze, descending like a judgment. Robert sets the guitar across the stool and shuffles out to where Beatrice lies on the floor. She rolls heavily to her side, laughing, muttering to herself. Robert catches her under the arms, helps her up, and guides her to a chair in the corner—and then it's over. The men start joking again, the bar gets busy, women tell stories, laugh.

Beatrice slumps in the chair, chin to chest, and begins to snore—delicate, jagged, the purr of a cat. Robert grins and pats her head—then turns to the bar. Ida Mae is there, measuring out drinks. Her eyes are moist. Robert squeezes the husk of a lemon over his glass, half fills it with rum, and presses a nickel into her palm. "What you got cooking, Ida Mae?" he says.

A thin silver chain hangs between her breasts, beneath the neckline of her cotton dress. It is ornamented with a wooden guitar pick, highly varnished, the shape of a seed.

"Got eggs," she says. "And beans."

Lubbock, Natchez, Pascagoula, Dallas, Eudora, Rosedale, Baton Rouge, Memphis, Friars Point, Vicksburg, Jonesboro, Mooringsport, Edwards, Chattanooga, Rolling Fork, Commerce, Itta Bena. Thelma, Betty Mae, Adeline, Harriet, Bernice, Ida Bell, Bertha Lee, Winifred, Maggie, Willie Mae. "Robert been driving too hard," people said. "Got to stumble."

In 1937 Franco laid siege to Madrid, the Japanese invaded Nanking, Amelia Earhart lost herself in the Pacific, and Robert made a series of recordings for Victrix Records. He was twenty-three at the time. Or twenty-two. A man from Victrix sent him train fare to New Orleans in care of the High Times Club in Biloxi. Robert slit the envelope with his penknife and ran his thumb over the green-and-silver singles while the bartender read him the letter. Robert was ecstatic. He kissed women, danced on the tables, bought a Havana cigar—but the bills whispered in his palm and he never made it to the station. A week later the man sent him a nonrefundable one-way ticket.

The man was waiting for him when the train pulled into the New Orleans station. Robert stepped off the day coach with his battered Harmony Sovereign and a cardboard valise. The stink of kerosene and coal blistered the air. Outside, automobiles stood at the curb like a dream of the twentieth century. "Walter Fagen," the man said, holding out his hand. Robert looked up at the wisps of white-blond hair, the pale irises, the red tie, and then down at a torn ticket stub on the platform. "Pleased to meet you," he mumbled. One hand was on the neck of the guitar, the other in his pocket. "Go ahead, shake," Fagen said. Robert shook.

Fagen took him to a boardinghouse, paid the big kerchief-headed woman at the door, instructed Robert to come around to the Arlington Hotel in the morning. Then he gave him a two-dollar advance. Three hours later Fagen's dinner was interrupted by a phone call from the New Orleans police: Robert was being held for disorderly conduct. Fagen hired a taxi, drove to the jailhouse, laid five silver dollars on the desk, and walked out with his recording artist. Robert's right eye was swollen closed; the guitar was gone. Robert had nothing to say. When the taxi stopped in front of the boardinghouse, Fagen gave him thirty-five cents for breakfast and told him to get a good night's sleep.

Back at the Arlington, Fagen took a seat in the dining room and reordered. He was sipping a gimlet when a boy paged him to the phone. It was Robert. "I'm lonesome," he said.

"Lonesome?"

"Yeah—there's a woman here wants forty cents and I'm a nickel short."

The voices wash around her like birds at dawn, a Greek chorus gone mad. Smoke and stale sweat, the smell of lemon. She grits her teeth. "Give me a plate of it, then, girl," he is saying. "Haven't eat in two days." Then she's in the back room, stirring beans, cracking eggs, a woman scorned. The eggs, four of them, stare up at her like eyes. Tiny embryos. On the shelf above the stove: can of pepper, saltcellar, a knife, the powder they use for rats and roaches.

Agamemnon, watch out!

Robert's dream is thick with the thighs of women, the liquid image of songs sung and songs to come, bright wire wheels and sloping fenders, swamps, trees, power lines, and the road, the road spinning out like string from a spool, like veins, blood and heart, distance without end, without horizon.

It is the last set. Things are winding down. Beatrice sags in the chair, skirt pulled up over her knees, her chest rising and falling with the soft rhythm of sleep. Beside her, a man in red suspenders presses a woman against the wall. Robert watches the woman's hands like dark animals on the man's hips. Earlier, a picker had been stabbed in the neck after a dispute over dice or women or liquor, and an old woman had fallen, drunk, and cut her head on the edge of a bench. But now things are winding down. Voices are hushed, cigarettes burn unattended, moonlight limns the windows.

Robert rests the guitar on his knee and does a song about a train station, a suitcase, and the eyes of a woman. His voice is mournful, sad as a steady rain, the guitar whining above it like a cry in the distance. "Yes!" they call out. "Robert!" Somebody whistles. Then they applaud, waves on the rocks, smoke rising as if from a rent in the earth. In response, the guitar reaches low for the opening bars of Robert's signature tune, his finale, but there is something wrong—the chords staggering like a seizure, stumbling, finally breaking off cold.

Cramps. A spasm so violent it jerks his fingers from the strings. He begins again, his voice quavering, shivered: "Got to keep moving, got to keep moving, / Hellbound on my trail." And then suddenly the voice chokes off, gags, the guitar slips to the floor with a percussive shock. His bowels are on fire. He stands, clutches his abdomen, drops to hands and knees. "Boy's had too much of that Mexican," someone says. He looks up, a sword run through him, panting, the shock waves pounding through his frame, looks up at the pine plank, the barrels, the cold, hard features of the girl with the silver necklace in her hand. Looks up, and snarls.

All Shook Up

About a week after the FOR RENT sign disappeared from the window of the place next door, a van the color of cough syrup swung off the blacktop road and into the driveway. The color didn't do much for me, nor the oversize tires with the raised white letters, but the side panel was a real eye-catcher. It featured a life-size portrait of a man with high-piled hair and a guitar, beneath which appeared the legend: *Young Elvis, The Boy Who Dared To Rock*. When the van pulled in I was sitting in the kitchen, rereading the newspaper and blowing into my eighth cup of coffee. I was on vacation. My wife was on vacation too. Only she was in Mill Valley, California, with a guy named Fred, and I was in Shrub Oak, New York.

The door of the van eased open and a kid about nineteen stepped out. He was wearing a black leather jacket with the collar turned up, even though it must have been ninety, and his hair was a glistening, blue-black construction of grease and hair spray that rose from the crown of his head like a bird's nest perched atop a cliff. The girl got out on the far side and then ducked round the van to stand gaping at the paint-blistered Cape Cod as if it were Graceland itself. She was small-boned and tentative, her big black-rimmed eyes like puncture wounds. In her arms, as slack and yielding as a bag of oranges, was a baby. It couldn't have been more than six months old.

I fished three beers out of the refrigerator, slapped through the screen door, and crossed the lawn to where they stood huddled in the driveway, looking lost. "Welcome to the neighborhood," I said, proffering the beers.

The kid was wearing black ankle boots. He ground the toe of the right one into the pavement as if stubbing out a cigarette, then glanced up and said, "I don't drink."

"How about you?" I said, grinning at the girl.

"Sure, thanks," she said, reaching out a slim, veiny hand bright with lacquered nails. She gave the kid a glance, then took the beer, saluted me with a wink, and raised it to her lips. The baby never stirred.

I felt awkward with the two open bottles, so I gingerly set one down on the grass, then straightened up and took a hit from the other. "Patrick," I said, extending my free hand.

The kid took my hand and nodded, a bright wet spit curl swaying loose over his forehead. "Joey Greco," he said. "Glad to meet you. This here is Cindy."

There was something peculiar about his voice—tone and accent both. For one thing, it was surprisingly deep, as if he were throwing his voice or doing an impersonation. Then too, I couldn't quite place the accent. I gave Cindy a big welcoming smile and turned back to him. "You from down South?" I said.

The toe began to grind again and the hint of a smile tugged at the corner of his mouth, but he suppressed it. When he looked up at me his eyes were alive. "No," he said. "Not really."

A jay flew screaming out of the maple in back of the house, wheeled overhead, and disappeared in the hedge. I took another sip of beer. My face was beginning to ache from grinning so much and I could feel the sweat leaching out of my armpit and into my last clean T-shirt.

"No," he said again, and his voice was pitched a shade higher. "I'm from Brooklyn."

Two days later I was out back in the hammock, reading a thriller about a double agent who turns triple agent for a while, is discovered, pursued, captured, and finally persuaded under torture to become a quadruple agent, at which point his wife leaves him and his children change their surname. I was also drinking my way through a bottle of Chivas Regal Fred had given my wife for Christmas, and contemplatively rubbing tanning butter into my navel. The doorbell took me by surprise. I sat up, plucked a leaf from the maple for a bookmark, and padded round the house in bare feet and paint-stained cutoffs.

Cindy was standing at the front door, her back to me, peering through the screen. At first I didn't recognize her: she looked waifish, lost, a Girl Scout peddling cookies in a strange neighborhood. Just as I was about to say something, she pushed the doorbell again. "Hello," she called, cupping her hands and leaning into the screen.

The chimes tinnily reproduced the first seven notes of "Camptown Races," an effect my wife had found endearing; I made a mental note to disconnect them first thing in the morning. "Anybody home?" Cindy called.

"Hello," I said, and watched her jump. "Looking for me?"

"Oh," she gasped, swinging round with a laugh. "Hi." She was wearing a halter top and gym shorts, her hair was pinned up, and her perfect little toes looked freshly painted. "Patrick, right?" she said.

"That's right," I said. "And you're Cindy."

She nodded, and gave me the sort of look you get from a haberdasher when you go in to buy a suit. "Nice tan."

I glanced down at my feet, rubbed a slick hand across my chest. "I'm on vacation."

"That's great," she said. "From what?"

"I work up at the high school? I'm in Guidance."

"Oh, wow," she said, "that's really great." She stepped down off the porch. "I really mean it—that's something." And then: "Aren't you kind of young to be a guidance counselor?"

"I'm twenty-nine."

"You're kidding, right? You don't look it. Really. I would've thought you were twenty-five, maybe, or something." She patted her hair tentatively, once around, as if to make sure it was all still there. "Anyway, what I came over to ask is if you'd like to come to dinner over at our place tonight."

I was half drunk, the thriller wasn't all that thrilling, and I hadn't been out of the yard in four days. "What time?" I said.

"About six."

There was a silence, during which the birds could be heard cursing one another in the trees. Down the block someone fired up a rotary mower. "Well, listen, I got to go put the meat up," she said, turning to leave. But then she swung round with an afterthought. "I forgot to ask: are you married?"

She must have seen the hesitation on my face.

"Because if you are, I mean, we want to invite her too." She stood there watching me. Her eyes were gray, and there was a violet clock in the right one. The hands pointed to three-thirty.

"Yes," I said finally, "I am." There was the sound of a stinging ricochet and a heartfelt guttural curse as the unseen mower hit a stone. "But my wife's away. On vacation."

I'd been in the house only once before, nearly eight years back. The McCareys had lived there then, and Judy and I had just graduated from the state teachers' college. We'd been married two weeks, the world had been freshly created from out of the void, and we were moving into our new house. I was standing in the driveway, unloading boxes of wedding loot from the trunk of the car, when Henry McCarey ambled across the lawn to introduce himself. He must have been around seventy-five. His pale, bald brow swept up and back from his eyes like a helmet, square and imposing, but the flesh had fallen in on itself from the cheekbones down, giving his face a mismatched look. He wore wire-rim

glasses. "If you've got a minute there," he said, "we'd like to show
you and your wife something." I looked up. Henry's wife, Irma,
stood framed in the doorway behind him. Her hair was pulled
back in a bun and she wore a print dress that fell to the tops of her
white sweat socks.

I called Judy. She smiled, I smiled, Henry smiled; Irma, smiling, held the door for us, and we found ourselves in the dark,
cluttered living room with its excess furniture, its framed photographs of eras gone by, and its bric-a-brac. Irma asked us if we'd
like a cup of tea. "Over here," Henry said, gesturing from the far
corner of the room.

We edged forward, smiling but ill at ease. We were twenty-two,
besotted with passion and confidence, and these people made our
grandparents look young. I didn't know what to say to them,
didn't know how to act: I wanted to get back to the car and the
boxes piled on the lawn.

Henry was standing before a glass case that stood atop a mound
of doilies on a rickety-looking corner table. He fumbled behind it
for a moment, and then a little white Christmas bulb flickered on
inside the case. I saw a silver trowellike thing with an inscription
on it and a rippled, petrified chunk of something that looked as if
it might once have been organic. It was a moment before I realized it was a piece of wedding cake.

"It's from our golden anniversary," Henry said, "six years ago.
And that there is the cake knife—can you read what it says?"

I felt numb, felt as if I'd been poking around in the dirt and
unearthed the traces of a forgotten civilization. I stole a look at
Judy. She was transfixed, her face drawn up as if she were about to
cry: she was so beautiful, so rapt, so moved by the moment and its
auguries, that I began to feel choked up myself. She took my
hand.

"It says 'Henry and Irma, 1926–1976, Semper Fidelis.' That last
bit, that's Latin," Henry added, and then he translated for us.

Things were different now.

I rapped at the flimsy aluminum storm door and Joey bobbed
into view through the dark mesh of the screen. He was wearing a
tight black sports coat with the collar turned up, a pink shirt, and

black pants with jagged pink lightning bolts ascending the outer seam. At first he didn't seem to recognize me, and for an instant, standing there in my cutoffs and T-shirt with half a bottle of Chivas in my hand, I felt more like an interloper than an honored guest—she *had* said tonight, hadn't she?—but then he was ducking his head in greeting and swinging back the door to admit me.

"Glad you could make it," he said without enthusiasm.

"Yeah, me too," I breathed, wondering if I was making a mistake.

I followed him into the living room, where spavined boxes and green plastic trash bags stuffed with underwear and sweaters gave testimony to an ongoing adventure in moving. The place was as close and dark as I'd remembered, but where before there'd been doilies, bric-a-brac, and end tables with carved feet, now there was a plaid sofa, an exercycle, and a dirty off-white beanbag lounger. Gone was the shrine to marital fidelity, replaced by a Fender amp, a microphone stand, and an acoustic guitar with capo and pickup. (Henry was gone too, dead of emphysema, and Irma was in a nursing home on the other side of town.) There was a stereo with great black monolithic speakers, and the walls were hung with posters of Elvis. I looked at Joey. He was posed beside a sneering young Elvis, rocking back and forth on the heels of his boots. "Pretty slick," I said, indicating his get-up.

"Oh, this?" he said, as if surprised I'd noticed. "I've been rehearsing—trying on outfits, you know."

I'd figured he was some sort of Elvis impersonator, judging from the van, the clothes, and the achieved accent, but aside from the hair I couldn't really see much resemblance between him and the King. "You, uh—you do an Elvis act?"

He looked at me as if I'd just asked if the thing above our heads was the ceiling. Finally he just said, "Yeah."

It was then that Cindy emerged from the kitchen. She was wearing a white peasant dress and sandals, and she was holding a glass of wine in one hand and a zucchini the size of a souvenir baseball bat in the other. "Patrick," she said, crossing the room to brush my cheek with a kiss. I embraced her ritualistically—you might have thought we'd known each other for a decade—and held her a moment while Joey and Elvis looked on. When she stepped back, I caught a whiff of perfume and alcohol. "You like zucchini?" she said.

"Uh-huh, sure." I was wondering what to do with my hands. Suddenly I remembered the bottle and held it up like a turkey I'd shot in the woods. "I brought you this."

Cindy made a gracious noise or two, I shrugged in deprecation—"It's only half full," I said—and Joey ground his toe into the carpet. I might have been imagining it, but he seemed agitated, worked up over something.

"How long till dinner?" he said, a reedy, adolescent whine snaking through the Nashville basso.

Cindy's eyes were unsteady. She drained her wine in a gulp and held out the glass for me to refill. With Scotch. "I don't know," she said, watching the glass. "Half an hour."

"Because I think I want to work on a couple numbers, you know?"

She gave him a look. I didn't know either of them well enough to know what it meant. That look could have said, "Go screw yourself," or, "I'm just wild about you and Elvis"—I couldn't tell.

"No problem," she said finally, sipping at her drink, the zucchini tucked under her arm. "Patrick was going to help me in the kitchen, anyway—right, Patrick?"

"Sure," I said.

At dinner, Joey cut into his *braciola,* lifted a forkful of tomatoes, peppers, and zucchini to his lips, and talked about Elvis. "He was the most photographed man in the history of the world. He had sixty-two cars and over a hundred guitars." Fork, knife, meat, vegetable. "He was the greatest there ever was."

I didn't know about that. By the time I gave up pellet guns and minibikes and began listening to rock and roll, it was the Doors, Stones, and Hendrix, and Elvis was already degenerating into a caricature of himself. I remembered him as a bloated old has-been in a white jumpsuit, crooning corny ballads and slobbering on middle-aged women. Besides, between the Chivas and the bottle of red Cindy had opened for dinner, I was pretty far gone. "Hmph," was about all I could manage.

For forty-five minutes, while I'd sat on a cracked vinyl barstool at the kitchen counter, helping slice vegetables and trading stories with Cindy, I'd heard Joey's rendition of half a dozen Elvis classics. He was in the living room, thundering; I was in the kitchen, drinking. Every once in a while he'd give the guitar a rest or step back from the microphone, and I would hear the real Elvis moaning faintly in the background: *Don't be cruel / To a heart that's true* or *You ain't nothin' but a hound dog.*

"He's pretty good," I said to Cindy after a particularly thunderous rendition of "Jailhouse Rock." I was making conversation.

She shrugged. "Yeah, I guess so," she said. The baby lay in a portable cradle by the window, giving off subtle emanations of feces and urine. It was asleep, I supposed. If it weren't for the smell, I would have guessed it was dead. "You know, we had to get married," she said.

I made a gesture of dismissal, tried for a surprised expression. Of course they'd had to get married. I'd seen a hundred girls just like her—they passed through the guidance office like flocks of unfledged birds flying in the wrong direction, north in the winter, south in the summer. Slumped over, bony, eyes sunk into their heads, and made up like showgirls or whores, they slouched in the easy chair in my office and told me their stories. They thought they were hip and depraved, thought they were nihilists and libertines, thought they'd invented sex. Two years later they were housewives with preschoolers and station wagons. Two years after that they were divorced.

"First time I heard Elvis, first time I remember, anyway," Joey was saying now, "was in December of '68 when he did that TV concert—the Singer Special? It blew me away. I just couldn't believe it."

"Sixty-eight?" I echoed. "What were you, four?"

Cindy giggled. I turned to look at her, a sloppy grin on my face. I was drunk.

Joey didn't bat an eye. "I was seven," he said. And then: "That was the day I stopped being a kid." He'd tucked a napkin under his collar to protect his pink shirt, and strands of hair hung loose over his forehead. "Next day my mom picked up a copy of *Elvis's Greatest Hits, Volume One,* and a week later she got me my first guitar. I've been at it ever since."

Joey was looking hard at me. He was trying to impress me; that much was clear. That's why he'd worn the suit, dabbed his lids with green eye shadow, greased his hair, and hammered out his repertoire from the next room so I couldn't help but catch every lick. Somehow, though, I wasn't impressed. Whether it was the booze, my indifference to Elvis, or the fear and loathing that had gripped me since Judy's defection, I couldn't say. All I knew was that I didn't give a shit. For Elvis, for Joey, for Fred, Judy, Little Richard, or Leonard Bernstein. For anybody. I sipped my wine in silence.

"My agent's trying to book me into the Catskills—some of the resorts and all, you know? He says my act's really hot." Joey patted his napkin, raised a glass of milk to his lips, and took a quick swallow. "I'll be auditioning up there at Brown's in about a week. Meanwhile, Friday night I got this warm-up gig—no big deal, just some dump out in the sticks. It's over in Brewster—you ever heard of it?"

"The sticks, or Brewster?" I said.

"No, really, why not drop by?"

Cindy was watching me. Earlier, over the chopping board, she'd given me the rundown on this and other matters. She was twenty, Joey was twenty-one. Her father owned a contracting company in Putnam Valley and had set them up with the house. She'd met Joey in Brooklyn the summer before, when she was staying with her cousin. He was in a band then. Now he did Elvis. Nothing but. He'd had gigs in the City and out on the Island, but he wasn't making anything and he refused to take a day job: nobody but hacks did that. So they'd come to the hinterlands, where her father could see they didn't starve to death and Cindy could work as a secretary in his office. They were hoping the Brewster thing would catch on—nobody was doing much with Elvis up here.

I chewed, swallowed, washed it down with a swig of wine. "Sounds good," I said. "I'll be there."

Later, after Joey had gone to bed, Cindy and I sat side by side on the plaid sofa and listened to a tape of *Swan Lake* I'd gone next door to fetch ("Something soft," she'd said. "Have you got something soft?"). We were drinking coffee, and a sweet yellowish cordial she'd dug out of one of the boxes of kitchen things. We'd been talking. I'd told her about Judy. And Fred. Told her I'd been feeling pretty rotten and that I was glad she'd moved in. "Really," I said, "I mean it. And I really appreciate you inviting me over too."

She was right beside me, her arms bare in the peasant dress, legs folded under her yoga-style. "No problem," she said, looking me in the eye.

I glanced away and saw Elvis. Crouching, dipping, leering, humping the microphone, and spraying musk over the first three rows, Elvis in full rut. "So how do you feel about all this"—I waved my arm to take in the posters, the guitar and amp, the undefined space above us where Joey lay sleeping—"I mean, living with the King?" I laughed and held my cupped hand under her chin. "Go ahead, dear—speak right into the mike."

She surprised me then. Her expression was dead serious, no time for levity. Slowly, deliberately, she set down the coffee cup and leaned forward to swing round so that she was kneeling beside me on the couch; then she kicked her leg out as if mounting a horse and brought her knee softly down between my legs until I could feel the pressure lighting up my groin. From the stereo, I could hear the swan maidens bursting into flight. "It's like being married to a clone," she whispered.

When I got home, the phone was ringing. I slammed through the front door, stumbled over something in the dark, and took the stairs to the bedroom two at a time. "Yeah?" I said breathlessly as I snatched up the receiver.

"Pat?"

It was Judy. Before I could react, her voice was coming at me, soft and passionate, syllables kneading me like fingers. "Pat, listen," she said. "I want to explain something—"

I hung up.

The club was called Delvecchio's, and it sat amid an expanse of blacktop like a cruise ship on a flat, dark sea. It was a big place, with two separate stages, a disco, three bars, and a game room. I recognized it instantly: teen nirvana. Neon pulsed, raked Chevys rumbled out front, guys in Hawaiian shirts and girls in spike heels stood outside the door, smoking joints and cigarettes and examining one another with frozen eyes. The parking lot was already beginning to fill up when Cindy and I pulled in around nine.

"Big on the sixteen-year-old crowd tonight," I said. "Want me to gun the engine?"

Cindy was wearing a sleeveless blouse, pedal pushers, and heels. She'd made herself up to look like a cover girl for *Slash* magazine, and she smelled like a candy store. "Come on, Pat," she said in a hoarse whisper. "Don't be that way."

"What way?" I said, but I knew what she meant. We were out to have a good time, to hear Joey on his big night, and there was no reason to kill it with cynicism.

Joey had gone on ahead in the van to set up his equipment and do a sound check. Earlier, he'd made a special trip over to my place to ask if I'd mind taking Cindy to the club. He stood just inside the door, working the toe of his patent-leather boot and gazing beyond me to the wreckage wrought by Judy's absence: the cardboard containers of takeout Chinese stacked atop the TV, the beer bottles and Devil Dog wrappers on the coffee table, the clothes scattered about like the leavings of a river in flood. I looked him in the eye, wondering just how much he knew of the passionate groping Cindy and I had engaged in while he was getting his beauty rest the other night, wondering if he had even the faintest notion that I felt evil and betrayed and wanted his wife because I had wounds to salve and because she was there, wanted her like forbidden fruit, wanted her like I'd wanted half the knocked-up, washed-out, defiant little twits that paraded through

my office each year. He held my gaze until I looked away. "Sure,"
I murmured, playing Tristan to his Mark. "Be happy to."

And so, come eight o'clock, I'd showered and shaved, slicked
back my hair, turned up the collar of my favorite gigolo shirt, and
strolled across the lawn to pick her up. The baby (her name was
Gladys, after Elvis's mother) was left in the care of one of the
legions of pubescent girls I knew from school, Cindy emerged
from the bedroom on brisk heels to peck my cheek with a kiss, and
we strolled back across the lawn to my car.

There was an awkward silence. Though we'd talked two or
three times since the night of the *braciola* and the couch, neither
of us had referred to it. We'd done some pretty heavy petting and
fondling, we'd got the feel of each other's dentition and a taste of
abandon. I was the one who backed off. I had a vision of Joey
standing in the doorway in his pajamas, head bowed under the
weight of his pompadour. "What about Joey," I whispered, and
we both swiveled our heads to gaze up at the flat, unrevealing
surface of the ceiling. Then I got up and went home to bed.

Now, as we reached the car and I swung back the door for her, I
found something to say. "I can't believe it"—I laughed, hearty,
jocular, all my teeth showing—"but I feel like I'm out on a date or
something."

Cindy just cocked her head and gave me a little smirk. "You
are," she said.

They'd booked Joey into the Troubadour Room, a place that
seated sixty or seventy and had the atmosphere of a small club.
Comedians played there once in a while, and the occasional folk
singer or balladeer—acts that might be expected to draw a slightly
older, more contemplative crowd. Most of the action, obviously,
centered on the rock bands that played the main stage, or the
pounding fantasia of the disco. We didn't exactly have to fight for a
seat.

Cindy ordered a Black Russian. I stuck with Scotch. We talked
about Elvis, Joey, rock and roll. We talked about Gladys and how
precocious she was and how her baby raptures alternated with
baby traumas. We talked about the watercolors Cindy had done in

high school and how she'd like to get back to them. We talked about Judy. About Fred. About guidance counseling. We were on our third drink—or maybe it was the fourth—when the stage lights went up and the emcee announced Joey.

"Excited?" I said.

She shrugged, scanning the stage a moment as the drummer, bass player, and guitarist took their places. Then she found my hand under the table and gave it a squeeze.

At that moment Joey whirled out of the wings and pounced on the mike as if it were alive. He was dressed in a mustard-colored suit spangled with gold glitter, a sheeny gold tie, and white patent-leather loafers. For a moment he just stood there, trying his best to radiate the kind of outlaw sensuality that was Elvis's signature, but managing instead to look merely awkward, like a kid dressed up for a costume party. Still, he knew the moves. Suddenly his right fist shot up over his head and the musicians froze; he gave us his best sneer, then the fist came crashing down across the face of his guitar, the band lurched into "Heartbreak Hotel," and Joey threw back his head and let loose.

Nothing happened.

The band rumbled on confusedly for a bar or two, then cut out as Joey stood there tapping at the microphone and looking foolish.

"AC/DC!" someone shouted from the darkness to my left.

"Def Leppard!"

The emcee, a balding character in a flowered shirt, scurried out onstage and crouched over the pedestal of the antiquated mike Joey had insisted on for authenticity. Someone shouted an obscenity, and Joey turned his back. There were more calls for heavy-metal bands, quips and laughter. The other band members—older guys with beards and expressionless faces—looked about as concerned as sleepwalkers. I stole a look at Cindy; she was biting her lip.

Finally the mike came to life, the emcee vanished, and Joey breathed "Testing, testing," through the PA system. "Ah'm sorry 'bout the de-lay, folks," he murmured in his deepest, backwoodsiest basso, "but we're 'bout ready to give it another shot. A-one,

two, three!" he shouted, and "Heartbreak Hotel," take two,
thumped lamely through the speakers:

> Well, since my baby left me,
> I found a new place to dwell,
> It's down at the end of Lonely Street,
> That's Heartbreak Hotel.

Something was wrong, that much was clear from the start. It
wasn't just that he was bad, that he looked nervous and maybe a
bit effeminate and out of control, or that he forgot the words to the
third verse and went flat on the choruses, or that the half-assed
pickup band couldn't have played together if they'd rehearsed
eight hours a day since Elvis was laid in his grave—no, it went
deeper than that. The key to the whole thing was in creating an
illusion—Joey had to convince his audience, for even an instant,
that the real flesh-and-blood Elvis, the boy who dared to rock,
stood before them. Unfortunately, he just couldn't cut it. Musi-
cally or visually. No matter if you stopped your ears and squinted
till the lights blurred, this awkward, greasy-haired kid in the
green eye shadow didn't come close, not even for a second. And
the audience let him know it.

Hoots and catcalls drowned out the last chord of "Heartbreak
Hotel," as Joey segued into one of those trembly, heavy-breathing
ballads that were the bane of the King's middle years. I don't
remember the tune or the lyrics—but it was soppy and out of key.
Joey was sweating now, and the hair hung down in his eyes. He
leaned into the microphone, picked a woman out of the audience,
and attempted a seductive leer that wound up looking more like
indigestion than passion. Midway through the song a female voice
shouted "Faggot!" from the back of the room, and two guys in
fraternity jackets began to howl like hound dogs in heat.

Joey faltered, missed his entrance after the guitar break, and
had to stand there strumming over nothing for a whole verse and
chorus till it came round again. People were openly derisive now,
and the fraternity guys, encouraged, began to intersperse their
howls with yips and yodels. Joey bowed his head, as if in defeat,

and let the guitar dangle loose as the band closed out the number. He picked up the tempo a bit on the next one—"Teddy Bear," I think it was—but he never got anywhere with the audience. I watched Cindy out of the corner of my eye. Her face was white. She sat through the first four numbers wordlessly, then leaned across the table and took hold of my arm. "Take me home," she said.

We sat in the driveway awhile, listening to the radio. It was warm, and with the windows rolled down we could hear the crickets and whatnot going at it in the bushes. Cindy hadn't said much on the way back—the scene at the club had been pretty devastating—and I'd tried to distract her with a line of happy chatter. Now she reached forward and snapped off the radio. "He really stinks, doesn't he?" she said.

I wasn't biting. I wanted her, yes, but I wasn't about to run anybody down to get her. "I don't know," I said. "I mean, with that band Elvis himself would've stunk."

She considered this a moment, then fished around in her purse for a cigarette, lit it, and expelled the smoke with a sigh. The sigh seemed to say: "Okay, and what now?" We both knew that the babysitter was hunkered down obliviously in front of the TV next door and that Joey still had another set to get through. We had hours. If we wanted them.

The light from her place fell across the lawn and caught in her hair; her face was in shadow. "You want to go inside a minute?" I said, remembering the way she'd moved against me on the couch. "Have a drink or something?"

When she said "Sure," I felt my knees go weak. This was it: counselor, counsel thyself. I followed her into the house and led her up the dark stairs to the bedroom. We didn't bother with the drink. Or lights. She felt good, and a little strange: she wasn't Judy.

I got us a drink afterward, and then another. Then I brought the bottle to bed with me and we made love again—a slow, easeful, rhythmic love, the crickets keeping time from beyond the windows. I was ecstatic. I was drunk. I was in love. We moved together and I was tonguing her ear and serenading her in a passionate whisper, mimicking Elvis, mimicking Joey. "Well-a bless-a my soul, what's-a wrong with me," I murmured, "I'm itchin' like a ma-han on a fuzzy tree . . . oh-oh-oh, oh, oh yeah." She laughed, and then she got serious. We shared a cigarette and a shot of sticky liqueur afterward; then I must have drifted off.

I don't know what time it was when I heard the van pull in next door. Downstairs the door slammed and I went to the window to watch Cindy's dark form hurrying across the lawn. Then I saw Joey standing in the doorway, the babysitter behind him. There was a curse, a shout, the sound of a blow, and then Joey and the babysitter were in the van, the brake lights flashed, and they were gone.

I felt bad. I felt like a dog, a sinner, a homewrecker, and a Lothario. I felt like Fred must have felt. Naked, in the dark, I poured myself another drink and watched Cindy's house for movement. There was none. A minute later I was asleep.

I woke early. My throat was dry and my head throbbed. I slipped into a pair of running shorts I found in the clutter on the floor, brushed my teeth, rinsed my face, and contemplated the toilet for a long while, trying to gauge whether or not I was going to vomit.

Half a dozen aspirin and three glasses of water later, I stepped gingerly down the stairs. I was thinking poached eggs and dry toast—and maybe, if I could take it, half a cup of coffee—when I drifted into the living room and saw her huddled there on the couch. Her eyed were red, her makeup smeared, and she was wearing the same clothes she'd had on the night before. Beside her, wrapped in a pink blanket the size of a bath towel, was the baby.

"Cindy?"

She shoved the hair back from her face and narrowed her eyes, studying me. "I didn't know where else to go," she murmured.

"You mean, he—?"

I should have held her, I guess, should have probed deep in my counselor's lexicon for words of comfort and assurance, but I couldn't. Conflicting thoughts were running through my head, acid rose in my throat, and the baby, conscious for the first time since I'd laid eyes on it, was fixing me with a steady, unblinking gaze of accusation. This wasn't what I'd wanted, not at all.

"Listen," I said, "can I get you anything—a cup of coffee or some cereal or something? Milk for the baby?"

She shook her head and began to make small sounds of grief and anguish. She bit her lip and averted her face.

I felt like a criminal. "God," I said, "I'm sorry. I didn't—" I started for her, hoping she'd raise her tear-stained face to me, tell me it wasn't my fault, rise bravely from the couch, and trudge off across the lawn and out of my life.

At that moment there was a knock at the door. We both froze. It came again, louder, booming, the sound of rage and impatience. I crossed the room, swung open the door, and found Joey on the doorstep. He was pale, and his hair was in disarray. When the door pulled back, his eyes locked on mine with a look of hatred and contempt. I made no move to open the storm door that separated us.

"You want her?" he said, and he ground the toe of his boot into the welcome mat like a ram pawing the earth before it charges.

I had six inches and forty pounds on him; I could have shoved through the door and drowned my guilt in blood. But it wasn't Joey I wanted to hurt, it was Fred. Or, no, down deep, at the root of it all, it was Judy I wanted to hurt. I glanced into his eyes through the flimsy mesh of the screen and then looked away.

"'Cause you can have her," he went on, dropping the Nashville twang and reverting to pure Brooklynese. "She's a whore. I don't need no whore. Shit," he spat, looking beyond me to where she sat huddled on the couch with the baby, "Elvis went through a hundred just like her. A thousand."

Cindy was staring at the floor. I had nothing to say.

"Fuck you both," he said finally, then turned and marched across the lawn. I watched him slam into the van, fire up the engine, and back out of the driveway. Then the boy who dared to rock was gone.

I looked at Cindy. Her knees were drawn up under her chin

and she was crying softly. I knew I should comfort her, tell her it
would be all right and that everything would work out fine. But
I didn't. This was no pregnant fifteen-year-old who hated her
mother or a kid who skipped cheerleading practice to smoke pot
and hang out at the video arcade—this wasn't a problem that
would walk out of my office and go home by itself. No, the problem was at my doorstep, here on my couch: I was involved—I was
responsible—and I wanted no part of it.

"Patrick," she stammered finally. "I-I don't know what to say. I
mean"—and here she was on the verge of tears again—"I feel as if
. . . as if—"

I didn't get to hear how she felt. Not then, anyway. Because at
that moment the phone began to ring. From upstairs, in the bedroom. Cindy paused in mid-phrase; I froze. The phone rang
twice, three times. We looked at each other. On the fourth ring I
turned and bounded up the stairs.

"Hello?"

"Pat, listen to me." It was Judy. She sounded breathless, as if
she'd been running. "Now don't hang up. Please."

The blood was beating in my head. The receiver weighed six
tons. I struggled to hold it to my ear.

"I made a mistake," she said. "I know it. Fred's a jerk. I left him
three days ago in some winery in St. Helena." There was a pause.
"I'm down in Monterey now and I'm lonely. I miss you."

I held my breath.

"Pat?"

"Yeah?"

"I'm coming home, okay?"

I thought of Joey, of Cindy downstairs with her baby. I glanced
out the window at the place next door, vacant once again, and
thought of Henry and Irma and the progress of the years. And
then I felt something give way, as if a spell had been broken.

"Okay," I said.

A Bird in Hand

No, jutty, frieze,
Buttress, nor coign of vantage, but this bird
Hath made his pendent bed and procreant cradle.
—*MACBETH*, I. vi.

1980

They come like apocalypse, like all ten plagues rolled in one, beating across the sky with an insidious drone, their voices harsh and metallic, cursing the land. Ten million strong, a flock that blots out the huge pale sinking sun, they descend into the trees with a protracted explosion of wings, black underfeathers swirling down like a corrupt snow. At dawn they vacate the little grove of oak and red cedar in a streaming rush, heading west to disperse and feed in the freshly seeded fields; at dusk they gather like storm clouds to swarm back to their roost. Ten million birds, concentrated in a stand of trees no bigger around than a city block—each limb, each branch, each twig and bole and strip of bark bowed under the weight of their serried bodies—ten million tiny cardiovascular systems generating a sirocco of heat, ten million digestive tracts processing seeds, nuts, berries, animal feed, and

streaking the tree trunks with chalky excrement. Where before
there had been leafspill, lichened rocks, sunlit paths beneath the
trees, now there are foot-deep carpets of bird shit.

"We got a problem, Mai." Egon Scharf stands at the window,
turning a worn paperback over in his hand. Outside, less than a
hundred feet off, ten million starlings squat in the trees, cursing
one another in a cacophony of shrieks, whistles, and harsh *check-
checks*. "Says here," holding up the book, "the damn birds carry
disease."

A muted undercurrent of sound buzzes through the house like
static, a wheezing, whistling, many-throated hiss. Mai looks up
from her crocheting: "What? I can't hear you."

"Disease!" he shouts, flinging the book down. "Stink, fungus,
rot. I say we got to do something."

"Tut," is all she says. Her husband has always been an alarmist,
from the day Jack Kennedy was shot and he installed bulletproof
windows in the Rambler, to the time he found a single tent-cater-
pillar nest in the cherry tree and set fire to half the orchard. "A
flock of birds, Egon, that's all—just a flock of birds."

For a moment he is struck dumb with rage and incomprehension, a lock of stained white hair caught against the bridge of his
nose. "Just a flock—? Do you know what you're saying? There's
millions of them out there, crapping all over everything. The
drains are stopped up, it's like somebody whitewashed the car—I
nearly broke my neck slipping in wet bird shit right on my own
front porch, for Christ's sake—and you say it's nothing to worry
about? *Just a flock of birds?*"

She's concentrating on a tricky picot stitch. For the first time, in
the silence, she becomes aware of the steady undercurrent of
sound. It's not just vocal, it's more than that—a rustling, a whisper whispered to a roar. She imagines a dragon, breathing fire,
just outside the house.

"Mai, are you listening to me? Those birds can cause disease."
He's got the book in his hand again—*The Pictorial Encyclopedia
of Birds*—thumbing through it like a professor. "Here, here it is:
histoplasmosis, it says. Wind-borne. It grows in bird crap."

She looks inexpressibly wise, smug even. "Oh, that? That's

nothing, no more serious than a cold," she says, coughing into her fist. "Don't you remember Permilla Greer had it two years back?"

"Can spread through the reticulo-something-or-other system," he reads, and then looks up: "with a high percentage of mortality."

Three days later a man in a blue Ford pickup with tires the size of tank treads pulls into the driveway. The bed of the truck is a confusion of wires and amplifiers and huge open-faced loudspeakers. Intrigued, Mai knots the belt of her housecoat and steps out onto the porch.

"Well, yes, sure," Egon is saying, "you can back it over that pile of fence posts there and right up under the trees, if you want."

A young man in mirror sunglasses is standing beside the open door of the pickup. He nods twice at Egon, then hoists himself into the truck bed and begins flinging equipment around. "Okay," he says, "okay," as if addressing a large and impatient audience, "the way it works is like this: I've got these tapes of starling distress calls, and when they come back tonight to roost I crank up the volume and let 'em have it."

"Distress calls?"

The man is wearing a T-shirt under his jacket. When he pauses to put his hands on his hips, Mai can make out the initials emblazoned across his chest—KDOG—red letters radiating jagged orange lightning bolts. "Yeah, you know, like we mike a cage full of starlings and then put a cat or a hawk or something in there with them. But that's not when we start the tape. We wait till the cat rips one up, then we set the reels rolling."

Egon looks dubious. Mai can see him pinching his lower lip the way he does when somebody tells him the Russians are behind high fertilizer prices or that a pack of coyotes chewed the udders off twenty dairy cows in New Jersey.

"Don't worry," the man says, a thick coil of electrical cord in his hand, "this'll shake 'em up."

For the next two weeks, at dusk, the chatter of the roosting birds is entirely obliterated by a hideous tinny death shriek, crackling with static and blared at apocalyptic volume. When the Bird Man, as Mai has come to think of him, first switches on the amplifier each night, thirty or forty starlings shoot up out of the nearest tree and circle the yard twice before settling back down again. These, she supposes, are the highstrung, flighty types. As for the rest—the great weltering black mass hunkered down in the trees like all the generations of God's creation stretching back from here to the beginning of time—they go about their business as if wrapped in the silence of the Ages. That is, they preen their wings, cackle, squawl, screech, warp the branches, and crap all over everything, as unruffled and oblivious as they were before the Bird Man ever set foot in the yard.

On this particular evening the racket seems louder than ever, the very windowpanes humming with it. Mai has not been feeling well—she's got a cough that makes her want to give up smoking, and her forehead seems hot to the touch—and she was lying down when the Bird Man started his serenade. Now she gets up and shuffles over to the window. Below, parked in the shadow of the nearest oak, the Bird Man sits in his truck, wearing a set of headphones and the sunglasses he never removes. The hammering shriek of the bird call sets Mai's teeth on edge, assaults her ears, and stabs at her temples, and she realizes in that instant that it is distressing her far more than it distresses the birds. She suddenly wants to bolt down the stairs, out the door, and into the pickup, she wants to pull the plug, rake the sunglasses from the Bird Man's face, and tell him to get the hell out of her yard and never come back again. Instead, she decides to have a word with Egon.

Downstairs the noise is even louder, intolerable, as if it had been designed to test the limits of human endurance. She rounds the corner into the den, furious, and is surprised to see Ed Bartro, from the McCracken Board of Supervisors, perched on the edge of the armchair. "Hello, Mai," he shouts over the clamor, "I'm just telling your husband here we got to do something about these birds."

Egon sits across from him, looking hunted. He's got two cigarettes going at once, and he's balancing a double gimlet on his knee. Mai can tell from the blunted look of his eyes that it isn't his first.

"It worked in Paducah," Ed is saying, "and over at Fort Campbell too. Tergitol. It's a detergent, like what you use on your dishes, Mai," he says, turning to her, "and when they spray it on the birds it washes the oil out of their feathers. Then you get them wet—if it rains, so much the better; if not, we'll have the fire department come out and soak down the grove—and they freeze to death in the night. It's not cheap, not by a long shot," he says, "but the county's just going to have to foot the bill."

"You sure it'll work?" Egon shouts, rattling the ice in his glass for emphasis.

"Nothing's for certain, Egon," Ed says, "but I'm ninety-nine and nine-tenths sure of it."

The following night, about seven o'clock, a pair of helicopters clatter over the house and begin circling the grove. Mai is hand-mashing potatoes and frying pork chops. The noise startles her, and she turns down the flame, wipes her hands on her apron, and steps out onto the porch to have a look. Angry suddenly, thinking, *Why must everything be so loud?*, she cups her hands over her ears and watches the searchlights gleam through the dark claws of the treetops. Gradually, she becomes aware of a new odor on the damp night air, a whiff of soap and alcohol undermining the sour ammoniac stench of the birds. It's like a dream, she thinks, like a war. The helicopters scream, the spray descends in a deadly fog, the pork chops burn.

An hour later the firemen arrive. Three companies. From Lone Oak, West Paducah and Woodlawn. The sequence is almost surreal: lights and shouts, black boots squashing the shoots in the garden, heavy-grid tires tearing up the lawn, the rattle of the pumps, coffee for thirty. By the time they leave, Mai is in bed, feeling as if she's been beaten with a shoe. She coughs up a ball of phlegm, spits it into a tissue and contemplates it, wondering if she should call the doctor in the morning.

When Egon comes in it is past midnight, and she's been dozing with the light on. "Mai," he says, "Mai, are you asleep?" Groggy, she props herself up on her elbows and squints at him. He is drunk, trundling heavily about the room as he strips off his clothes. "Well, I think this is going to do it, Mai," he says, the words thick on his tongue. "They knocked off six million in one shot with this stuff over at Russellville, so Ed tells me, and they only used half as much."

She can't make out the rest of what he says—he's muttering, slamming at a balky bureau drawer, running water in the bathroom. When she wakes again the house is dark, and she can feel him beside her, heavy and inert. Outside, in the trees, the doomed birds whisper among themselves, and the sound is like thunder in her ears.

In the morning, as the sun fires the naked fingers of the highest branches, the flock lifts up out of the trees with a crash of wings and a riot of shrieks and cackles. Mai feels too weak to get out of bed, feels as if her bones have gone soft on her, but Egon is up and out the door at first light. She is reawakened half an hour later by the slam of the front door and the pounding of footsteps below. There is the sound of Egon's voice, cursing softly, and then the click-click-click of the telephone dial. "Hello, Ed?" The house is still, his voice as clear as if he were standing beside her. A cough catches in her throat and she reaches for the bottle of cough syrup she'd fished out of the medicine cabinet after the firemen had left.

". . . nothing at all," her husband says below. "I think I counted eighty-six or -seven birds . . . uh-huh, uh-huh . . . yeah, well, you going to try again?"

She doesn't have to listen to the rest—she already knows what the county supervisor is saying on the other end of the line, the smooth, reasonable politician's voice pouring honey into the receiver, talking of cost overruns, uncooperative weather, the little unpleasantries in life we just have to learn to live with. Egon will be discouraged, she knows that. Over the past few weeks he's become increasingly touchy, the presence of the birds an ongoing ache, an open wound, an obsession. "It's not bad enough that the drought withered the soybeans last summer or that the damned government is cutting out price supports for feed corn," he'd shouted one night after paying the Bird Man his daily fee, "Now I can't even enjoy the one stand of trees on my property. Christ," he roared, "I can't even sit down to dinner without the taste of bird piss in my mouth." Then he'd turned to her, his face flushed, hands shaking with rage, and she'd quietly reminded him what the doctor had said about his blood pressure. He poured himself a drink and looked at her with drooping eyes. "Have I done something to deserve this, Mai?" he said.

Poor Egon, she thinks. He lets things upset him so. Of course the birds are a nuisance, she'll admit that now, but what about the man with the distress calls and the helicopters and firemen and all the rest? She tilts back the bottle of cough syrup, thinking she ought to call him in and tell him to take it easy, forget about it. In a month or so, when the leaves start to come in, the flock will break up and head north: why kill yourself over nothing? That's what she wants to tell him, but when she calls his name her voice cracks and the cough comes up on her again, racking, relentless, worse than before. She lets the spasm pass, then calls his name again. There is no answer.

It is then that she hears the sputter of the chainsaw somewhere beyond the window. She listens to the keening whine of the blade as it engages wood—a sound curiously like the starling distress call—and then the dry heaving crash of the first tree.

1890

An utter stillness permeates the Tuxedo Club, a hush bred of money and privilege, a soothing patrician quiet insisted upon by the arrases and thick damask curtains, bound up in the weave of the rugs, built into the very walls. Eugene Schiefflin, dilettante, portraitist, man of leisure, and amateur ornithologist, sits before the marble fireplace, leafing through the *Oologist Monthly* and sipping meditatively at a glass of sherry. *The red-eyed vireo*, he reads, *nests twice a year, both sexes participating in the incuba-*

tion of the eggs. The eggs, two to four in number, are white with brown maculations at the larger extremity, and measure ⁵/₁₆ by ⅔ of an inch. . . . When his glass is empty, he raises a single languid finger and the waiter appears with a replacement, removes the superfluous glass, and vanishes, the whole operation as instantaneous and effortless as an act of the will.

Despite appearances to the contrary—the casually crossed legs, the proprietary air, the look of dignity and composure stamped into the seams of his face—Eugene is agitated. His eyes give him away. They leap from the page at the slightest movement in the doorway, and then surreptitiously drop to his waistcoat pocket to examine the face of the gold watch he produces each minute or so. He is impatient, concerned. His brother Maunsell is half an hour late already—has he forgotten their appointment? That would be just like him, damn it. Irritated, Eugene lights a cigar and begins drumming his fingertips on the arm of the chair while the windows go gray with dusk.

At sixty-three, with his great drooping mustache and sharp, accipiter's nose, Eugene Schiefflin is a salient and highly regarded figure in New York society. Always correct, a master of manners and a promoter of culture and refinement, a fixture of both the Society List and the Club Register, he is in great demand as commencement speaker and dinner guest. His grandfather, a cagey, backbiting immigrant, had made a fortune in the wholesale drug business, and his father, a lawyer, had encouraged that fortune to burgeon and flower like some clinging vine, the scent of money as sweet as bougainvillaea. Eugene himself went into business when he was just out of college, but he soon lost interest. A few years later he married an heiress from Brooklyn and retired to hold forth at the Corinthian Yacht Club, listen to string quartets, and devote himself to his consuming passions—painting, Shakespeare, and the study of birds.

It wasn't until he was nearly fifty, however, that he had his awakening, his epiphany, the moment that brought the disparate threads of his life together and infused them with import and purpose. He and Maunsell were sitting before the fire one evening in his apartment at Madison and Sixty-fifth, reading aloud from

Romeo and Juliet. Maunsell, because his voice was pitched higher, was reading Juliet, and Eugene, Romeo. "Wilt thou be gone?" Maunsell read, "it is not yet near day: / It was the nightingale, and not the lark, / That pierc'd the fearful hollow of thine ear." The iambs tripped in his head, and suddenly Eugene felt as if he'd been suffused with light, electrocuted, felt as if Shakespeare's muse had touched him with lambent inspiration. He jumped up, kicking over his brandy and spilling the book to the floor. "Maunsell," he shouted, "Maunsell, that's it!"

His brother looked up at him, alarmed and puzzled. He made an interrogatory noise.

"The nightingale," Eugene said, "and, and . . . woodlarks, siskins, linnets, chaffinches—and whatever else he mentions!"

"What? Who?"

"Shakespeare, of course. The greatest poet—the greatest man —of all time. Don't you see? This will be our enduring contribution to culture; this is how we'll do our little bit to enrich the lives of all the generations of Americans to come—"

Maunsell's mouth had dropped open. He looked like a classics scholar who's just been asked to identify the members of the Chicago White Stockings. "What in Christ's name are you talking about?"

"We're going to form the American Acclimatization Society, Maunsell, here and now—and we're going to import and release every species of bird—every last one—mentioned in the works of the Bard of Avon."

That was thirteen years ago.

Now, sitting in the main room of the Tuxedo Club and waiting for his brother, Eugene has begun to show his impatience. He jerks round in his seat, pats at his hair, fiddles with his spats. He is imbibing his fourth sherry and examining a table enumerating the stomach contents of three hundred and fifty-nine bay-breasted warblers when he looks up to see Maunsell in the vestibule, shrugging out of his overcoat and handing his hat and cane over to the limp little fellow in the cloakroom.

"Well?" Eugene says, rising to greet him. "Any news?"

Maunsell's face is flushed with the sting of the March wind.

"Yes," he says, "yes," the timbre of his voice instantly soaked up in the drapes and rugs and converted to a whisper. "She's on schedule as far as they know, and all incoming ships have reported clear weather and moderate seas."

Any irritation Eugene may have shown earlier has vanished from his face. He is grinning broadly, the dead white corners of his mustache lifted in exultation, gold teeth glittering. "That's the best news I've heard all week," he says. "Tomorrow morning, then?"

Maunsell nods. "Tomorrow morning."

At eight the following morning, the two brothers, in top hats and fur-lined overcoats, are perched anxiously on the edge of the broad leather seat of Maunsell's carriage, peering out at the taper-ing length of the Fourteenth Street pier and the Cunard steamer edging into the slips. Half an hour later they are on deck, talking animatedly with a man so short, pale, and whiskerless he could be mistaken for a schoolboy. It is overcast, windy, raw, the tempera-ture lurking just below the freezing mark. "They seem to have held up pretty well, sir," the little fellow is shouting into the wind. "Considering the Cunard people made me keep them in the hold."

"What? In the hold?" Both brothers look as if they've been slapped, indignation and disbelief bugging their eyes, mad wisps of silver hair foaming over their ears, hands clutching savagely at the brims of their hats.

"'Loive cargo goes in the 'old,'" the little fellow says, his voice pinched in mockery, "'and Oy'm vewy sowwy, Oy am, but them's the regelations.'" He breaks into a grin. "Oh, it was awful down there—cold, and with all those horses stamping and whinnying and the dogs barking it's a wonder any of the birds made it at all."

"It's a damned outrage," Eugene sputters, and Maunsell clucks his tongue. "How many did you say made it, Doodson?"

"Well, as you'll see for yourself in a minute, sir, the news is both good and bad. Most of the thrushes and skylarks came through all right, but there was a heavy mortality among the nightingales—and I've got just three pairs still alive. But the starlings, I'll tell you, they're a hardy bird. Didn't lose a one, not a single one."

Eugene looks relieved. In what has become a reflex gesture over the past few days, he consults his pocket watch and then looks up at Doodson. "Yes, they're a glorious creature, aren't they?"

Maunsell directs the driver to Central Park East—Fifth and Sixty-fifth—and then settles back in the seat beside his brother. Two cabs fall in behind them, the first containing Doodson and a portion of the transatlantic aviary, the second packed to the roof with bird cages. There is the steady adhesive clap of hoofs, the rattling of the springs. Eugene glances over his shoulder to reassure himself that the cabs—and birds—are still there, and then turns to his brother, beaming, his fingers tapping at the stiff crown of the hat in his lap, an aureole of hair radiating from his head. "When birds do sing, hey ding a ding, ding: / Sweet lovers love the spring," he recites with a laugh, unscrewing the cap of his flask and nudging Maunsell. "I think we've really got it this time," he says, laughing again, the sound of his voice softening the cold clatter of the coach. "I can feel it in my bones."

Outwardly, his mood is confident—celebratory, even—but in fact his high hopes are tempered by the Acclimatization Society's history of failure over the course of the thirteen years since its inception. Eugene has released thrushes, skylarks, and nightingales time and again. He has released siskins, woodlarks, and common cuckoos. All have failed. Inexplicably, the seed populations disappeared without a trace, as if they'd been sucked up in a vacuum or blown back to Europe. But Eugene Schieffelin is not a man to give up easily—oh no. This time he's got a new ace in the hole, *Sturnus vulgaris*, the starling. Certainly not the Bard's favorite bird—in all the countless lines of all the sonnets, histories, comedies, and tragedies it is mentioned only once—but legitimate to the enterprise nonetheless. And hardy. Doodson's report has got to be looked upon as auspicious: *not a single bird lost in the crossing*. It's almost too good to be true.

He is musing with some satisfaction on the unexected beauty of

the bird—the stunning metallic sheen of the plumage and the
pale butter pat of the beak revealed to him through the mesh of
the cage—when the carriage pulls up along the curb opposite the
park. Before the percussive echo of the horses' hoofs has faded,
Eugene is out of the carriage and shouting directions to Doodson,
the two cabbies, and Maunsell's driver. In one hand he clutches a
pry bar; in the other, a bottle of Moët et Chandon. "All right," he
calls, rigorous as a field marshal, "I want the cages laid side by
side underneath those elms over there." And then he strikes out
across the grass, Maunsell bringing up the rear with three long-
stemmed glasses.

It is still cold, a crust of ice stretched over the puddles in the
street, the cabbies' breath clouding their faces as they bend to
negotiate the wooden cages. "Here," Eugene barks, striding
across the field and waving his arm impatiently, "hurry it along,
will you?" Well tipped, but muttering nonetheless, the cabbies
struggle with one cage while Doodson—his nose red with
cold and excitement—helps Maunsell's chauffeur with another.
Within minutes all eight cages are arranged in parallel rows beneath the elms, laid out like coffins, and Eugene has begun his
customary rambling speech outlining his and the society's pur-
poses, eulogizing Shakespeare and reciting quotations relevant to
the caged species. As he stoops to pry the lid from the first cage of
thrushes, he shouts out an injunction from *Hamlet:* "Unpeg the
baskets on the house's top," he calls, liberating the birds with a
magisterial sweep of his arm, "Let the birds fly."

The cabbies, paid and dismissed, linger at a respectful distance
to watch the mad ceremony. Deliberate, methodical, the old fellow in the top hat and silk muffler leans down to remove the tops
of the cages and release the birds. There is a rustle of wings, a cry
or two, and then the appearance of the first few birds, emerging at
random and flapping aimlessly into the branches of the nearest
tree. The pattern is repeated with each box in succession, until
the old man draws up to the single remaining cage, the cage of
starlings. The other old fellow, the rickety one with the drawn
face and staring eyes, steps forward with the glasses, and then
there's the sound of a cork popping. "A toast," the first one shouts,

and they're raising their glasses, all three of them, the two old duffers and the young cub with the red nose. "May these humble creatures, brought here with good will and high expectation, breed and prosper and grace the land with beauty and song."

"Hear, hear!" call the others, and the chauffeur as well, though he hasn't been offered any wine.

Behind the mesh of their cage, the big dull birds crouch in anticipation, stuffed like blackbirds in a pie, their voices wheezing with a sound of metal on metal. The cabbies shake their heads. A cold wind tosses the dead, black limbs of the trees. Then the old gentleman bends to the cage at his feet, his hair shining in the pale sunlight, and there is a sudden startling explosion as the birds stream from the opening as if propelled, feathers rasping, wings tearing at the air, a single many-voiced shriek of triumph issuing from their throats. En masse, almost in precision formation, they wheel past the spectators like a flock of pigeons, and then, banking against the sun, they wing off over the trees, looking for a place to roost.

Two Ships

I saw him today. At the side of the road, head down, walking. There were the full-leafed trees, the maples, elms, and oaks I see every day, the snarl of the wild berry bushes, sumac, milkweed, and thistle, the snaking hot macadam road, sun-flecked shadows. And him. An apparition: squat, bow-legged, in shorts, T-shirt, and sandals, his head shaved to the bone, biceps like legs of lamb. I slowed with the shock of seeing him there, with the recognition that worked in my ankles and fingertips like sap, and for a stunned second or two I stared, fixated, as the car pulled me closer and then swept past him in a rush. I was dressed in white, on my way to crack stinging serves and return treacherous backhands in sweet arcing loops. He never looked up.

When I got home I made some phone calls. He was back in the country—legally—the government forgiving, his mind like damaged fruit. Thirty-one years old, he was staying with his parents, living in the basement, doing God knows what—strumming a guitar, lifting weights, putting pieces of wood together—the things he'd been doing since he was fourteen. Erica listened as I pried information from the receiver, a cigarette in the corner of her mouth, polished surfaces behind her.

I was pouring Haig & Haig over a hard white knot of ice cubes. The last of my informants had got off the subject of Casper and was filling me in on the pains in her neck, lips, toes, and groin as I cradled the receiver between ear and shoulder. The smile I gave Erica was weak. When the whiskey-cracked voice on the other end of the line paused to snatch a quick breath, I changed the subject, whispered a word of encouragement and hung up.

"Well?" Erica was on her feet.

"We've got to move," I said.

I was overdramatizing. For effect. Overdramatizing because humor resides in exaggeration, and humor is a quick cover for alarm and bewilderment. I *was* alarmed. He could stay indefinitely, permanently. He could show up at the tennis courts, at the lake, at my front door. And then what would I do? Turn my back, look through him, crouch behind the door and listen to the interminable sharp intercourse of knuckle and wood?

"Is it really that bad?" Erica said.

I sipped at my Scotch and nodded. It was really that bad.

Twelve years ago we'd been friends. Close friends. We'd known each other from the dawn of consciousness on. We played in the cradle, in the schoolyard, went to camp together, listened to the same teachers, blocked and batted for the same teams. When we were sixteen we declared war on the bourgeois state and its material and canonical manifestations. That is, we were horny adolescents sublimating glandular frustrations in the most vicious and mindless acts of vandalism. We smoked pot, gulped stolen vodka, and drove our parents' cars at a hundred miles an hour. Each night we cruised the back streets till three or four, assaulting religious statues, churches, the slick curvilinear windshields of Porsches and Cadillacs. Indiscriminate, we burned crosses and

six-pointed stars. We tore down fences, smashed picture windows, filled Jacuzzis with sand. Once we climbed a treacherous
three-hundred-foot cliff in utter darkness so we could drop raw
eggs on the patrons of the chic restaurant nestled at its base.
We committed secretive acts of defiance the way Crazy Horse
counted coup. We lacked perspective.

Casper saw the whole thing as a crusade. He was given to di-
atribe, and his diatribes had suddenly begun to bloom with the
rhetoric of Marxism. We would annihilate a dentist's plaster lawn
ornaments—flamingoes and lantern-wielding pickaninnies—and
he'd call it class warfare. Privately, I saw our acts of destruction as
a way of pissing in my father's eye.

We ran away from home at one point—I think we were fifteen
or so—and it was then that I had my first intimation of just how
fanatical and intransigent Casper could be. I'd never considered
him abnormal, had never thought about it. There was his obsession with the bodily functions, the vehement disgust he felt over
his parents' lovemaking—*I could hear them,* he would say, his
features pinched with contempt, *grunting and slobbering, humping like pigs*—the fact that he went to a shrink twice a week. But
none of this was very different from what other fifteen-year-olds
did and said and felt, myself included. Now, running away, I saw
that Casper's behavior went beyond the pale of wise-guyism or
healthy adolescent rebellion. I recognized the spark of madness in
him, and I was both drawn to it and repelled by it. He was
serious, he was committed, his was the rapture of saints and
martyrs, both feet over the line. He went too far; I drew back
from him.

We'd planned this excursion with all the secrecy and precision
of prison breakers. Twenty miles away, tucked deep in the leafy
recesses of Fahnestock State Park, was a huge cache of canned
food, an ax, two sixpacks of Jaguar malt liquor, sleeping bags, and
a tent. We signed in at school, ducked out the back door, hitchhiked the twenty miles, and experienced freedom. The following
day, while we were exploring the park, my father stalked up to the
campsite (my brother had broken down under interrogation and
given us away) and settled down to wait. My father is a powerful

and unforgiving man. He tapped a birch switch against a rock for an hour, then packed up everything he could carry—food, tent, sleeping bags, canteens—and hiked out to the highway. The sight of the barren campsite made my blood leap. At first I thought we were in the wrong spot, the trees all alike, dusk falling, but then Casper pointed out the blackened circle of rocks we'd cooked a triumphant dinner over the night before. I found my father's note pinned to a tree. It was curt and minatory, the script an angry flail.

Casper refused to give in. Between us we had four dollars and twenty cents. He dragged me through swamps and brambles, the darkening stalks of the trees, past ponds, down hills, and out to the highway. Afraid to hitch—my father could be glaring behind each pair of headlights—we skirted the road and made our way to a clapboard grocery where we purchased a twenty-five-pound bag of Ken-L Ration. Outside, it was 29°F. We hiked back up into the woods, drank from a swamp, crunched the kibbled nuggets of glyceryl monostearate and animal fat preserved with BHA, and slept in our jackets. In the morning I slipped away, walked out to the road, and hitchhiked back home.

The state police were called in to track Casper down. They employed specially trained trackers and bloodhounds. Casper's parents hired a helicopter search team for eighty-five dollars an hour. The helicopter spotted Casper twice. Whirring, kicking up a cyclone, the machine hovered over the treetops while Casper's mother shouted stentorian pleas through a bullhorn. He ran. Two weeks later he turned up at home, in bed, asleep.

It was just after this that Casper began to talk incessantly of repression and the police state. He shuffled round the corridors at school with a huge, distended satchel full of poorly printed pamphlets in faded greens and grays: *The Speeches of V. I. Lenin, State and Anarchy, Das Kapital.* The rhetoric never appealed to me, but the idea of throwing off the yoke, of discounting and discrediting all authority, was a breath of fresh air.

He quit college at nineteen and went to live among the revolutionary workers of the Meachum Brothers Tool & Die Works in Queens. Six months later he was drafted. How they accepted him or why he agreed to report, I'll never know. He was mad as a loon, fixated in his Marxist-Leninist phase, gibbering nonstop about imperialist aggressors and the heroic struggle of the revolutionary democratic peoples of the Republic of Vietnam. It was summer. I was living in Lake George with Erica and he came up for a day or two before they inducted him.

He was worked up—I could see that the minute he got off the bus. His feet shuffled, but his limbs and torso danced, elbows jerking as if they were wired, the big knapsack trembling on his back, a cord pulsing under his left eye. He was wearing a cap that clung to his head like something alive, and the first thing he did was remove it with a flourish to show off his bald scalp: he'd shaved himself—denuded himself—every hair plucked out, right down to his mustache and eyebrows. From the neck up he looked like a space invader; from the neck down, rigidly muscled, he was Charles Atlas.

He couldn't stop talking. Couldn't sit down, couldn't sleep, couldn't eat. Said he was going into the army all right, but that he'd do everything in his power to subvert them, and that when they shipped him to Vietnam he'd turn his weapon on his own platoon and then join the NLF. I tried to joke with him, distract him—if only for a moment. But he was immovable. He played his one note till Erica and I just wanted to jump into the car and leave him there with the house, the books, the stereo, everything. Someone pulled a knife out of my ribs when he left.

I never saw him again. Until today.

Rumor had it that he'd disappeared from Fort Dix the first week. He was in Canada, he was in Sweden. The Finns had jailed him for entering the country illegally, the Swiss had expelled him. He was in Belize City stirring up the locals, the British had got hold of him and the United States was pressing for his extradition. Rumors. They sifted back to me through my mother, friends, people who claimed they'd seen him or talked to someone who had. I was in law school, student-deferred. There were exams, the seasons changed, Erica visited on weekends, and there were long breathy phone calls in between. In my second year, the packages began to show up in my mailbox. Big, crudely bundled manuscripts—manuscripts the size of phone books—sent from an address in London, Ontario.

There were no cover letters. But, then, cover letters would have been superfluous: the moment I saw the crabbed scrawl across the flat surface of the first package (lettering so small it could have been written with the aid of magnification), I knew who had sent it. Inside these packages were poems. Or, rather, loosely organized snatches of enjambed invective in strident upper-case letters:

> THE FASCIST NAZI ABORTIONIST LOBBY THAT FEEDS
> ON THE TATTERED FLESH OF ASIAN ORPHANS
> MUST BE CIRCUMVENTED FROM ITS IMPERIALIST EXPANSIONIST
>   DESIGN
> TO ENSLAVE THE MASSES AND TURN ARTIFICIALLY NATIONALIZED
> PROLETARIANS AGAINST BROTHER AND SISTER PROLETARIANS
> IN THE INTERNECINE CONFLICT THAT FEEDS
> THE COFFERS
> OF THE REVISIONIST RUNNING DOGS
> OF BOURGEOIS COMPLACENCY!

The poems went on for hundreds of pages. I couldn't read them. I wondered why he had sent them to me. Was he trying to persuade me? Was he trying to justify himself, reach out, recapture some sympathy he'd deluded himself into thinking we'd once shared? I was in law school. I didn't know what to do. Eventually, the packages stopped coming.

Erica and I married, moved back to Westchester, built a house, had a daughter. I was working in a law firm in White Plains. One night, 2:00 A.M., the phone rang. It was Casper. "Jack," he said, "it's me, Casper. Listen, listen, this is important, this is vital—" Phone calls in the night. I hadn't spoken to him in seven years, gulfs had opened between us, I was somebody else—and yet here he was, with the same insistent, demanding voice that wraps you up in unasked-for intimacies like a boa constrictor, talking as if we'd just seen each other the day before. I sat up. He was nearly crying.

"Jack: you've got to do something for me, life and death, you got
to promise me—"

"Wait a minute," I said, "wait, hold on—" I didn't want to hear
it. I was angry, puzzled; I had to be at work in five and a half
hours.

"Just this one thing. You know me, right? Just this: if anybody
asks, you stick up for me, okay? No, no: I mean, tell them I'm all
right, you know what I mean? That I'm good. There's nothing
wrong with me, understand?"

What could I say? The phone went dead, the room was dark.
Beside me, in bed, Erica shifted position and let out a sigh that
would have soothed all the renegades in the world.

I was busy. The incident slipped my mind. Three days later a
man in an elaborately buckled and belted trench coat stepped into
the anteroom at Hermening & Stinson, the firm that had given me
my tenuous foothold in the world of corporate law. No one paid
much attention to him until he announced that he was from the
FBI and that he wanted to speak with me. The typist stopped
typing. Charlie Hermening looked up at me like a barn owl scanning the rafters. I shrugged my shoulders.

The man was big and fleshy and pale, his irises like water, wisps
of white hair peeping out from beneath the fedora that hugged his
bullet head. When I showed him into my office he flashed his
credentials, and I remember wondering if TV producers had studied FBI men, or if FBI men had learned how to act from watching
TV. He took a seat, but declined to remove either his hat or
trench coat. Was I acquainted with a Casper R. Hansen, he
wanted to know. Did I know his whereabouts? When had I seen
him last? Had he telephoned, sent anything in the mail? What did
I think of his mental state?

"His mental state?" I repeated.

"Yes," the man said, soft and articulate as a professor, "I want to
know if you feel he's mentally competent."

I thought about it for a minute, thought about Lake George, the
poems, Casper's tense and frightened voice over the phone. I almost asked the FBI man why he wanted to know: Was Casper in
trouble? Had he done something illegal? I wanted to gauge the

man's response, listen for nuances that might give me a clue as to what I should say. But I didn't. I simply leaned across the desk, looked the man in the eye, and told him that in my estimation Casper was seriously impaired.

That was a year ago. I'd forgotten the man from the FBI, forgotten Casper. Until now. Now he was back. Like a slap in the face, like a pointed finger: he was back.

"What are you afraid of?" Erica asked. "That he'll say hello or shake your hand or something?"

It was dark. Moths batted against the screens; I toyed with my asparagus crêpes and spinach salad. The baby was in bed. I poured another glass of French Colombard. "No," I said, "that's not it." And then: "Yes. That would be bad enough. Think of the embarrassment."

"Embarrassment? You were friends, you grew up together."

"Yes," I said. That was the problem. I sipped at the wine.

"Look, I'm not exactly thrilled about seeing him either—the weekend at Lake George was enough to last me a lifetime—but it's not the end of the world or anything. . . . I mean, nothing says you've got to invite him over for dinner so he can lecture us on the wisdom of Mao Tse-tung or tell us how miserable he is."

She was in the kitchen area, spooning the foam off a cup of cappuccino. "Are you afraid he'll vandalize the house—is that it?"

"I don't know," I said. "I mean, we're not kids any more—he's not that crazy." I thought about it, listening to the hiss of the coffee maker. The house we'd put up was pretty cozy and dramatic. Modern. With decks and skylights and weathered wood and huge sheets of glass. It called attention to itself, stylish and unique, a cut above the slant-roofed cottages that lined the road. It was precisely the sort of house Casper and I had sought out and violated when we were sixteen. I looked up from my wine. "He might," I admitted.

Erica looked alarmed. "Should we call the police?"

"Don't be ridiculous, we can't—" I broke off. It was futile. I wasn't really afraid of that sort of thing—no, my fears went deeper, deeper than I wanted to admit. He would look at me and

he would condemn me: I'd become what we'd reacted against together, what he'd devoted his mad, misguided life to subverting.
That was the problem. That's why I didn't want to see him at the
tennis courts or at the lake or even walking along the road with his
shoulders hunched under the weight of his convictions.

"Hey"—she was at my side, massaging the back of my neck—
"why not forget about it, you've got enough worries as it is." She
was right. The EPA was filing suit against one of our clients—a
battery company accused of dumping toxic waste in the Hudson—
and I'd been poring over the regulations looking for some sort of
loophole. I was meeting with Charlie Hermening in the morning
to show him what I'd come up with.

"You know something—didn't Rose say he'd been back nearly a
month already?" She was purring, the cappuccino smelled like a
feast, I could feel the alcohol loosening my knotted nerves. "And
you only saw him today for the first time? If he was going to come
over, wouldn't he have done it by now?"

I was about to admit she was right, finish my coffee, and take a
look at the newspaper when there was a knock at the door. A
knock at the door. It was nine-thirty. I nearly kicked the table
over. "I'm not here," I hissed. "No matter who it is," and I slipped
into the bedroom.

There were voices in the hallway. I heard Erica, and then the
polite but vaguely querulous tones of—a woman?—and then
Erica's voice, projecting: "Jack. Jack, will you come out here,
please?"

Mrs. Shapiro, our next-door neighbor, was standing in the
doorway. "Sorry to bother you," the old woman said, "but your
garbitch is all over the driveway—I can't even get the car
through."

Garbage? Her driveway was at least fifty feet from ours. What
was she talking about?

The night was warm, redolent of flowers and grass clippings.
There was a moon, and the crickets seemed to be serenading it,
chirring in the trees like a steel band locked in a groove. I walked
beside Mrs. Shapiro to where her car sat rumbling and sputtering,

lights flooding the gumbo of vegetable peels, papers, milk car-
tons, and diapers strewn across her driveway. The cans had been
deliberately hauled down the street, upended and dumped—no
dog or raccoon could have been so determined or efficient. This
was deliberate. As I bent to the mess, I thought of Casper.

"Kids." Mrs. Shapiro, arms folded, stood silhouetted against
the headlights. She spat the words out as if she were cursing.
"Things just seem to get worse and worse, don't they?"

I worked in silence, embarrassed, digging into the slop with my
bare hands, trying not to think about baby stool, maggots, the
yielding wet paste of coffee grounds and canteloupe shells, scoop-
ing it up by the armload. When I was finished I told Mrs. Shapiro
that I'd have Erica hose down the driveway for her in the morning. The elderly woman merely raised her hand as if to say "Forget about it," tumbled into the car seat, and set the car in motion
with a shriek of the steering mechanism and a rumble of rotten
exhaust. I watched the taillights trace the arc of her driveway,
then hauled the garbage cans back to my own yard, all the while
expecting Casper to pop out at me with a laugh. Or maybe he was
crouching in the bushes, giggling to himself like a half-witted adolescent. That was about his speed, I thought.

Inside, I washed up, fumed at Erica—"It was deliberate," I
kept saying, "I know it was"—and then shut myself up in the
study with the brief I'd prepared on the battery manufacturer. I
couldn't read a word of it. After a while—it must have been
twenty minutes or so—I heard Erica getting ready for bed—running water, brushing her teeth—and then the house went silent. I
knew I should go over the brief a couple of times, have a mug of
hot Ovaltine, and get a good night's rest. But I was rooted to the
chair, thinking about Casper—a grown man, thirty-one years
old—sneaking around in the dark dumping people's garbage.
What could he be thinking of?

A muffled sound was pulsing through the house. At first it
didn't register, and then, with a flash of anger, I realized what it
was: someone was knocking at the door. This was too much. If
there was garbage in the neighbors' driveway they could damn

well clean it up themselves, I thought, storming down the hallway. I wrenched the door back, expecting Mrs. Shapiro.

It was Casper.

He stood there, his head bowed, the moon blanching the stiff
bristle of his crown. He was wearing a sleeveless T-shirt, shorts,
sandals. The veins stood out in his arms. When he looked up at
me his eyes were soft and withdrawn. "Jack," was all he said.

I was at a loss. The worst possible scenario was playing itself out
on my doorstep, and I was caught up in it, against my will, suddenly forced to take a part. I felt like an unrehearsed actor shoved
out onstage; I felt exhausted and defeated. My initial impulse had
been to slam the door shut, but now, with Casper standing there
before me, I could only clear my throat, wipe my features clean,
and ask him in.

He hesitated. "No," he said, "no, I couldn't do that. I mean, I
just came to . . . to say hello, that's all."

"Don't be silly," I said, insistent, already ushering him in.
"Here, the living room. Have a seat. Can I get you something:
beer? brandy? 7-Up?"

We were standing beside each other in the center of the living
room. He took in the potted plants, the umbrella tree, the little
Paul Klee my mother had given me. The nearest piece of furniture was the loveseat; he perched on the edge of it, apologetic.
"No thanks," he said, eyes on the floor.

I was halfway to the kitchen, needing a brandy. "You sure? It's
no trouble at all. I've got liqueur—how about a Drambuie?" It
had suddenly become crucially important that I give him something, an offering of some sort, a peace pipe, the communal leg of
lamb. "Are you hungry? I've got Brie and crackers—I could make
a sandwich—?"

He was still staring at the floor. "Milk," he said, so softly I
wasn't sure I'd heard him.

"You want a glass of milk?"

"Yes, thanks—if it's not too much trouble."

I made some deprecatory noises, poured out a brandy and a
milk, arranged some Danish flatbread on a platter around the
cheese. Two minutes later we were sitting across the room from

each other. I was looking into my brandy snifter; he was studying the glass of milk as if he'd never seen anything like it before. "So," I said, "you're back."

He didn't answer. Just sat there, looking at his milk. There was something monkish about him—perhaps it was the crewcut. I thought of acolytes, nuns, the crop-headed Hare Krishnas in airport lounges. "It's been a long time," I offered. No response. It occurred to me to ask about the garbage cans—perhaps we could share the intimacy of the joke—but then I thought better of it: no sense in embarrassing him or stirring up any rancor.

"About the garbage cans," he said, as if reading my thoughts, "I did it."

I waited for an explanation. He stared at me so fixedly I finally looked away, and more as a means of breaking the silence than satisfying my curiosity, I asked him why.

He seemed to consider this. "I don't know," he said finally, took a tentative sip of milk, then downed the glass in a single gulp. He belched softly and settled back in the chair.

I was losing my patience. I had work in the morning. The last thing I wanted to do was sit here with this wacko, on edge in my own living room, mouthing the little platitudes of social formality when I knew both of us were seething. I made another stab at conversation, just because the silence was so inadmissible. "So," I said, "we've wondered about you from time to time, Erica and I. . . . We have a daughter, did you know that? Her name's Tricia."

His arms were rigid, tense with muscle. He was staring down at his interlocked fingers, straining with the tension, as if he were doing an isometric exercise. "I was in the hospital," he said.

The hospital. The syllables bit into me, made something race round the edge of my stomach. I did not want to hear it.

I got up to pour another brandy. "More milk?" I asked, the rigorous host, but he ignored me. He was going to tell me about the hospital. He raised his voice so I could hear him.

"They said it was a condition of giving me a clean slate. You know, they'd rehabilitate me. Eleven months. Locked up with the shit-flingers and droolers, the guys they'd shot up in the war. That was the hospital."

I stood in the kitchen doorway, the brandy in my hand. He was accusing me. I'd started the war, oppressed the masses, wielded the dollar like an ax; I'd deserted him, told the FBI the truth, created the American Nazi Party, and erected the slums, stick by stick. What did he want from me—to say I was sorry? Sorry he was crazy, sorry he couldn't go to law school, sorry Marx's venom had eaten away the inside of his brain?

He was on his feet now. The empty glass flashed in his hand as he crossed the room. He handed it to me. We were inches apart. "Jack," he said. I looked away.

"I've got to go now," he whispered.

I stood at the door and watched him recede into the moonlight that spilled across the lawn like milk. He turned left on the macadam road, heading in the direction of his parents' house.

Erica was behind me in her robe, squinting against the light in the hallway. "Jack?" she said.

I barely heard her. Standing there in the doorway, watching the shadows close like a fist over the lawn, I was already packing.

Rara Avis

It looked like a woman or a girl perched there on the roof of the furniture store, wings folded like a shawl, long legs naked and exposed beneath a skirt of jagged feathers the color of sepia. The sun was pale, poised at equinox. There was the slightest breeze. We stood there, thirty or forty of us, gaping up at the big motionless bird as if we expected it to talk, as if it weren't a bird at all but a plastic replica with a speaker concealed in its mouth. Sidor's Furniture, it would squawk, loveseats and three-piece sectionals.

I was twelve. I'd been banging a handball against the side of the store when a man in a Studebaker suddenly swerved into the parking lot, slammed on his brakes, and slid out of the driver's seat as if mesmerized. His head was tilted back, and he was shading his eyes, squinting to focus on something at the level of the roof. This was odd. Sidor's roof—a flat glaring expanse of crushed

stone and tar relieved only by the neon characters that irradiated
the proprietor's name—was no architectural wonder. What could
be so captivating? I pocketed the handball and ambled round to
the front of the store. Then I looked up.

There it was: stark and anomalous, a relic of a time before shopping centers, tract houses, gas stations, and landfill, a thing of
swamps and tidal flats, of ooze, fetid water, and rich black festering muck. In the context of the minutely ordered universe of sub-
urbia, it was startling, as unexpected as a downed meteor or the
carcass of a woolly mammoth. I shouted out, whooped with surprise and sudden joy.

Already people were gathering. Mrs. Novak, all three hundred
pounds of her, was lumbering across the lot from her house on the
corner, a look of bewilderment creasing her heavy jowls. Robbie
Matechik wheeled up on his bike, a pair of girls emerged from the
rear of the store with jump ropes, an old man in baggy trousers
struggled with a bag of groceries. Two more cars pulled in, and
a third stopped out on the highway. Hopper, Moe, Jennings,
Davidson, Sebesta: the news echoed through the neighborhood as
if relayed by tribal drums, and people dropped rakes, edgers, pru-
ning shears, and came running. Michael Donadio, sixteen years
old and a heartthrob at the local high school, was pumping gas at
the station up the block. He left the nozzle in the customer's tank,
jumped the fence, and started across the blacktop, weaving under
his pompadour. The customer followed him.

At its height, there must have been fifty people gathered there
in front of Sidor's, shading their eyes and gazing up expectantly,
as if the bird were the opening act of a musical comedy or an
ingenious new type of vending machine. The mood was jocular,
festive even. Sidor appeared at the door of his shop with two
stockboys, gazed up at the bird for a minute, and then clapped his
hands twice, as if he were shooing pigeons. The bird remained
motionless, cast in wax. Sidor, a fleshless old man with a monk's
tonsure and liver-spotted hands, shrugged his shoulders and
mugged for the crowd. We all laughed. Then he ducked into the
store and emerged with an end table, a lamp, a footstool, motioned to the stockboys, and had them haul out a sofa and an arm-

chair. Finally he scrawled BIRD WATCHER'S SPECIAL on a strip of cardboard and taped it to the window. People laughed and shook their heads. "Hey, Sidor," Albert Moe's father shouted, "where'd you get that thing—the Bronx Zoo?"

I couldn't keep still. I danced round the fringe of the crowd, tugging at sleeves and skirts, shouting out that I'd seen the bird first—which wasn't strictly true, but I felt proprietary about this strange and wonderful creature, the cynosure of an otherwise pedestrian Saturday afternoon. Had I seen it in the air? people asked. Had it moved? I was tempted to lie, to tell them I'd spotted it over the school, the firehouse, the used-car lot, a hovering shadow, wings spread wider than the hood of a Cadillac, but I couldn't. "No," I said, quiet suddenly. I glanced up and saw my father in the back of the crowd, standing close to Mrs. Schlecta and whispering something in her ear. Her lips were wet. I didn't know where my mother was. At the far end of the lot a girl in a college sweater was leaning against the fender of a convertible while her boyfriend pressed himself against her as if he wanted to dance.

Six weeks earlier, at night, the community had come together as it came together now, but there had been no sense of magic or festivity about the occasion. The Novaks, Donadios, Schlectas, and the rest—they gathered to watch an abandoned house go up in flames. I didn't dance round the crowd that night. I stood beside my father, leaned against him, the acrid, unforgiving stink of the smoke almost drowned in the elemental odor of his sweat, the odor of armpit and crotch and secret hair, the sematic animal scent of him that had always repelled me—until that moment. Janine McCarty's mother was shrieking. Ragged and torn, her voice clawed at the starless night, the leaping flames. On the front lawn, just as they backed the ambulance in and the crowd parted, I caught a glimpse of Janine, lying there in the grass. Every face was shouting. The glare of the fire tore disordered lines across people's eyes and dug furrows in their cheeks.

There was a noise to that fire, a killing noise, steady and implacable. The flames were like the waves at Coney Island—ghost waves, insubstantial, yellow and red rather than green, but waves all the same. They rolled across the foundation, spat from the windows, beat at the roof. Wayne Sanders was white-faced. He was a tough guy, two years older than I but held back in school because of mental sloth and recalcitrance. Police and firemen and wild-eyed neighborhood men nosed round him, excited, like hounds. Even then, in the grip of confusion and clashing voices, safe at my father's side, I knew what they wanted to know. It was the same thing my father demanded of me whenever he caught me—in fact or by report—emerging from the deserted, vandalized, and crumbling house: What were you doing in there?

He couldn't know.

Spires, parapets, derelict staircases, closets that opened on closets, the place was magnetic, vestige of an age before the neat rows of ranches and Cape Cods that lined both sides of the block. Plaster pulled back from the ceilings to reveal slats like ribs, glass pebbled the floors, the walls were paisleyed with aerosol obscenities. There were bats in the basement, rats and mice in the hallways. The house breathed death and freedom. I went there whenever I could. I heaved my interdicted knife end-over-end at the lintels and peeling cupboards, I lit cigarettes and hung them from my lower lip, I studied scraps of pornographic magazines with a fever beating through my body. Two days before the fire I was there with Wayne Sanders and Janine. They were holding hands. He had a switchblade, stiff and cold as an icicle. He gave me Ex-Lax and told me it was chocolate. Janine giggled. He shuffled a deck of battered playing cards and showed me one at a time the murky photos imprinted on them. My throat went dry with guilt.

After the fire I went to church. In the confessional the priest asked me if I practiced self-pollution. The words were formal, unfamiliar, but I knew what he meant. So, I thought, kneeling there in the dark, crushed with shame, there's a name for it. I looked at the shadowy grill, looked toward the source of the soothing voice of absolution, the voice of forgiveness and hope, and I lied. "No," I whispered.

And then there was the bird.

It never moved, not once, through all the commotion at its feet, through all the noise and confusion, all the speculation regarding its needs, condition, origin, species: it never moved. It was a statue, eyes unblinking, only the wind-rustled feathers giving it away for flesh and blood, for living bird. "It's a crane," somebody said. "No, no, it's a herring—a blue herring." Someone else thought it was an eagle. My father later confided that he believed it was a stork.

"Is it sick, do you think?" Mrs. Novak said.

"Maybe it's broke its wing."

"It's a female," someone insisted. "She's getting ready to lay her eggs."

I looked around and was surprised to see that the crowd had thinned considerably. The girl in the college sweater was gone, Michael Donadio was back across the street pumping gas, the man in the Studebaker had driven off. I scanned the crowd for my father: he'd gone home, I guessed. Mrs. Schlecta had disappeared too, and I could see the great bulk of Mrs. Novak receding into her house on the corner like a sea lion vanishing into a swell. After a while Sidor took his lamp and end table back into the store.

One of the older guys had a rake. He heaved it straight up like a javelin, as high as the roof of the store, and then watched it slam down on the pavement. The bird never flinched. People lit cigarettes, shuffled their feet. They began to drift off, one by one. When I looked around again there were only eight of us left, six kids and two men I didn't recognize. The women and girls, more easily bored or perhaps less interested to begin with, had gone home to gas ranges and hopscotch squares: I could see a few of the girls in the distance, on the swings in front of the school, tiny, their skirts rippling like flags.

I waited. I wanted the bird to flap its wings, blink an eye, shift a foot; I wanted it desperately, wanted it more than anything I had ever wanted. Perched there at the lip of the roof, its feet clutching the drainpipe as if welded to it, the bird was a coil of possibility, a muscle relaxed against the moment of tension. Yes, it was magnificent, even in repose. And, yes, I could stare at it, examine its every line, from its knobbed knees to the cropped feathers at the back of its head, I could absorb it, become it, look out from its

unblinking yellow eyes on the street grown quiet and the sun
sinking behind the gas station. Yes, but that wasn't enough. I had
to see it in flight, had to see the great impossible wings beating in
the air, had to see it transposed into its native element.

Suddenly the wind came up—a gust that raked at our hair and
scattered refuse across the parking lot—and the bird's feathers
lifted like a petticoat. It was then that I understood. Secret, raw,
red, and wet, the wound flashed just above the juncture of the
legs before the wind died and the feathers fell back in place.

I turned and looked past the neighborhood kids—my playmates
—at the two men, the strangers. They were lean and seedy, unshaven, slouching behind the brims of their hats. One of them was
chewing a toothpick. I caught their eyes: they'd seen it too.

I threw the first stone.

The Overcoat II

There was a commotion near the head of the queue, people shouting, elbowing one another, wedging themselves in, and bracing for the inevitable shock wave that would pulse through the line, tumbling children, pregnant women, and unsuspecting old pensioners like dominoes. Akaky craned his neck to see what was happening, but he already knew: they were running out of meat. Two and a half hours on line for a lump of gristly beef to flavor his kasha and cabbage, nearly a hundred people ahead of him and Lenin knows how many behind, and they had to go and run out.

It was no surprise. The same thing had happened three days ago, last week, last month, last year. A cynic might have been led to grumble, to disparage the farmers, the truckers, the butchers and butchers' assistants, to question their mental capacity and cast

aspersions on their ancestry. But not Akaky. No, he was as patient
and enduring as the limes along the Boulevard Ring, and he
knew how vital personal sacrifice was to the Soviet socialist workers' struggle against the forces of Imperialism and Capitalist Ex-
ploitation. He knew, because he'd been told. Every day. As a boy
in school, as an adolescent in the Young Pioneers, as an adult in
on-the-job political-orientation sessions. He read it in *Pravda* and
Izvestia, heard it on the radio, watched it on TV. Whizz, whir,
clack-clack-clack: the voice of Lenin was playing like a tape recording inside his head. "Working People of the Soviet Union!
Struggle for a Communist attitude toward labor. Hold public
property sacred and multiply it!"

"Meat," cried a voice behind him. He squirmed round in disbelief—how could anyone be so insensitive as to voice a complaint
in public?—and found himself staring down at the shriveled husk
of an old woman, less than five feet tall, her babushkaed head
mummy-wrapped against the cold. She was ancient, older than
the Revolution, a living artifact escaped from the Museum of Serf
Art. Akaky's mouth had dropped open, the word "Comrade" flying to his lips in gentle remonstrance, when the man in front of
him, impelled by the estuarine wash of the crowd, drove him up
against the old woman with all the force of a runaway tram. Akaky
clutched at her shoulders for balance, but she was ready for him,
lowering her head and catching him neatly in the breastbone with
the rock-hard knot in the crown of her kerchief. It was as if he'd
been shot. He couldn't breathe, tried to choke out an apology,
found himself on the pavement beneath a flurry of unsteady feet.
The old woman towered over him, her face as stolid and impassive
as the monumental bust of Lenin at the Party Congress. "Meat,"
she cried, "meat!"

Akaky stayed on another quarter of an hour, until a cordon of
policemen marched up the street and superintended the closing
of the store. It was 9:00 P.M. Akaky was beat. He'd been standing
in one line or another since 5:30, when he left the ministry where
he worked as file clerk, and all he had to show for it was eight
russet potatoes, half a dozen onions, and twenty-six tubes of
Czechoslovakian toothpaste he'd been lucky enough to blunder

across while looking for a bottle of rubbing alcohol. Resigned, he started across the vacant immensity of Red Square on his way to Herzen Street and the Krasnaya Presnya district where he shared a communal apartment with two families and another bachelor. Normally he lingered a bit when crossing the great square, reveling in the majesty of it all—from the massive blank face of the Kremlin wall to the Oriental spires of Pokrovsky Cathedral—but now he hurried, uncommonly stung by the cold.

One foot after the next, a sharp echo in the chill immensity, ice in his nostrils, his shoulders rattling with the cold that clutched at him like a hand. What was it: twenty, twenty-five below? Why did it seem so much colder tonight? Was he coming down with something? One foot after the next, rap-rap-rap, and then he realized what it was: the overcoat. Of course. The lining had begun to come loose, peeling back in clumps as if it were an animal with the mange—he'd noticed it that morning, in the anteroom at the office—balls of felt dusting his shoes and trouser cuffs like snow. The coat was worthless, and he'd been a fool to buy it in the first place. But what else was there? He'd gone to the Central Department Store in response to a notice in the window—"Good Quality Soviet Made Winter Coats"—at a price he could afford. He remembered being surprised over the shortness and sparseness of the line, and over the clerk's bemused expression as he handed him the cloth coat. "You don't want this," the clerk had said. The man was Akaky's age, mustachioed. He was grinning.

Akaky had been puzzled. "I don't?"

"Soviet means shoddy," the man said, cocky as one of the American delinquents Akaky saw rioting on the televised news each night.

Akaky's face went red. He didn't like the type of person who made light of official slogans—in this case, "Soviet Means Superior"—and he was always shocked and embarrassed when he ran across one of these smug apostates.

The man rubbed his thumb and forefingers together. "I'll have something really nice here, well made, stylish, a coat that will hold up for years after this *shtampny* is in the rubbish heap. If you want to meet me out back, I think I can, ah, arrange something for you—if you see what I mean?"

The shock and outrage that had seized Akaky at that moment were like an electric jolt, like the automatic response governed by electrodes implanted in the brains of dogs and monkeys at the State Lab. He flushed to the apex of his bald spot. "How dare you insinuate—" he sputtered, and then choked off, too wrought up to continue. Turning away from the clerk in disgust he snatched up the first overcoat at random and strode briskly away to join the swollen queue on the payment line.

And so he was the owner of a shabby, worthless garment that fit him about as snugly as a circus tent. The lining was in tatters and the seam under the right arm gaped like an open wound. He should have been more cautious, he should have controlled his emotions and come back another day. Now, as he hurried up Herzen Street, reflexively clutching his shoulders, he told himself that he'd go to see Petrovich the tailor in the morning. A stitch here, a stitch there, maybe a reinforced lining, and the thing would be good as new. Who cared if it was ill-fitting and outdated? He was no fashion plate.

Yes, he thought, Petrovich. Petrovich in the morning.

Akaky was up at 7:00 the next morning, the faintly sour odor of a meatless potato-onion soup lingering in unexpected places, the room numb with cold. It was dark, of course, dark till 9:00 A.M. this time of year, and then dark again at 2:30 in the afternoon. He dressed by candlelight, folded up the bed, and heated some kasha and spoiled milk for breakfast. Normally he had breakfast in his corner of the kitchen, but this morning he used the tiny camp stove in his room, reluctant to march down the hallway and disturb the Romanovs, the Yeroshkins or old Studniuk. As he slipped out the door ten minutes later, he could hear Irina Yeroshkina berating her husband in her pennywhistle voice: "Up, Sergei, you drunken lout. Get up. The factory, Sergei. Remember, Sergei? Work? You remember what that is?"

It was somewhere around thirty below, give or take a degree. Akaky was wearing two sweaters over his standard-brown serge suit (the office wags called it "turd brown"), and still the cold made him dance. If it was any consolation, the streets were alive with other dancers, shudderers, sprinters, and vaulters, all in a delirious headlong rush to get back inside before they shattered like cheap glass. Akaky was not consoled. His throat was raw and his eyelids crusted over by the time he flung himself into Petrovich's shop like Zhivago escaped from the red partisans.

Petrovich was sitting beneath a single brown light bulb in a heap of rags and scraps of cloth, the antique pedal sewing machine rising up out of the gloom beside him like an iron monster. He was drunk. Eight o'clock in the morning, and he was drunk. "Well, well, well," he boomed, "an early customer, eh? What's it this time, Akaky Akakievich, your cuffs unraveling again?" And then he was laughing, choking away like a tubercular horse.

Akaky didn't approve of drinking. He lived a quiet, solitary existence (as solitary as the six Yeroshkin brats would allow), very rarely had occasion to do any social drinking, and saw no reason to drink alone. Sure, he had a shot of vodka now and again to ward off the cold, and he'd tasted champagne once when his sister had got married, but in general he found drinking repugnant and always got a bit tongue-tied and embarrassed in the presence of someone under the influence. "I . . . I . . . I was, uh, wondering if—"

"Spit it out," Petrovich roared. The tailor had lost an eye when he was eighteen, in the Hungarian police action—he'd poked his head up through the top hatch of his tank and a Magyar patriot had nailed him with a dexterously flung stone—and his good eye, as if in compensation, seemed to have grown to inhuman proportions. He fixed Akaky with this bulging protoplasmic mass and cleared his throat.

"—wondering if you could, ah, patch up the lining of my, ah, overcoat."

"Trash," Petrovich said.

Akaky held the coat open like an exhibitionist. "Look: it's not really that bad, just peeling back a litle. Maybe you could, ah, reinforce the lining and—"

"Trash, *shtampny, brak*. You're wearing a piece of Soviet-

bungled garbage, a fishnet, rotten through to the very thread of
the seams. I can't fix it."

"But—"

"I won't. It wouldn't last you the winter. Nope. The only thing
to do is go out and get yourself something decent."

"Petrovich." Akaky was pleading. "I can't afford a new coat.
This one cost me over a month's salary as it is."

The tailor had produced a bottle of vodka. He winked his eye
closed in ecstasy as he took a long pull at the neck of it. When he
righted his head he seemed to have trouble focusing on Akaky,
addressing himself to a point in space six feet to the left of him.
"I'll make you one," he said, pounding at his rib cage and belching
softly. "Down-lined, fur collar. Like they wear in Paris."

"But, but . . . I can't afford a coat like that—"

"What are you going to do, freeze? Listen, Akaky Akakievich,
you couldn't get a coat like this for five hundred rubles on the
black market."

Black market. The words made Akaky cringe, as if the tailor had
spouted some vile epithet: faggot, pederast, or CIA. The black
market was flourishing, oh yes, he knew all about it, all about the
self-centered capitalist revisionists who sold out the motherland
for a radio or a pair of blue jeans or—or an overcoat. "Never," he
said. "I'd rather wear rags."

"Hey, hey: calm down, Akaky, calm down. I said I *could* get
you one, not that I would. No, for five-fifty I'll make you one."

Five hundred and fifty rubles. Nearly three months' salary. It
was steep, it was outrageous. But what else could he do? Go back
to the department store for another piece of junk that would fall
apart in a year? He stepped back into the tailor's line of vision.
"Are you absolutely sure you can't fix this one?"

Petrovich shook his massive head. "No way."

"All right," Akaky said, his voice a whisper. "When could you
have it done?"

"One week from today."

"One week? Isn't that awfully fast work?"

The tailor grinned at him, and winked his bloated eye. "I have
my methods," he said. "Rely on me."

At the office that morning, while he crouched shuddering over the radiator in his worn overcoat, ragged sweaters, and standard-brown serge suit, Akaky became aware of a disturbance at his back: strident whispers, giggling, derisive laughter. He turned to look up into the grinning, wet-lipped faces of two of the younger clerks. They were wearing leather flight jackets with fur collars and blue jeans stamped prominently with the name of an American Jewish manufacturer, and they were staring at him. The shorter one, the blond, tossed his head arrogantly and made an obscene comment, something to do with mothers, sexual intercourse, and Akaky's Soviet-made overcoat. Then he put a finger to his head in a mock salute and sauntered through the main door, closely tailed by his tall cohort. Akaky was puzzled at first, then outraged. Finally, he felt ashamed. Was he really such a sight? Shoulders hunched, he ducked down the hallway to the lavatory and removed overcoat and sweaters in the privacy of one of the stalls.

Akaky took his afternoon break in the window of a gloomy downstairs hallway rather than endure the noisy, overcrowded workers' cafeteria. He munched a dry onion sandwich (he hadn't seen butter in weeks), drank weak tea from a thermos, and absently scanned the *Izvestia* headlines: RECORD GRAIN HARVEST; KAMA RIVER TRUCK PLANT TRIPLES OUTPUT; AMERICAN NEGROES RIOT. When he got back to his desk he knew immediately that something was wrong—he sensed it, and yet he couldn't quite put a finger on it. The others were watching him: he looked up, they looked down. What was it? Everything was in place on his desk— the calendar, the miniature of Misha the Olympic bear, his citation from the Revolutionary Order of United Soviet File Clerks for his twenty-five years of continuous service . . . and then it occurred to him: he was late. He'd dozed over lunch, and now he was late getting back to his desk.

Frantic, he jerked round to look at the clock, and saw in that instant both that he was as punctual as ever and that a terrible, shaming transformation had come over the lifesize statue of Lenin that presided over the room like a guardian angel. Someone, some jokester, some flunky, had appropriated Akaky's overcoat and draped it over the statue's shoulders. This was too much. The bastards, the thoughtless, insensitive bastards. Akaky was on his feet, his face splotched with humiliation and anger. "How could you?" he shouted out. A hundred heads looked up. "Comrades: how could you do this to me?"

They were laughing. All of them. Even Turpentov and Moronov, so drunk they could barely lift their heads, even Rodion Mishkin, who sometimes played a game of chess with him over lunch. What was wrong with them? Was poverty a laughing matter? The overcoat clung to Lenin's shoulders like a growth, the underarm torn away, a long tangled string of felt depending from the skirts like a tail. Akaky strode across the room, mounted the pedestal and retrieved his coat. "What is it with you?" he sputtered. "We're all proletarians, aren't we?" For some reason, this fired up the laughter again, a wave of it washing over the room like surf. The blond tough, the punk, was smirking at him from the safety of his desk across the room; Moronov was jeering from beneath his red, vodka-swollen nose. "Citizens!" Akaky cried. "Comrades!" No effect. And then, shot through with rage and shame and bewilderment, he shouted as he had never shouted in his life, roared like an animal in a cage: "Brothers!" he bellowed.

The room fell silent. They seemed stunned at his loss of control, amazed to see that this little man who for twenty-five years had been immovable, staid as a statue, was made of flesh and blood after all. Akaky didn't know what he was doing. He stood there, the coat in one hand, the other clutching Lenin's shoulder for support. All at once something came over him—he suddenly felt heroic, an orator, felt he could redeem himself with words, shame them with a spontaneous speech, take to the pulpit like one of the revolutionary sailors of the *Potemkin*. "Brothers," he said, more softly, "don't you realize—"

There was a rude noise from the far side of the room. It was the blond tough, razzing him. The tall one took it up—his accomplice—and then Turpentov, and in an instant they were all laughing and jeering again. Akaky stepped down from the pedestal and walked out the door.

As rooms go—even in apartment-starved Moscow—Akaky's was pretty small, perhaps half a size larger than the one that drove Raskolnikov to murder. Actually, it was the foyer of the gloomy four-room apartment he shared with the eight Yeroshkins, five Romanovs, and old Studniuk. The room's main drawback, of course, was that anyone entering or leaving the apartment had to troop through it: Sergei Yeroshkin, on the tail end of a three-day drunk; Olga Romanov, necking with her boyfriend at the door while a whistling draft howled through the room and Akaky tried fitfully to sleep; old Studniuk's ancient, unsteady cronies lurching through the door like elephants on their way to the burial ground. It was intolerable. Or at least it would have been, had Akaky given it any thought. But it never occurred to him to question his lot in life or to demand that he and Studniuk switch rooms on a rotating basis or to go out and look for more amenable living quarters. He was no whining, soft-in-the-middle bourgeois, he was a hard-nosed revolutionary communist worker and an exemplary citizen of the Union of Soviet Socialist Republics. When industrial production goals were met, the party leaders would turn their attention to housing. Until then, there was no sense in complaining. Besides, if he really wanted privacy, he could duck into the coat closet.

Now, coming up the steps and into the still, darkened apartment, Akaky felt like an intruder in his own home. It was two-fifteen in the afternoon. He hadn't been home at this hour in thirteen years, not since the time he'd come down with a double attack of influenza and bronchitis, and Mother Gorbanyevskaya (she'd had Studniuk's room then) had nursed him with lentil soup and herb tea. He closed the door on silence: the place was deserted, the dying rays of the sun suffusing the walls with a soft eerie light, the samovar a lurking presence, shadows in the corners like spies and traducers. Without a pause, Akaky unfolded his bed, undressed, and pulled the covers up over his head. He had never felt more depressed and uncertain in his life: the injustice of it, the pettiness. He was a good man, true to the ideals of

the Revolution, a generous man, inoffensive, meek: why did they
have to make him their whipping boy? What had he done?

His thoughts were interrupted by the sound of a key turning in
the lock. What now? he thought, stealing a glance at the door. The
lock rattled, the bolt slid back, and old Studniuk was standing
there in the doorway, blinking in bewilderment, a swollen string
bag over his shoulder. "Akaky Akakievich?" he said. "Is that you?"

From beneath the blankets, Akaky grunted in assent.

"Blessed Jesus," the old man shouted, "what is it: have you
gone rotten in the stomach, is that it? Have you had an accident?"
Studniuk had shut the door and was standing over the bed now:
Akaky could feel the old man's trembling fingertips on the bed-
spread. "Talk to me, Akaky Akakievich—are you all right? Should
I call a doctor?"

Akaky sat up. "No, no, Trifily Vladimirovich, no need. I'm ill,
that's all. It'll pass."

With a crack of his ancient knees, old Studniuk lowered himself
to the corner of the bed and peered anxiously into Akaky's face.
The string bag lay at his feet, bulging with cabbages, carrots,
cheese, butter, bread, bottles of milk, and squarish packages
wrapped in butcher's paper. After a long moment, the old man
pulled a pouch of tobacco from his shirt pocket and began to roll a
cigarette. "You don't look sick," he said.

All his life, Akaky had put a premium on truthfulness. When he
was fifteen and assistant treasurer of the Young Pioneers, two of
his co-workers had misappropriated the funds from a collection
drive and no one in the group would expose them until Akaky
came forward. The group leader had given him a citation for revolutionary rectitude which he still kept in a box with his school
diploma and a photograph of his mother at the Tolstoi Museum.
He looked Studniuk in the eye. "No," he said, "I'm not sick. Not
physically anyway."

The old man rolled another cigarette with his clonic fingers,
tucked the finished product behind his ear along with the first,
and produced a handkerchief the size of a dish towel. He thoughtfully plumbed his nostrils while Akaky, in a broken voice, nar-
rated the sad tale of his humiliation at the office. When Akaky was

finished, the old man carefully folded up the handkerchief, tucked it in his shirt pocket, and extracted a paring knife from his sleeve. He cut the rind from a round of cheese and began sucking at bits of it while slowly shaking his head back and forth. After a while he said, "I've got some advice for you."

Studniuk was the patriarch of the apartment complex, ageless, a man who didn't have to look at newsreels to see history: it played in his head. He'd been there. For fifty-two years he'd worked at the First State Bearing Plant, present at its opening, a face in the crowd while successive generations of leaders came and went— Kerensky, Lenin, Trotsky, Stalin, Khrushchev. No one knew how old he was, or how he managed to live so well. He was jaunty, big-shouldered, bald as a fire hydrant; his nose had been broken so many times it looked like a question mark. Suddenly he was laughing, a sound like wind in the grass.

"You know," the old man said, fighting for control, "you're a good man, Akaky Akakievich, but you're an ass." Studniuk looked him full in the face, as hard and squint-eyed as a snapping turtle. "An ass," he repeated. "Don't you know that nobody gives half a shit about all this party business any more? Huh? Are you blind, son, or what? Where do you think I got all this?" he said, nodding at the sack of food with a belligerent jerk of his neck.

Akaky felt as if he'd been slapped in the face. The words were on his lips—"Betrayer, backslider"—but the old man cut him off. "Yes, that's right: wheeling and dealing on the black market. And you're a damn fool and an ass if you don't go out there and get everything you can, because it's for shit sure there ain't no comrade commissioner going to come round and give it to you."

"Get out of my room, Studniuk," Akaky said, his heart pounding wildly at his rib cage. "I'm sorry. But, please get out."

Wearily, the old man got to his feet and gathered up his things. He hesitated in the hallway, the ravaged nose glowing in the shadows like something made of luminescent wax. "I'll tell you why they hate you, Akaky Akakievich, you want to know why? Because you're a stick in the mud, because you're a holier than thou, because you're a party tool, that's why. Because you go around in that goddamned flapping overcoat like a saint or something, that's

why." The old man shook his head, then turned and receded into
the gloom of the hallway.

Akaky didn't hear him leave. He was biting his lip and pressing
his hands to his ears with a fierce, unrelenting pressure, with the
strict stoic rectitude of saints and martyrs and revolutionary
heroes.

Petrovich was true to his word: the overcoat was ready in a
week. It was a week to the day, in fact, that Akaky appeared at the
tailor's shop, full of misgivings and clutching a wad of ruble notes
as if he expected them to wriggle through his fingers like worms or
sprout wings and flutter up in his face. He'd exhausted his savings
and sold his antique Tovstonogov Star TV set to come up with the
money, a real hardship considering how inflexible his budget was.
(For the past twenty-two years he'd been sending half of each
paycheck to his invalid mother in the Urals. It seemed there'd
been some sort of mysterious calamity in the area and the author-
ities had had to relocate her entire village. Ever since, she'd been
pale and listless, her hair had fallen out, and she complained that
her bones felt as if they'd gone hollow, like a bird's.) The tailor
was expecting him. "Akaky Akakievich," he shouted, rubbing
his hands together and ushering him into the shop, "come in,
come in."

Akaky shook Petrovich's hand and then stood uneasily in the
center of the shop while the tailor ducked into the back room to
fetch the coat. Left alone, Akaky found himself surveying the
place with a discerning eye, as if it were the shop he was buying
and not merely an overcoat. The place was shabby, no question
about it. Cracks rent the plaster like fault lines, soiled rags and
odd scraps of cloth puddled up round his ankles like the aftermath
of an explosion in a textile plant, a dish of roach poison glistened in
the corner, pincushioned with the yellow husks of dead and dying
insects. Could a man who worked in such squalor produce anything worthwhile—anything worth five hundred and fifty rubles?

There was a rustle of wrapping paper and Petrovich was at his
side, holding out a loosely wrapped package in both arms, as if it
were an offering. Akaky felt his stomach sink. The tailor swept an

armful of half-finished garments to the floor and laid the package on the table. It was wrapped in soft white tissue paper, the sort of paper you see at Christmas, but then only in the store windows. Akaky reached out to touch it, and the tailor swept back the paper with a flourish.

Akaky was stunned. He was staring down at the overcoat of a prince, as fine as the one the Secretary himself wore, so handsome it was almost indecent. "You can't—" he began, but he couldn't find the words.

"Camel's hair," Petrovich said, winking his enormous eye. "That's genuine fox, that collar. And look at the lining."

Akaky looked. The lining was quilted with down.

"You don't think you'll be warm in that?" Petrovich said, breathing vodka fumes in his face and nudging him, "eh, Akaky Akakievich, eh?"

It's such a small thing, an overcoat, a necessity of life—what's to be so excited about? Akaky told himself as he slid into the coat and followed Petrovich into the back room to stand before the speckled mirror. What he saw reflected there drove the last vestige of composure from his body. . . . He looked . . . magnificent, dignified, like a member of the Politburo or the manager of the National Hotel, like one of the bigwigs themselves. He couldn't help himself, he was grinning, he was beaming.

Akaky was late to work that morning for the first time in anyone's memory. He strolled in at quarter past the hour, as though oblivious of the time, nodding benignly at this clerk or that. What was even more remarkable, from his fellow clerks' point of view, was the way he was dressed—they recognized the cracked imitation vinyl gloves, the standard-brown serge trousers, and the great woolly black hat that clung to his head like an inflated rodent—but the overcoat, the fox-trimmed camel's-hair overcoat, really threw them. Was this Akaky A. Bashmachkin, party tool and office drudge, strutting through the corridors like a coryphee with the Bolshoi, like an Olympic shot putter, like one of the *apparatchiki?* Had he been elevated to a supervisory position, was that it? Had he come into a fortune, held up a bank? A few heads turned toward the door, half expecting a cordon of KGB men to burst in and lead him away in disgrace.

No one had said a word to Akaky since the incident of a week before, but now, with furtive glances over their shoulders for the supervisor, Turpentov, Moronov, and Volodya Smelyakov—the elder statesman of the office, hoary-headed, toothless, and two months from retirement—gathered round Akaky's desk. "Good morning, Akaky Akakievich," Moronov slurred, his tongue already thickening from his morning pick-me-up, "nice day, isn't it?" Moronov's eyes were red as a pearl diver's. Beyond the windows the sky was like steel wool, the wind was raging, and the temperature rapidly plunging from a high of minus twenty-eight degrees.

Akaky had no reason to be cordial to Moronov, nor did he approve of his drinking, but instead of fixing him with his usual bland and vaguely disapproving stare, he smiled, the upper lip drawing back from his teeth as if by the operation of some hidden, uncontrollable force. He couldn't help it. He felt marvelous, felt like a new man, and not even Moronov, not even the jeering blond tough, could sour his mood. The fact was, he was late because he'd lingered on the streets, despite the cold, to examine his reflection in shop windows and try out his new, magnanimous big-shot's grin on strangers in Red Square. On a whim, he'd stopped in at a tourist shop for an outrageously overpriced cup of coffee and sweet bun. So what if he was late one morning out of five thousand? Would the world collapse round him?

Old man Smelyakov cleared his throat and smacked his gums amicably. "Well, well, well," he said in the voice of a throttled bird, "what a lovely, lovely, ah"—the word seemed to stick in his throat—"overcoat you have there, Akaky Akakievich."

"Yes," Akaky said, slipping out of the coat and hanging it reverently on the hook beside the desk, "yes it is." Then he sat down and began shuffling through a sheaf of papers.

Turpentov tugged at his knuckles. His voice was harsh, like a great whirring mill saw bogged down in a knotty log. "You wouldn't want to trust that to the workers' cloakroom, now would you," he said, making a stab at jocularity. "I mean, it's so ritzy and all, so expensive-looking."

Akaky never even glanced up. He was already cranking the first report into his antiquated Rostov Bear typewriter. "No," he said, "no, I wouldn't."

During the afternoon break, Akaky took his lunch amid the turmoil of the workers' cafeteria, rather than in the solitary confines of the lower hallway. On the way in the door, he'd nearly run head-on into the surly blond youth and had stiffened, expecting some sort of verbal abuse, but the blond merely looked away and went about his business. Akaky found a spot at one of the long imitation Formica tables and was almost immediately joined by Rodion Mishkin, his sometime chess partner, who squeezed in beside him with a lunchbox in one hand and a copy of *Novy Mir* in the other. Mishkin was a thin, nervous man in wire-rimmed spectacles, who carried a circular yellow patch of hardened skin on his cheek like a badge and looked as if he should be lecturing on molecular biology at the Academy of Sciences. He had a habit of blowing on his fingertips as he spoke, as if he'd just burned them or applied fresh nail polish. "Well," he said with a sigh as he eased down on the bench and removed a thickly buttered sausage sandwich from his lunchbox, "so you've finally come around, Akaky Akakievich."

"What do you mean?" Akaky said.

"Oh come on, Akaky, don't be coy."

"Really, Rodion Ivanovich, I have no idea what you're talking about."

Mishkin was grinning broadly, his gold fillings glistening in the light, grinning as if he and Akaky had just signed some nefarious pact together. "The overcoat, Akaky, the overcoat."

"Do you like it?"

Mishkin blew on his fingers. "It's first-rate."

Akaky was grinning now too. "You wouldn't believe it—I had it custom-made, but I suppose you can see that in the lines and the distinction of it. A tailor I know, lives in squalor, but he put it together for me in less than a week."

It was as if Mishkin's fingertips had suddenly exploded in flame: he was puffing vigorously at them and waving his hands from the wrist. "Oh, come off it, Akaky—you don't have to put on a show for me," he said, simultaneously flailing his fingers and nudging Akaky with a complicitous elbow.

"It's the truth," Akaky said. And then: "Well, I guess it wouldn't be fair to say *less* than a week—it took him a full seven days, actually."

"All right, all right," Mishkin snapped, bending to his sandwich, "have it any way you want. I don't mean to pry."

Puzzled at his friend's behavior, Akaky looked up to see that a number of heads were turned toward them. He concentrated on his sandwich: raw turnip and black bread, dry.

"Listen," Mishkin said after a while, "Masha and I are having a few people from the office over tonight—for some dinner and talk, maybe a hand or two at cards. Want to join us?"

Akaky never went out at night. Tickets to sporting events, films, concerts, and the ballet were not only beyond his means but so scarce that only the *apparatchiki* could get them in any case, and since he had no friends to speak of, he was never invited for dinner or cards. In all the years he'd known Rodion Ivanovich the closest they'd come to intimacy was an occasional exchange on sports or office politics over a lunchtime game of chess. Now Rodion was inviting him to his house. It was novel, comradely. The idea of it—of dinner out, conversation, the company of women other than the dreary Romanov wife and daughter or the vituperative Mrs. Yeroshkina—suddenly burst into flower in his head and flooded his body with warmth and anticipation. "Yes," he said finally, "yes, I'd like that very much."

After work, Akaky spent two hours in line at the grocery, waiting to buy a small box of chocolates for his hostess. He had only a few rubles left till payday, but remembered reading somewhere that the thoughtful dinner guest always brought a little gift for the hostess—chocolates, flowers, a bottle of wine. Since he wasn't a drinker, he decided against the wine, and since flowers were virtually impossible to obtain in Moscow at this time of year, he settled on candy—a nice little box of chocolates with creme centers would be just the thing. Unfortunately, by the time he got to the head of the line, every last chocolate in the store had been bought up, and he was left with a choice between penny bubble gum and a rock-hard concoction of peppermint and butterscotch coated in a vaguely sweet soya substance that sold for two to the penny. He took ten of each.

As he hurried up Chernyshevsky Street, clutching the scrap of paper on which Mishkin had scrawled his address, Akaky was surprised by a sudden snow squall. He'd thought it was too cold for snow, but there it was, driving at him like a fusillade of frozen needles. Cocking the hat down over his brow and thrusting his hands deep in his pockets, he couldn't help smiling—the overcoat was marvelous, repelling the white crystals like a shield, and he was as warm as if he were home in bed. He was thinking of how miserable he'd have been in the old overcoat, shivering and stamping, dashing in and out of doorways like a madman, his bones rattling and nose running—when suddenly he felt an arm slip through his. Instinctively, he jerked back and found himself staring into the perfect oval of a young woman's face; she had hold of his arm and was matching him stride for stride as if they were old acquaintances out for an evening stroll. "Cold night," she breathed, looking up into his eyes.

Akaky didn't know what to do. He stared into her face with fascination and horror—what was happening to him?—captivated by her candid eyes and mascaraed lashes, the blond curls fringing her fur cap, the soft wet invitation of her Western lipstick. "I—I beg your pardon?" he said, trying to draw his hand from his pocket.

She had a firm grip on him. "You're so handsome," she said. "Do you work at the ministry? I love your coat. It's so, so elegant."

"I'm sorry," he said, "I've—"

"Would you like to take me out?" she said. "I'm available tonight. We could have a drink and then later—" She narrowed her eyes and squeezed his hand, still buried in the overcoat pocket.

"No, no," he said, his voice strained and unfamiliar in his ears,

as if he'd suddenly been thrust into a stranger's body, "no, you see
I can't really, I—I'm on my way to a dinner engagement."

They were stopped now, standing as close as lovers. She looked
up at him imploringly, then said something about money. The
snow blew in their faces, their breath mingled in clouds. Suddenly Akaky was running, hurtling headlong up the street as if a
legion of gypsy violinists and greedy yankee moneylenders were
nipping at his heels, his heart drumming beneath the standard-
brown serge suit, the layers of down, and the soft, impenetrable
elegance of his camel's-hair overcoat.

"Akaky Akakievich, how good to see you." Rodion stood at the
door, blowing on his fingertips. Beside him, a short, broad-faced
woman in an embroidered dressing gown, whom Akaky took to be
his wife. "Masha," Rodion said by way of confirmation, and Akaky
made a quick little bow and produced the bag of sweets. To his
consternation, he saw that in the confusion on the street it had
gotten a bit crushed, and that some of the soya substance had
begun to stain the bottom of the white confectioner's bag. Masha's
smile bloomed and faded as quickly as an accelerated film clip of
horticultural miracles. "You shouldn't have," she said.

The apartment was magnificent, stunning, like nothing Akaky
could have imagined. Three and a half rooms, abundantly fur-
nished, with oil paintings on the walls—and they had it all to
themselves. Rodion showed him around the place. There was a
new stove and refrigerator, a loveseat in the front room. Little
Ludmila lay sleeping on a cot in the bedroom. "Really, Rodion
Ivanovich, I'm impressed," Akaky said, wondering how his friend
managed to live so well. It was true that Rodion, as Deputy Assistant to the Chief File Clerk of the Thirty-second Bureau, made
somewhat more than he did, and true too that Akaky was effec-
tively operating on half pay because of his mother, but still, this
was real opulence as far as he was concerned. Rodion was showing
him the Swiss cuckoo clock. "It's very kind of you to say that,
Akaky. Yes"—puffing at his fingers—"we find it comfortable."

There were a number of courses at dinner: a clear broth; fish in
cream sauce; pickled sausages, white bread, and cheese; chicken,

galushki, and Brussels sprouts. Rodion poured vodka and French wine throughout the meal, and afterward served a cherry cake and coffee. Akaky recognized some of the other guests from the office—faces but not names—and found himself engaged in a conversation with a man beside him over the melodic virtues of Dixieland jazz as opposed to the dissonance of free jazz. Akaky had never heard of either variety of jazz—in fact, he only vaguely knew what jazz was, a degenerate Negro sort of thing from America, with blaring horns and saxophones—but he smiled agreeably and asked an occasional question, while the man expatiated on one school of musical thought or another. Timidly, Akaky began to sip at the glass of wine before him; each time he turned around the glass was full again, and Rodion was beaming at him from the head of the table. He began to feel a depth of warmth and gratitude toward these people gathered around him, his comrades, men and women whose interests and knowledge ranged so far, whose wit flowed so easily: at one point he realized how much he'd been missing, felt that until now life had been passing him by. When Rodion proposed a toast to Masha—it was her birthday—Akaky was the first to raise his glass.

After the coffee, there was more vodka, a few hands of cards, and a good uproarious sing-along, all the old tunes Akaky had sung as a boy rising up for some deep hollow in him to burst forth as if he rehearsed them every day. He never missed a beat. When, finally, he thought to look at his watch, he was shocked to see that it was past one in the morning. Rodion's eyes were bloodshot, and the patch of skin on his cheek seemed to have concentrated all the color in his face; Masha was nowhere to be seen, and only one other guest remained—the jazz man—snoring peaceably in the corner. Akaky leaped to his feet, thanked Rodion profusely— "Best time I've had in years, in *years,* Rodion Ivanovich"—and hurried out into the desolate streets.

It was still snowing. Silently, stealthily, while Akaky had been pulling strips of chicken from the bone, raising his glass and singing "How high the shrubless crags!" the snow had been steadily accumulating, until now it spread a flat, even finish over streets, stairways, and rooftops and clung like dander to the hoods of automobiles and the skeletons of neglected bicycles. Whistling, Akaky kicked through the ankle-deep powder, for once unmindful of his cracked imitation plastic galoshes and disintegrating gloves, the fox collar as warm as a hand against the back of his neck. As he turned into Red Square, he was thinking how lucky he was.

It was ghostly, the square, as barren as the surface of the moon, trackless and white. Behind him, Pokrovsky Cathedral, like some shrouded Turkish dream; ahead the dark bank of the Lenin Mausoleum and the soft, snow-blurred lights of the city. He was just passing the mausoleum when two men materialized before him. The one was tall, cheekbones like slashes, with a fierce Oriental mustache that disappeared in the folds of his muffler; the other was hooded and slight. "Comrade," snarled the taller man, rushing at him out of the gloom, "that's my coat you've got there."

"No," Akaky said, "no, you must be mistaken," but the man had already taken hold of his collar and presented him with a bare fist the size of a football. The fist wavered under Akaky's nose for an instant, then dropped into the darkness and hammered him three or four times in the midsection. Suddenly Akaky was on the ground, crying out like an abandoned infant, while the big man rolled him over and his accomplice tugged at the sleeve of the overcoat. Ten seconds later it was over. Akaky lay on the ground in his standard-brown serge suit and imitation plastic galoshes, doubled up in the fetal position, gasping for breath. The thugs were gone. In the near distance, the Kremlin wall drew a white line across the night. The snow sifted down with a hiss.

How he made it home that night, Akaky will never know. For a long while he merely lay there in the snow, stunned by the enormity of the crime against him, some last fiber of his faith and conviction frayed to the breaking point. He remembered the feel of the snowflakes brushing his lips and melting against his eyelids, remembered feeling warm and cozy despite it, remembered the overwhelming, seductive craving for oblivion, for sleep and surcease. As he lay there, drifting between consciousness and absence, the words of the First Secretary began to echo in his ears, over and over, a record stuck in the groove: "Our goal is to make the life of the Soviet people still better, still more beautiful, and still more happy." Oh yes, oh yes, he thought, lying there on the ground. And then the man and woman had come along—or was it two men and a woman?—practically tripping over him in the dark. "My God," the woman had gasped, "it's a poor murdered man!"

They helped him to his feet, brushed the snow from his clothes. He was mad with the cold, with the hunger for justice—who said the world was fair or that everyone played by the same rules?—delirious with the fever of purpose. "The police!" he sputtered as a gloved hand held a flask of vodka to his lips. "I've been robbed." They were solicitous, these people, faces and voices emerging dreamlike from the banks of swirling snow, but they were cautious too—distant even. (It was as though they weren't quite sure what to make of his story—was he the victimized citizen he claimed to be, or merely a gibbering kopeck wheedler on the tail end of a drinking spree?) They guided him to the nearest precinct station and left him on the steps.

Pockets and cuffs heavy with snow, his eyebrows frosted over and lower lip quivering with indignation, Akaky burst through the massive double doors and into the cavernous anteroom of the Bolshaya Ordynka police station. It was about 3:00 A.M. Four patrolmen stood in the corner beneath the Soviet flag, drinking tea and joking in low tones; another pair sat together in the front row of an interminable file of benches, playing backgammon. At the far end of the chamber, on a dais, a jowly officer with thickly lidded eyes sat behind a desk the size of a pickup truck.

Akaky trotted the length of the room, a self-generated wind flapping round him, bits of compacted snow flying from his suit. "I've been beaten and robbed!" he cried, his voice strangely constricted, as if someone had hold of his windpipe. "In a public place. In Red Square. They took, they took"—here he felt himself racked by deep quaking bursts of sorrow so that he had to fight back the tears—"they took my overcoat!"

The desk sergeant looked down at him, immense, inscrutable, his head as heavy and shaggy as a circus bear's. Behind him, a great faded mural depicted Lenin at the helm of the ship of state.

After a long moment of absolute, drenching silence, the sergeant pressed a chubby hand to his eyes, then rattled some papers and waited for the clerk to appear at his side. The clerk, also in uniform, looked to be about eighteen or nineteen, his face cratered with acne. "You will fill out this form, comrade, delineating the salient details," the clerk said, handing Akaky eight or ten pages of printed matter and an imitation ballpoint pen, "and then you will return at ten o'clock sharp tomorrow morning."

Akaky sat over the form—Place of Employment, Birthdate, Mother's Name and Shoe Size, Residence Permit Number, Previous Arrest Record—until past four in the morning. Then he handed it to the clerk, absently gathered up his hat and gloves, and wandered out into the teeth of the storm, as dazed and unsteady as the sole survivor of a shipwreck.

Akaky woke with a start at quarter past nine the following morning, the Ukrainian-made alarm clock having failed to go off on schedule. He was late for work, late for his appointment at the police station; his throat ached, a phlegmy cough clenched at his chest, and, worst of all, his overcoat was gone—gone, vanished, pilfered, three months' salary down the drain. It hit him all at once, in the instant of waking, and he fell back against the pillow, paralyzed, crushed under the weight of catastrophe and loss of faith. "Vladimir Ilyich Lenin!" he cried, taking the great man's name in vain as the six smirking Yeroshkin brats trundled by his bed on their way to school, "what am I going to do now?"

If he could have buried himself then and there, piled the dirt eight feet high atop his bed, he would have done it. What was the sense in going on? But then he thought of the police—perhaps they'd apprehended the thieves, put them behind bars where they belonged; perhaps they'd recovered his overcoat. He pictured the bearlike sergeant handing it to him with his apologies, and then commending him for his alert description of the crime's perpetrators and the swift and unhesitating way in which he'd filled out the crime report. As he pulled on the standard-brown serge trousers and imitation plastic boots, the image of the coat filled his consciousness and for a minute he was lost in reverie, remembering its softness, its lines, its snug and simple elegance. How long had he owned it—less than twenty-four hours? He wanted to cry.

His hand trembled as he knotted the olive-drab tie, finger-combed his hair, and tried to reach the office on Irina Yeroshkina's telephone. "Hello? Kropotkin's Laundry. May I be of assistance?" He hung up, dialed again. A voice immediately came over the wire, no salutation or identification, reading a list of numbers in a harsh, consonant-thick accent: "*dva-dyevyat-odin-chyetirye-dva-dva*—" Akaky's stomach was on fire, his head pumped full of helium. He slammed down the receiver, snatched up the sad, ragged tatters of his Soviet-made overcoat, and hurried out the door.

It was three minutes past ten when he hurtled through the doors of the police station like a madman, out of breath, racked with shivers and trailing a dirty fringe of knotted felt lining. He ran headlong into a hunched old grandmother in a bábushka— what was it about her that looked so familiar?—and realized with a start that the room that had been so empty just six hours ago was now thronged with people. The old woman, who called him a rude name and set down a bag of beets to give him a clean two-armed shove, was standing in an endless, snaking line that cut back on itself and circled the room twice. Akaky followed the line to the end and asked a man in knee boots and Tatar hat what was going on. The man looked up from the chess puzzle he'd been studying and fixed Akaky with a cold eye. "I assume you have a crime to report, comrade?"

Akaky bit his lower lip. "They took my overcoat."

The man held up a closely inscribed form. "Have you picked up your report yet?"

"Well, no, I—"

"First door to your left," the man said, turning back to his puzzle. Akaky looked in the direction the man had indicated and saw that a line nearly as long as the first was backed up outside the door. His stomach turned over like an egg in a skillet. This was going to be a wait.

At four-thirty, just when Akaky had begun to despair of gaining admission to the inner sanctum of the police headquarters or of ever seeing his overcoat again, a man in the uniform of the OBKhSS marched down the line to where Akaky was standing, snapped his heels together, and said: "Akaky A. Bashmachkin?" The OBKhSS was a branch of the Ministry of Internal Security, officially designated "The Department for the Struggle Against the Plundering of Socialist Property." Its job, as Akaky was reminded each day in the newspapers and on TV, was to curtail black-market activities by cracking down on the pirating of the people's goods to pay for foreign luxury items smuggled into the country. "Yes." Akaky blinked. "I—I've lost an overcoat."

"Come with me, please." The man spun on one heel and stamped off in the direction from which he'd come, Akaky hurrying to keep up. They breezed by the sixty or so scowling citizens who made up the forward section of the line, passed through the heavy wooden door into a room swarming with victims, suspects, police officers, and clerks, and then through a second door, down a hallway, and finally into a long, low-ceilinged room dominated by a glossy conference table. A single man sat at the head of the table. He was bald-headed, clean-shaven, dressed in slippers, slacks, and sports shirt. "Have a seat," he said, indicating a chair at the near end of the table. And then, to the OBKhSS man: "Watch the door, will you, Zamyotov?"

"Now," he said, clearing his throat and consulting the form on the table before him, "you're Akaky A. Bashmachkin, is that right?" His voice was warm, fraternal, spilling over the room like sugared tea. He could have been a country physician, a writer of children's books, the genial veterinarian who'd tended the old cow Akaky's grandmother had kept tethered outside the door when he was a boy in the Urals. "I'm Inspector Zharyenoye, Security Police," he said.

Akaky nodded impatiently. "They've taken my overcoat, sir."

"Yes," said Zharyenoye, leaning forward, "why don't you tell me about it."

Akaky told him. In detail. Told him of the mockery he'd been exposed to at the office, of Petrovich's promise, of the overcoat itself, and of the brutal, uncommunist spirit of the men who'd taken it from him. His eyes were wet when he was finished.

Zharyenoye had listened patiently throughout Akaky's recitation, interrupting him only twice—to ask Petrovich's address and to question what Akaky was doing in Red Square at one-thirty in the morning. When Akaky was finished, Zharyenoye snapped his fingers and the antiplunderer from the OBKhSS stepped into the room and laid a package on the table. The inspector waved his hand, and the man tore back the wrapping paper.

Akaky nearly leaped out of his chair: there, stretched out on the table before him, as pristine and luxurious as when he'd first laid eyes on it, was his overcoat. He was overjoyed, jubilant, he was delirious with gratitude and relief. Suddenly he was on his feet, pumping the OBKhSS man's hand. "I can hardly believe it," he exclaimed. "You've found it, you've found my overcoat!"

"One moment, Comrade Bashmachkin," the inspector said. "I wonder if you might positively identify the coat as the one you were deprived of early this morning. Has your name been sewed into the lining perhaps? Can you tell me what the pockets contain?"

Akaky wanted to kiss the inspector's bald pate, dance him round the room: how good the policemen were, how efficient and dedicated and clever. "Yes, yes, of course. Um, in the right front pocket there's an article clipped from the paper on cheese production in Chelyabinsk—my grandmother used to make her own."

Zharyenoye went through the pockets, extracting seven kopecks, a pocket comb, and a neatly folded page of newsprint. He read the headline: "'Cheese Production Up.' Well, I guess that proves ownership incontrovertibly, wouldn't you say, Mr. Zamyotov?—unless Comrade Bashmachkin is a clairvoyant." The inspector gave a little laugh; Zamyotov, humorless as a watchdog, grunted his concurrence.

Akaky was grinning. Grinning like a cosmonaut on parade, like a schoolboy accepting the Karl Marx solidarity prize before the assembled faculty and student body. He stepped forward to thank the inspector and collect his overcoat, but Zharyenoye, suddenly stern-faced, waved him off. He had a penknife in his hand, and he was bending over the coat. Akaky looked on, bewildered, as the inspector carefully severed a number of stitches fastening the lining to the inner collar of the coat. With an impeccably manicured thumbnail, Zharyenoye prized a label from beneath the lining. Akaky stared down at it. Black thread, white acetate: MADE IN HONG KONG.

The animation had gone out of the inspector's voice. "Perhaps you'd better sit down, comrade," he said.

From that moment on, Akaky's life shifted gears, lurching into a rapid and inexorable downward spiral. The inspector had finally let him go—but only after a three-hour grilling, a lecture on civic duty, and the imposition of a one-hundred-ruble fine for receiving smuggled goods. The overcoat, of course, became the property of the Soviet government. Akaky left the conference room in a daze—he felt as if he'd been squeezed like a blister, flattened like a fly. His coat was gone, yes—that was bad enough. But everything he believed in, everything he'd worked for, everything he'd been taught from the day he took his first faltering steps and gurgled over a communal rattle—that was gone too. He wandered the streets for hours, in despair, a stiff, relentless wind poking fingers of ice through the rotten fabric of his Soviet-made overcoat.

The cold he'd picked up in Red Square worsened. Virulent, opportunistic, the microbes began to work in concert, and the cold became flu, bronchitis, pneumonia. Akaky lay in his bed, ravaged with fever, unable to breathe—he felt as if someone had stuffed a sock down his throat and stretched him out on the stove to simmer. Mrs. Romanova tried to feed him some borscht; Irina Yeroshkina berated him for letting himself go. Her husband called a doctor, a young woman who'd been trained in Yakutsk and seemed to have a great deal of trouble inserting the thermometer and getting a temperature reading. She prescribed rest and a strong emetic.

At one point in his delirium Akaky imagined that three or four of the Yeroshkin children were having a game of darts over his bed; another time he was certain that the blond tough from the office was laughing at him, urging him to pull on his cracked imitation plastic galoshes and come back to work like a man. Old Studniuk was with him when the end came. The patriarch was leaning over him, his head blazing like the summer sun, his voice tense and querulous—he was lecturing: "Oh, you ass, you young ass—didn't I tell you so? The blindness, the blindness." The old gums smacked like thunder; the whole world shrieked in Akaky's ears. "I suppose you think they built that wall in Berlin to keep people out, eh? Eh?" Studniuk demanded, and suddenly Akaky was crying out, his voice choked with terror and disbelief—he must have been reliving the scene in Red Square, his feet pounding the pavement, fingers clutching at the Kremlin wall, the thieves at his heels—"Faster!" he shouted, "faster! Someone get me a ladder!" And then he was quiet.

There were no ghosts haunting Moscow that winter, no vengeful, overcoat-snatching wraiths driven from uneasy graves to settle the score among the living. Nor was there any slowdown in the influx of foreign-made overcoats pouring across the Finnish border, channeled through the maze of docks at Odessa, packed like herring in the trunks of diplomats' wives and the baggage of party officials returning from abroad. No, life went on as usual. Zhigulis hummed along the streets, clerks clerked and writers wrote, old Studniuk unearthed an antediluvian crony to take over Akaky's room and Irina Yeroshkin found herself pregnant again. Rodion Mishkin thought of Akaky from time to time, shaking his head over a tongue sandwich or pausing for a moment over his lunchtime chess match with Grigory Stravrogin, the spunky blond lad they'd moved up to Akaky's desk, and Inspector Zharyenoye had a single nightmare in which he imagined the little clerk storming naked into the room and repossessing his overcoat. But that was about it. Rodion soon forgot his former colleague—Grigory's gambits were so much more challenging—and Zharyenoye opened his closet the morning after his odd little dream to find the overcoat where he'd left it—hanging undisturbed between a pair of sports shirts and his dress uniform. The inspector never had another thought of Akaky Akakievich as long as he lived, and when he wore the overcoat in the street, proud and triumphant, people invariably mistook him for the First Secretary himself.

Acknowledgment is made to the following in which some of the stories in this book originally appeared: *Antaeus*: "Caviar" and "Rara Avis"; *Antioch Review*: "Rupert Beersley and the Beggar Master of Sivani-Hoota" and "A Bird in Hand"; *Atlantic Monthly*: "The Overcoat II"; *Esquire*: "On for the Long Haul"; *Iowa Review*: "Two Ships"; *Oui*: "Whales Weep"; *Paris Review*: "Greasy Lake," "Ike and Nina," and "The Hector Quesadilla Story"; *TriQuarterly*: "Stones in My Passway, Hellhound on My Trail" and "The New Moon Party." "Caviar" also appeared in *Pushcart Prize Stories IX*.

Grateful acknowledgment is made to the following for permission to reprint copyrighted material:
CBS Songs, a Division of CBS Inc.: Lyrics from "Don't Be Cruel," by Otis Blackwell and Elvis Presley. Copyright © 1956 by Unart Music Corporation. Rights assigned to CBS Catalogue Partnership. All rights controlled and administered by CBS Unart Catalog Inc. All rights reserved. International copyright secured.
Chappell/Intersong Music Group—USA: Lyrics from "Hound Dog," by Jerry Leiber and Mike Stoller. Copyright © 1956 by Elvis Presley Music and Lion Publishing Company, Inc. Copyright renewed, assigned to Gladys Music, Inc., and MCA Music. Administered in the U.S.A. by Chappell & Co., Inc. (Intersong Music, Publisher). International copyright secured. All rights reserved.
Kenneth Johnson/Horoscope Music Publishing Co.: Lyrics from "Stones in My Passway," "Phonograph Blues," and "Hellhound on My Trail," composed by Robert Johnson. All rights reserved.
Paramount Music Corporation: A selection from the song "That's Amore," by Jack Brooks and Harry Warren. Copyright © 1953 by Paramount Music Corporation and Four Jays Music. Copyright renewed 1981 by Paramount Music Corporation and Four Jays Music.
Bruce Springsteen/Jon Landau Management, Inc.: Lyrics from "Spirit in the Night," by Bruce Springsteen. Copyright © 1972 by Bruce Springsteen. All rights reserved.
Tree Publishing Co., Inc.: Lyrics from "Heartbreak Hotel," by Elvis Presley, Mae Boren Axton, and Tommy Durden. Copyright © 1956 by Tree Publishing Co., Inc. Copyright renewed. International copyright secured. All rights reserved.
Viking Penguin Inc.: Lines from "Whales Weep Not!" from *The Complete Poems of D. H. Lawrence*, collected and edited with an Introduction and Notes by Vivian de Sola Pinto and F. Warren Roberts. Copyright © 1964, 1971 by Angelo Ravagli and C. M. Weekley, Executors of the Estate of Frieda Lawrence Ravagli.